HIGH BLUE SKY

VICTORIA CONNELLY

Cover design by The Brewster Project
Photos copyright © Depositphotos

Author photo © Roy Connelly

Published by Cuthland Press

ISBN: 978-1-910522-17-2

To Jo and India with love

CHAPTER ONE

Spring is beautiful everywhere, but there's a quality to the air and a special lucidness to the light in the county of Sussex. Is it the proximity to the sea or the rolling beauty of the South Downs? Abigail Carey still hadn't decided even though she'd lived here for almost a year.

As she walked over the ridge of the hill and gazed down at the Georgian splendour of Winfield Hall, she found it hard to believe that this was her home now. She could still feel those clouds of butterflies in her stomach every time she saw it. It was a magical place to live and she never tired of gazing at its golden stone façade, its large sash windows which let in so much light and its walled garden that she had helped to restore and which, in the summer, had been full of flowers and produce for the kitchen. Abi had never been happier. Giving up her home in London and selling the company she'd built had been a tough decision, but starting again and finding out what she really wanted from her life had been wonderfully freeing.

Descending the hill, she thought about the seasons that had passed. Autumn had brought fiery golds and soft ambers to the countryside. The lanes had filled with leaves and had shone with showers. Then winter had come with its frosts silvering the trees and riming the grassy slopes of the downs. The air had been scented with wood smoke from the cottages in the village and Abi had brought piles of logs inside, stacking them neatly into baskets and lighting her wood burner. What a joy it had been to curl up next to it on those chilly winter evenings when the sun left your company so early. Abi might have missed the long evenings of summer in her garden, but she took solace in sketching the gifts of nature, bringing in great pine cones from the woods and pretty pebbles and shells from her trips to the sea.

To ward off the winter blues, she had recently treated herself to an old Albion printing press which had been fully restored. It had been a total extravagance and had taken a whole day to be assembled, but the huge black and gold iron beast looked so wonderful in her home and she had been learning how to use it to create linocuts and woodblock prints over the long winter months.

Now, spring was here and Abi could feel the life force of it surging through the air. The first primroses were decorating the banks along the village lane and Abi had spotted violets peeping through the grass in the churchyard. And work on Winfield was progressing at a good pace. As she made her way back towards the hall now, she thought about just how much work had been done in the last few months. The scaffolding that had been erected during the summer for work on the windows had been taken down just the week before, part of the wall in the garden had been repointed and two new apartments were now ready to let, one with a tenant in already.

Abi now made her way towards the vacant one adjacent to

her own, opening the door and standing in the middle of the living room, sighing in appreciation.

'They've done a good job,' a voice said from behind her. It was Edward Townsend, the man who owned the other half of Winfield Hall.

Abi turned to smile at him as he came in from the hallway 'They really have, haven't they?'

'My second one's going to be ready sometime over the summer,' Edward told her.

'When will you start advertising?'

'Immediately.'

'Me too.'

'It's going to be strange sharing this place with more new people,' Edward confessed.

'Well, it's not like we've ever had it to ourselves,' Abi pointed out. 'We've been sharing it with builders for months now.'

'True.'

'And Harry's been here since August.'

Edward nodded. 'What do you think of him?'

'He seems great! I haven't really spoken to him much. He's always rushing off somewhere.'

'He's been setting up his firm's new office in Brighton.'

'Ah,' Abi said, now understanding why the young man she'd seen coming and going always looked slightly frazzled around the edges.

'Any idea who you'll rent yours out to?' Edward asked.

Abi looked closely at his face. 'You're still worried about that, aren't you?'

'What? No!'

'Yes you are! You're worried I'm going to fill the hall with hopeless artists who can't pay their rent, little as I'm charging, and that the whole place will fall back into ruin.'

'I'm not worried. I trust you,' he said.

'You do?'

He cleared his throat. 'Mostly.'

Abi laughed. Edward was notoriously rational when it came to business matters. He'd thoroughly vetted each of his applicants, deciding that the apartments on his side of the hall were only to be let to professionals on good solid incomes. It was thoroughly sensible, of course, but Abi had other ideas. She wanted to let her side out to artists and creatives – people who were trying to make a difference in the world. Maybe they were struggling and would never have been able to afford to live somewhere like Winfield. Well, Abi wanted to step in and give them the opportunity to live somewhere beautiful and inspirational while they found their footing. It was her way of passing on a little of the luck she felt had come her way with her design business: paying it forward, sharing the joy. And although Edward claimed that he approved of her idea, she couldn't help thinking that he was harbouring some misgivings about it. But she liked him all the more for that. She liked that he was different from her with his serious notions about how people should earn a living. He was so thoroughly old-fashioned and she rather enjoyed teasing him.

'I've already had a trapeze artist apply,' Abi told him now, 'only she wanted to set a rope up between the roof and the top of the walled garden.'

'You're kidding!' Edward had turned white.

Abi giggled. 'Yes, I'm kidding.'

Edward shook his head. 'My heart nearly stopped then.'

'I'm sorry. I couldn't resist!'

They left the apartment together.

'Just let me know who you decide on, won't you?'

'So you can vet them?' she asked.

'So I can come and say hello and welcome them to Winfield,' he countered.

She smiled. 'I promise.'

Harry Freeman loved his new home, but he found he wasn't spending as much time there as he'd hoped he would. Giving up his place in London hadn't been as much of a wrench as he'd thought it would be. When his boss had told him that the new office for their advertising company was opening in Brighton and he was one of the chosen to make the transition, Harry was flattered, even though there were rumours among some of his colleagues that the newly-appointed Brighton team were as good as being ex-communicated. But Harry didn't see it like that at all. For him, it was a chance for a fresh start.

There was also the added bonus of living in the country which had always appealed to him. He'd grown up in the London suburbs in several smart terraced houses with small neat back gardens enclosed by fences. He hadn't minded the limited space in London until recently when he'd felt the need for something more. Then the job opportunity had arisen and he'd started looking at property in Sussex and had found Winfield. He'd never forget his first view of it as he'd driven into the village and he'd had to pinch himself that living in such a place was possible. It was so – well – palatial compared to the flats on offer in the city.

It all seemed to be right somehow. Harry's parents had moved out of London to live in Sussex a few years ago and it would be nice to be a closer to them and see them more often.

He just hadn't had the time when he'd been working in London. His hours had pretty much been round the clock and he'd often found himself taking little jobs home with him, working into the early hours and feeling permanently shattered. And that didn't seem to be changing now that he was living at Winfield. So much for a slower pace of life in the country, he thought. Mind you, it was early days at the Brighton office and the teething problems wouldn't go on forever. Then, he would have time to enjoy Winfield properly. He wouldn't feel bone-shatteringly tired all the time. He could sit in his beautiful apartment, gazing out at that view, maybe browse a newspaper or even pick up a book. When was the last time he'd done that? He really couldn't remember. It was all work and no play these days, and everybody knew what that made you: a very dull boy. He recalled Edward Townsend's kindness when he'd first moved in.

'Remember to enjoy this place,' Edward had told him. 'It's a great place for doing nothing in.'

Nothing.

Harry couldn't quite imagine himself doing nothing. He'd spent one weekend trying to relax, sitting on a new chair he'd bought for himself and which he'd placed next to one of the great sash windows that looked out over the downs. He'd made himself a cup of tea and had sat down. He'd even switched his phone off for the occasion and had taken a few deep breaths. And then his mind had kicked in. *I've got to do this,* he thought. *I should ring that person. I ought to start that new spreadsheet and invoice that company.* The voice in his head was relentless. His cup of tea had gone cold and he hadn't spent more than two minutes admiring the view before he'd reached for his phone and switched it back on.

Clearly, he still had some work to do when it came to doing nothing.

Aurora Arden looked out of her basement flat window on the outskirts of Lewes and couldn't help grimacing at the view that greeted her. She might have been able to do something to make the tiny courtyard garden pretty, but it was home to no less than six wheelie bins, a bicycle belonging to the woman who lived in the flat above hers, and a couple of old car wheels that belonged to the man in the flat above that.

The woman in the flat upstairs, Sophie, was a nice enough sort. She always smiled politely whenever they saw each other, and Aurora wasn't really one to complain, but Sophie did like her music. Loud. She liked her TV loud too so that Aurora was able to clearly hear all the questions and answers on the daytime TV quizzes Sophie watched. Didn't she have a job to go to or, if she worked from home, how on earth did she concentrate with all that noise?

Then there was the guy in the top flat. He came and went at odd hours and she'd hear him thumping up the stairs and slamming his door. Aurora despaired. In her ideal world, stairs were rarely thumped and doors were never slammed. But even more than peace and quiet, Aurora longed for somewhere beautiful. Beauty was important, she believed. Beauty fed the soul. But here, in her basement flat, she was beginning to feel soul-starved and that upset her because it went against everything she believed in and everything she taught others too – that true happiness came from within and that you created it yourself; you didn't need any outside stimuli to make you happy – you were enough.

Aurora had really done her best to live by those words and she had filled her tiny basement home with beautiful things like plants and the crystals she so adored. She lit candles, turned on her salt lamps to brighten the dark corners and scented her small home with essential oils and played soft music. But her personal blend of oils couldn't combat the smell of fried onions from Sophie's flat, and it was difficult to find inner peace and stillness in her meditation sessions when doors were being slammed and stairs were being thumped.

Whenever she could, Aurora sought refuge in her local park or at the beach, sitting on the cool grass or soft sand, filling her senses with the peace she so needed. As a healer, she always remembered that she needed to heal herself first in order to be in a good space to help others and so she soaked it all in – the birdsong, the wind and the waves, and the sound of children's laughter.

Then, on the way home, she would pop into the newsagents on the corner of her road to look at the notices in the window before glancing at the magazines on the shelves. There was a New Age magazine that she loved but it was the best part of five pounds and so she would try to sneak a look at it when the shop was busy and she could glance at it undisturbed. It was naughty and she knew she risked being banned from the shop, but she really didn't mean any harm and she always opened the pages carefully.

Today, she saw that there was an article about rose quartz which was one of her favourite crystals. She flipped to the page and skimmed the piece, making a note of a website it recommended for some meditations she wanted to try. Putting down the magazine, she checked her purse to see if she could actually afford to buy it this week as well as the local paper she always bought, but there wasn't enough. Maybe she didn't need to buy the paper. If she didn't buy the paper for a month, she could treat herself to the magazine. She hesitated, her hand hovering over the magazine. Then sense prevailed. She always liked to scan the rentals in the paper to see if there was something she could afford that was prettier and quieter than her rented digs at Highfield Terrace. So she left the magazine and bought the paper.

It was when she was back home, sipping a wild cherry herbal tea that she saw the advertisement.

ARE YOU A CREATIVE SOUL IN NEED OF A BEAUTIFUL AND PEACEFUL PLACE TO LIVE? IF YOU ARE, WINFIELD HALL NEEDS YOU!

Aurora read the rest of the advert and then did a double take. Had she read that right? Was this some kind of joke? Maybe it was a reality TV show and anyone who dared to reply to the ad would be filmed and mercilessly ribbed in front of thousands of viewers.

Quickly, she switched her laptop on and googled Winfield Hall, gasping when she saw the photos of it. It had sold at auction, she learned, and sat in the heart of the South Downs in a pretty village. How Aurora longed to live in a village!

She looked at the phone number and bit her lip. There were bound to be dozens of applicants for such a place. What made her think that she stood a chance of being successful?

Hey, a little voice said. *What happened to positive thinking? What happened to channelling your energy out into the universe? If you don't put good thoughts out there, how can you expect good things to find their way to you?*

There was only one thing to do. She rang the number.

CHAPTER TWO

Abi was pacing in the new apartment adjacent to hers. She was never one to pace, but she was so anxious about this whole interviewing business and she really shouldn't be because she'd run her own company and had endless experience of interviewing people. But this felt different. She wasn't giving a job here; she was sharing her home and it seemed even more important to get the right match. So far, she'd met a singer who'd smelt of tobacco and whisky; an artist who confessed that she owned five cats, two talking parrots and a boa constrictor; and a sculptor who said she did most of her work at night and would a bit of chiselling bother anyone?

When Abi had told Edward of her adventures, he'd turned quite pale.

'There'll be someone who's right,' she'd assured him even though she was still feeling nervous as well as excited at the prospect of sharing their home with new people.

She was also a little anxious about how things would change between her and Edward. Over the last year, their tentative friendship had grown. They still weren't living in each other's pockets – neither wanted that – but they had learned to live happily alongside each other, sharing a few jokes and anecdotes whenever they ran into one another as well as the occasional swim.

Abi still couldn't believe that Edward had persuaded her to go wild swimming with him and, so far, they'd had four outings together although none so far this year. As Abi waited for her next viewer to arrive, she thought back to the previous summer and the trips to the river with Edward. It was as if they shared a very special secret. Abi would never have thought to swim in a river and would probably never have found that particular spot without Edward. Having grown up in a nearby village, he'd known of it for years and she felt privileged that he'd shared it with her. It had helped them to become closer somehow, even though they still knew relatively little about each other, but there was definitely an ease between them from that shared experience of cold water swimming.

Walking around the apartment one last time, imagining what the unfurnished rooms would look like to the latest viewer, Abi couldn't help wondering if she was doing the right thing. She'd had this romantic notion about sharing her space with fellow creatives but, so far, she'd been sorely disappointed by the calibre of applicant.

She picked up her printed notes about the woman who was due any minute now. Her name was Aurora Arden. She was twenty-eight and was a healer. Abi had liked the sound of her when they'd spoken on the phone and had looked up her website which showed that she taught yoga classes and meditation sessions and that she was a crystal healer. Abi had never heard of that before, but it sounded rather beautiful and, unlike the sculptress, it also sounded wonderfully quiet.

~

Was it possible to want something too much? Aurora thought that it must be because she couldn't stop thinking about Winfield Hall. She'd even dreamed of it the night before her interview – if that's what it was called. She'd spoken to Abigail Carey on the phone and she'd seemed warm and friendly which almost made things worse because Aurora wanted the apartment more than ever now, even before seeing it.

Driving her old silver Mini, Aurora arrived well before her appointment time. She parked in the village and walked around the narrow lanes with their high banks, breathing in the downland air and marvelling at the peace of it all. Then, when it was time, she drove up the lane towards Winfield, parking in front of the golden house and sitting almost stupefied a moment later.

This can't possibly happen, a little voice said. *This is too much. You're not the kind of person who gets to live in a place like this.*

She took a deep breath as she told her clients to when they needed to centre themselves and quieten the voice of doubt in their minds. *Why shouldn't somebody like me live here*, she asked herself instead? Surely she'd served her time in the noisy dark basement flat. Perhaps this was her reward.

Aurora reached into her handbag and brought out two oval-shaped stones the size of small eggs: a smooth red carnelian which she held in her right hand and a waxy orange calcite which felt comforting in the palm of her left. Together, these two stones ensured confidence, courage and strength of purpose. With their help, she could call upon her own personal reservoirs of self-belief and so she held them both for a moment until she felt calmer. She could do this.

A moment later, after flattening her flyaway red hair and giving her lips a quick slick of pink gloss, she left the safety of her car, her stones in the pocket of her jacket. She'd worn one of her slightly less colourful lacy dresses in an attempt to look businesslike, but the one she had on now billowed in the late spring wind and inflated like a hot air balloon. Her hands patted the unruly garment down and she rang the doorbell, hoping nobody had spied the incident from one of the many windows.

A moment later, a woman opened the door, a huge smile on her face, her blonde hair blowing back as the wind rushed into the hall.

'Miss Arden?' she said.

'It's Aurora, but I usually shorten it to Aura.'

'Aura? Oh, I love that. Come on in! I'm Abigail, but it usually gets shortened to Abi.'

They shook hands and Aura immediately felt at ease, instinctively liking this woman. She had a lightness around her and a gentle warmth that was so welcoming that Aura silently chastised herself for her earlier nerves, although now she was even more anxious to make the right impression.

'You've not come far, have you?' Abi asked.

'Lewes. I have a flat there. Rented.'

'And you're looking for something like this – in the country?'

'Oh, yes. Somewhere quiet.'

It was just then that there was a huge bang from upstairs and a spiral of dust fell down the stairwell.

'We still have builders in, I'm afraid,' Abi explained. 'But it's not as bad as it was a few months ago. You should have seen the place then.'

'So you're restoring it all?'

'Pretty much. It was a bit of a shell when it was up for sale.'

Abi then proceeded to tell Aura about how the house was sold at auction to Edward Townsend and how she came in later when he decided to divide the house in two. Aura admired them both greatly for taking on such a daunting task.

Abi led the way across the enormous expanse of hallway to a white door on the right, opening it into the apartment.

'Well, this is it. There's a bedroom and bathroom over there, kitchen over here and, as you can see, an open-plan living area.'

Aura walked into the room.

'Those French doors are wonderful,' she said. 'I like to be able to get outside easily.'

'Me too,' Abi told her as Aura looked outside, 'and you'll love the garden.'

'It's wonderful. I've not had an outdoor space of my own yet.' She looked into the walled garden which she could see had been lovingly restored like the hall. There were no wheelie bins here and no car wheels dumped in a corner.

'I often keep my windows open all night here,' Abi confessed. 'Now that was something I'd never have done in London!'

'You moved here from London?'

Abi nodded. 'I sometimes have to pinch myself that I'm actually here.'

Aura gave a little sniff and quickly reached for a tissue from her dress pocket. 'Oh, dear.'

'What's the matter?' Abi asked.

'I'm afraid I'm going to make a spectacle of myself and cry!'

'Are you all right?' Abi asked, moving closer and gently touching her shoulder.

'It's silly of me,' Aura said. 'It's just, well, everything! I didn't know such places existed. Not outside of a magazine. Not in *real* life.'

'I felt the same way when I first saw it. It kind of grips your heart, doesn't it?'

Aura nodded.

'I'll give you a few minutes, okay? Take a look around – go out into the garden,' Abi said, motioning to the French doors. 'Take your time. Enjoy it.'

As Abi left the apartment, Aura took a deep breath. She felt so silly welling up like that, but it had been so spontaneous a feeling that she hadn't been able to control it. This place – it was more than a place – it was a living, breathing thing, and she knew with all her heart that she wanted to be a part of it.

Looking around the rooms just confirmed that feeling. The bedroom was as light and airy as the living space and the bathroom was pretty yet practical. It was almost too much because it wasn't hers yet, and seeing it and knowing that she could live somewhere like this, given a little bit of luck, would make it all the more unbearable if it wasn't going to happen. The thought of returning to that basement flat with the smell of other people's fried onions and the sound of other people's televisions would be trying indeed. No amount of meditating would see her through this disappointment.

Instinctively, Aura's hand plunged into her pocket and she felt the comforting weight of the carnelian and orange calcite. Take a moment, she told herself, venturing into the garden. Just as she'd expected, the outside was as perfect as the inside and she couldn't believe that the apartment came with such a wonderful space. Aura tried to imagine coming home after work and stepping out into the garden, perhaps sitting and watching the bees dancing among the flowers or meditating under the light of a full moon.

It isn't yours yet, a little voice said, *and it might never be.*

Aura banished the voice to the back of her mind, took one last look around the garden and then went back inside.

Abi was there waiting for her when she returned.

'Like it?' she asked.

'I *love* it,' Aura said.

'And have you got any questions about it? Anything you want to know?'

'Actually, I was wondering if I would be able to do some of my healing work here – I don't have many clients and I see most of them in a little room I rent in town. But it would be such a perfect place to see them.'

'You'd be able to use the place as you want. As long as there's nothing that would disturb other residents.'

'Of course.'

'So,' Abi said, 'I've had a few viewers round.'

'I can imagine.'

'And – well – listen, there's no point messing around and making you wait for my decision.' Abi paused.

'I see,' Aura said. So Abi had found somebody she preferred to her, had she? She tried to smile, but knew that her disappointment would be etched right across her face.

'No – you don't understand,' Abi said quickly, obviously seeing her distress. 'You can have the apartment. If you want it.'

'*If* I want it?' Aura said, barely able to contain her excitement. 'Oh, I *want* it!'

Abi beamed her a smile. 'Oh, good! I'm so glad!'

'I hope I didn't – well – bribe you with the waterworks earlier!' Aura said, 'because that wouldn't be fair if there are other viewers you're considering.'

'Not at all,' Abi told her. 'Between you and me, there have been some simply *shocking* viewers!'

'Really?'

'Really! You're the first I've met who I feel really belongs here.'

Aura gasped. 'I can't thank you enough.'

'You don't need to thank me. I feel *I* should thank *you!*'

They smiled at one another.

'Do you mind if I ask something?' Aura said at last.

'Of course not. Ask anything.'

'Why is the rent so low? I mean, this place is amazing. You could easily ask double what you are. Not that I'm objecting because I wouldn't be able to afford it if it was.'

'And there you've answered your own question,' Abi said. 'I wanted to share this place with people who maybe couldn't afford to live here because I know what it's like to struggle when you're trying to do something creative, and I know how important it is to be somewhere that inspires you.'

Aura was too stunned to speak. It was as if Abi was able to see right inside her and knew exactly what she needed.

'I don't know what to say,' Aura said. 'This is all... it's all...'

'I'll send you the paperwork, okay?' Abi said.

'Please.'

'And I look forward to you joining us here at Winfield.'

Life was a whirlwind after that for Aura. She gave her landlord her required month's notice, happy to pay the rent money even though she was moving out before the end of the lease. It would be worth it. Abi had told her that the apartment at Winfield was hers as soon as she was ready to take it and Aura wasn't going to waste a moment longer than she had to in the basement flat. So she packed everything up, which wasn't much really for her twenty-eight years on the planet. Other than her furniture, there were some old pieces of mismatched crockery she'd bought at a car boot sale, her clothes which were always bought in sales or from charity shops, her books, plants and her crystals. There wasn't anything in the way of ornaments because they just got in the way. Besides, her crystals were her ornaments from Mother Earth. As well as being vital for her work and for her own private use, her crystals were placed around her tiny home, imbuing it with light and positive energy from the clear quartz clusters to the large amethyst point she loved to wrap her hands around. Each one was now taken down from its home and lovingly cleaned before being carefully wrapped for the short journey to Winfield.

Then there was that wonderful sensation of doing everything for the last time: the last time she would put her bin bag out, the last time she'd have to clear the outside drain of her neighbour's noodles which were always tipped into the sink, the last time she'd be woken by the man upstairs after his pub crawl on a Friday night.

And then there was all the admin. Aura worked methodically through it all, sorting out all her utility bills and council tax and giving her new address to her bank, her friends and family members. But there was one family member she hesitated over. Johnny. It entered her mind for a blissful moment that this might be the perfect chance to escape from him – to leave him and his problems far behind her because, surely, she had dealt with them enough over the years. He could take care of himself now, couldn't he? He didn't need his big sister anymore, did he?

But, as soon as she had envisioned a peaceful life without him, guilt flooded her and she found herself writing to him, sending her love, as she always did, and telling him her new address, popping the letter in an envelope and enclosing a tiny jade stone for good luck. She then wrote his address on it.

She would post it to the prison first thing in the morning.

Abi had watched as Aura drove away after her viewing. As they'd left the apartment together, Abi had done her best not to laugh at Aura's stunned expression. The young woman was smitten, Abi could tell – well and truly, deeply and thoroughly smitten with Winfield, and who could blame her? And, luckily, Abi was just a bit smitten with Aura too. She'd liked her as soon as they'd met. There was something innately sweet about her, almost angelic, as if she didn't quite belong to this realm. With her long red hair, pale face and bright eyes that had sparkled with joy at everything Winfield had to offer, Abi couldn't think of a more fitting or deserving neighbour and she was so looking forward to her moving in. She was sure that Edward would be happy with her choice too. He'd been so nervous about who Abi was going to choose, hadn't he? Well, he needn't have worried because there was nothing about Aura that had set off any alarm bells whatsoever.

CHAPTER THREE

Aura moved into Winfield Hall on the first of May which she thought very propitious as it marked the festival of Beltane between the spring equinox and summer solstice – a time to celebrate the coming of the summer, the time of fertility, of welcoming the longer, warmer days and revelling in the beauty that nature had to offer. And Aura was revelling. She'd never been happier.

The first of May gave everything it could that year. The woods were full of bluebells and wild garlic, the cherry and apple trees were bursting with blooms, and deep blue irises and pale pink roses filled the gardens in the village. Aura felt such delight at being a part of it all.

The removal men didn't take long to bring in her meagre pieces of furniture but, as soon as they had, she suddenly realised how shabby all her bits looked in the pristine whiteness of her new apartment. They'd looked perfectly fine in the dreary basement flat, but they were quite out of place here. Still, she thought, she could take care of that with some tactfully-placed shawls and blankets in pretty, bright colours and textures. The main thing was she was in. She'd made it. This was a new start for her after years of renting substandard flats with dodgy plumbing, moth-eaten carpets and noisy neighbours. Winfield was going to be like heaven.

It didn't take Aura long to feel at home. Abi had been kind in welcoming her with dinner at the pub on her first night and told her that Edward Townsend, the other owner, had done the same for her when she'd first arrived. She'd introduced Aura to him the next day when they'd all been in the garden at the same time, soaking up the warm spring sunshine. But she hadn't yet met the other tenant, Harry Freeman.

'He's one of life's busy people,' Abi had told her. 'I've not really had a proper chat with him myself yet.'

But the next day, Aura saw him in the garden. He was obviously just back from work. His crisp white shirt was unbuttoned at the top and it looked as if he'd taken a tie off before coming outside. He was still wearing a pair of highly-polished shoes that looked so out of place in the garden. Aura longed for him to take them off and to feel the earth beneath his feet. He looked as if he needed a good grounding session.

She watched him for a moment as he sat on a bench, slumped over as though all the air had been knocked out of him. His skin was pale as if he didn't spend enough time outdoors and had rarely seen the sun, and his brow was furrowed. She thought about approaching him, but then he closed his eyes against the brightness and she didn't want to disturb his moment of peace.

It had been one of those weeks, Harry thought as he threw his head back and closed his eyes against the evening sun. He felt like he'd poured his full self into it, but had only got half back – if that. Work had been very trying indeed. He'd come up with one of the best product slogans in the whole of his career, had worked on his pitch for weeks and then the client had pulled out and gone with another company. Of course, his boss had looked at Harry as if it was his fault. Then, one of his favourite colleagues had announced he was leaving. Off to see South America, he'd said. Walking the Inca Trail. Canoeing down the Amazon. Camping out in rainforests. Things you couldn't do in Sussex apparently.

Then there was the small problem of Letitia Stevens. She was smart, hardworking and ambitious. She also appeared to have a crush on Harry although it was hard to tell because she played this push and pull game with him – flirting one moment and then swiping him with a barbed comment the next. He couldn't work her out. He certainly wasn't attracted to her. She scared him if he was absolutely honest.

He thought of the way she'd smiled as she came into his office with a box of doughnuts the other day.

'It's Pete's birthday so I bought these,' she'd said with a seductive smile as she pushed the box towards him.

'Oh, I'm not really into doughnuts,' he'd said.

'*Not* into doughnuts?' She'd thrown her head back and laughed and then she'd pouted at him, her red lipstick looking somehow predatory. 'You *have* to have one. Here – the one with the purple icing.' She was perching on the edge of his desk now like a cat.

Harry had stared at the vivid purple doughnut which had looked positively radioactive, but his hand dipped into the box to take it.

'There – that's better,' Letitia had said before sashaying out of his office.

He'd given the doughnut to Pete when he was quite sure Letitia wasn't around.

Harry suspected that it would be easy to fall under the spell of Letitia Stevens. With that dark glossy bob and beautiful figure, she was certainly attractive and he knew she had half the men in the company at her beck and call, but Harry hadn't fallen. He'd had his share of girlfriends and he missed having a woman in his life since breaking up with his last girlfriend, but he'd known they weren't right together. Colette had been sweet and kind and a lot of fun to be around, but there just hadn't been that spark between them and they'd kind of fizzled. He'd known that leaving London for the Brighton office would be a catalyst in their relationship and that it wouldn't survive the transition and he'd been right. Dates had turned into phone calls which had morphed into texts and then just slowly faded into nothing.

Life, he thought. What was it all about? You worked. You worked some more. You dated, but you were always too caught up in work for it to go anywhere. And then, when you were finally home from work, you could do nothing but *think* about work. How was that living?

He took a deep breath. He needed to learn how to relax properly because this sitting in a garden business was all very well, but his mind was still going at a hundred miles an hour. But at least the day was over. Even if he couldn't switch off completely, there was still something about Winfield that was deeply comforting. It was like a refuge – a special place where the outside world couldn't touch you. If you made sure you switched your phone off, that was.

He sat for a little longer before getting up and looking down the length of the walled garden. And that's when he saw her. She was sitting on a bench near the lean-to greenhouse, her eyes closed as if in meditation. He couldn't help envying her the peace which seemed to be radiating from her. She looked so at ease with life. She knew how to sit in a garden, he thought. And how pretty she was. She looked like a kind of flower fairy with her fine red hair billowing out behind her in the breeze and her legs stretched out in front of her. Harry was instantly captivated and slowly approached, noticing the delicate freckles on her porcelain skin as he got closer.

'Hello,' he said.

Her eyes snapped open and she gasped.

'Sorry – I didn't mean to disturb you,' he said quickly, hands in the air in heartfelt apology.

'That's okay,' she said with a shy smile.

'Are you sure? You looked so peaceful sitting there.'

'It's a good place to be peaceful in.'

Harry looked around and nodded. 'I guess it is,' he replied. 'I don't really have much time to sit out here, I'm afraid.'

She frowned at him as if he was completely mad. 'Really?' He shook his head. 'But that's such a shame. To live somewhere like this and not have the time to just sit and enjoy it.'

Harry motioned to the bench and she nodded and he sat down beside her.

'I'm Harry. Harry Freeman.'

'Aurora,' she said, 'but I usually go by Aura.'

They shook hands.

'I have to say, I've never met an Aurora before. Or an Aura. It's wonderfully unusual.'

She smiled.

'You've just moved in, haven't you?' he said.

'That's right. I have the apartment just there.' She pointed across the garden.

'I'm round the other side.'

'How long have you been here?'

'Since August.'

'Lucky you!'

'Yes. I had the honour of renting the very first apartment available.'

'It's a magical place, isn't it?' she said.

He sighed and he could feel her eyes upon him as he nodded.

'What do you do?' she asked. 'As a job?'

'I'm in advertising.'

'And you enjoy it?'

'Yes. I do. I mean, sure. The creative side, you know? But there's a lot of other stuff. Stuff that gets in the way. Stressful stuff.'

'I guess that's the same with most jobs.'

'I guess,' he said and he sighed again.

'You sigh a lot,' she said gently.

'Pardon?'

'I said you sigh a lot.'

'Do I?'

She nodded and he laughed at her unashamed honesty.

'I guess it's been one of those sighing days,' he confessed.

'It's fine to sigh,' she said. 'In fact, it's good. It's an exhale. Our exchange of life forces with the universe.'

He watched as she took a deep breath in and then slowly released it in a beautifully long exhale, her whole body seeming to relax as she did so. Then she fixed him with her bright eyes and he found himself taking a deep breath in and then releasing it into the depths of the garden.

She smiled. 'Good?'

'Yeah!'

She repeated the process as did he and, the more he did it, the better he felt.

'Hey, I feel really good,' he said after a few rounds.

'You sound surprised.'

'I am. I was sitting over there for the longest time,' he said, nodding towards the other bench in the garden.

'The longest?' she asked, not looking convinced.

'Well, ten minutes perhaps, but that's a pretty long time for me to just sit and do nothing. But I couldn't seem to relax. Not properly. Not like now. How come you've fixed that in like two minutes?'

A little smile danced across her mouth. 'I'm betting you were thinking while you were sitting.'

'Of course.'

'Then you should try not to.'

He could feel his forehead crease in a frown. 'What do you mean? How do you stop thinking?'

'You should distract your mind by focusing on your breath. Doing nothing but breathing – in and out – takes the attention away from all those thoughts that crowd our mind and vie for our attention.'

Harry considered this for a moment. 'There might be something in that.'

'You've just forgotten how to breathe,' she told him, matter-of-factly. 'Most people have and it's a terrible thing to forget because it's the very essence of us.'

Harry had been looking across the garden, but he turned to face his companion again.

'You're really into this, aren't you?' he said.

'You could say that.'

'Is it what you do for a living?'

She smiled and he couldn't help noticing how her eyes

sparkled.

'I teach yoga, meditation and mindfulness. Among other things.'

'Really? As your job?'

'Yes, as my job!' She laughed.

'Sorry! I didn't mean to sound rude. It's just that I didn't know you could do something like that as a job.'

'Well, you can.'

There was that smile again, Harry noticed, so pure and radiant. He couldn't remember when he'd seen somebody smile like that. The smiles he saw at work were always so loaded. They were a kind of an exchange – if you do this job right, I'll reward you with a smile. But this woman sitting next to him wasn't asking anything of him. She was giving smiles freely as if her soul was loaded with an excess of them.

'Tell me more,' he found himself saying.

'About what? My job?'

'Yes. How does one get into meditating for a living?'

'Well, I suppose it all began with the diamond brooch.'

It was Harry's turn to smile. He'd never heard an opening like that before.

'I was living in this place that was pretty ugly. It had these flats and office blocks that seemed to suck all the life and light out of the place. But there was this one shop – a jewellers – and that was like a beacon of beauty. I remember walking past it one day on the way home from school. I always stopped to look at the pieces on display and one day I saw the most amazing thing. It was a large diamond brooch – one of those Victorian pieces of showy jewellery shaped like a starburst. But it wasn't the brooch that mesmerised me – it was what it was sitting on.'

'What was it sitting on?' Harry asked, leaning a little closer.

'I didn't know at the time. I'd never seen anything like it so I dared to go in the shop and ask. I remember the lady laughed and told me it was an amethyst cluster. She brought it out of the window for me and I'll never forget the way it twinkled and winked so darkly at me under the lights of the shop. It was the most beautiful thing I'd ever seen. It was like a little piece of heaven had landed in that ugly corner of the world just for me to see. It was an instant connection.'

'And how does that fit in with you teaching meditation?' Harry asked.

'Well, shortly after the amethyst encounter, we moved to Brighton and there was a crystal shop,' she told him. 'I was just wandering the backstreets one day when I saw it. It was called Rainbow Crystals.'

'Is it still there?' he asked.

'It is! And I'll never forget my first visit. I walked though the door and was just hit by the smell of incense and the sight of all these different coloured crystals. The lady who ran it, Sylvie, looked like something out of a fairytale. She must have been in her fifties, but had all this long blonde hair tied up with coloured scarves and her fingers were adorned with huge crystal rings and there were crystal beads on her wrists and round her neck. I'd never seen anyone like her before and, well, I never have since.' Aura smiled at the memory of her.

'She had this catchphrase,' Aura went on and then stopped. 'Sorry, am I boring you with all this?'

'Not at all!' Harry said. 'Go on – what was her catchphrase?'

'It was, "There's a crystal for that!" Whatever your problem was, she'd have a crystal that could help you through it,' Aura told him. 'Can you imagine that? I'd walk in there after school with all the woes of the world on my teenage shoulders and she'd hand me this beautiful crystal and the tension of the day would just melt away.'

'You're saying they really work?'

'They do if you want them to.'

Harry took this information in. 'Then what happened?'

'Well, you know the saying, "like a kid in a candy store"? Well, crystals are even better. The stones were so much prettier than any sweet and they wouldn't get me into trouble with my dentist. But I never had enough pocket money. I bought little tumbled stones to begin with, collecting them in a bowl at home, but that only satisfied me for a little while and I longed to own larger pieces. So I begged Sylvie to give me a Saturday job. It wasn't much money, but it helped me start my own crystal collection and I learned so much working alongside her, and it was such a joy to spend the whole day surrounded by crystals. I learned how ancient civilisations used crystals for healing and in ceremonies and were even buried with them. I learned about geology and geography – discovering where different rocks and crystals came from and how they were formed. And I learned about the properties of colour and how we can tune into that and how we can use crystals as tools to help us find inner peace.'

Harry nodded and Aura cocked her head to one side, studying him.

'You're looking sceptical.'

'Am I?' he said.

'Yes, and believe me – I know what sceptical looks like in my line of work.'

'I didn't mean to offend you.'

'You didn't.'

'It's just – well – this is all new to me. I thought crystals were – well – just rocks.'

'Hold out your hand,' she told him. He frowned. 'Trust me!'

'Okay,' he said, doing as he was told.

'And close your eyes.'

He waited a moment, feeling the warmth of the evening air whisper gently over his face and the vulnerability of his open hand presented to this woman. A few seconds later, he felt a small weight upon it.

'You can touch it,' she said. 'How does it feel?'

Harry's fingers closed around it. 'Rough,' he said. 'A little sharp here and there.'

'Anything else?'

'It feels cool. Comfortable. There's a ridge – just here – where my thumb can rest.'

He heard Aura laugh. 'You've plugged into it.'

'I have?'

'That's the term I use. That comfortable feeling when you physically connect with a stone or crystal.'

'Can I open my eyes now?'

'Yes.'

He did so and looked at the crystal he'd been holding and getting to know.

'It's an amethyst, isn't it?' he said.

'Hold it up to the light. Is it just purple?' she asked him.

He gazed into its translucent depths. 'Oh, wow! There's yellow in it too.'

'That's citrine – a lovely yellow stone. But, here, it's mixed with amethyst so it's called ametrine.'

'Ametrine? Amethyst and citrine.'

'That's right. It's very popular in jewellery. If you can cut a ring so that you get both the yellow and the purple, it can be worth a lot of money.'

'And this piece?'

'It's just a cheap rough piece. One of the first I bought in fact. I just adore that flash of warm yellow glowing deep inside the purple.'

'It is lovely.'

'So, not just a rock then?'

He grinned. 'I see I have a lot to learn.'

'When I worked in the shop, I didn't realise how much I was learning just by listening to Sylvie and reading a few books. At first, I was too shy to test my new knowledge out on customers but, slowly, Sylvie began to push me towards them so that I wasn't just in there dusting shelves and working on the till. She expected me to listen to the customers and guide them in their purchases. It was terrifying at first. What if a customer needed a crystal for a specific thing and I gave them the wrong one? Sylvie would laugh at me and tell me to relax. Let my intuition be my guide. So I grew in confidence and then a strange thing happened. When I gave myself permission to relax, I noticed how the customers seemed to respond. If I wasn't around, Sylvie told me they would ask for me. "See!" she told me. "They have confidence in you." And that was a real boost. They believed in me in a way that my own family and teachers at school never had. It didn't take long before I was leading meditation sessions with crystals. There was a tiny room at the back of the shop for treatments and, well, that was the beginning.'

Harry took another look at the ametrine before passing it back to her and watching as she popped it into a pocket in her dress.

'Have you got a crystal that will give me more energy?' he half-joked. 'I've been feeling like I've got a slow puncture or something.'

'You'd like a crystal?'

Harry shrugged. 'Maybe.'

'I've got a piece of carnelian you can have.' She got up from the bench and gave him an encouraging smile as if to follow her, which he did.

They crossed the garden and entered the hall via an open French door into her apartment.

'It's a little messy, I'm afraid. I haven't unpacked everything yet. But I think I might just have a little something you can have...'

Harry looked around the room as she searched through a couple of boxes. Like all the rooms he'd seen at Winfield, it was bright and spacious with white-washed walls that bounced the light around making you feel as if you'd discovered heaven right here on earth. But Aura had already made this place her own and Harry took in the colourful mandala wall hanging and a framed print of the full moon. And, everywhere, there were candles and lamps and crystals – an Aladdin's cave of colour and light.

'And here it is!' Aura said a moment later, presenting him with a small red stone. Just a small carnelian, I'm afraid, but very nice to hold in your hand. It's a palm stone.'

Harry held it up to the light and noticed not only the rich claret-red, but faint white lines running through it too.

'It's a lovely thing, but what do I do with it?'

'You hold it whenever you need that little hit of energy or to remind yourself that you are strong and capable and that you can handle whatever life throws at you.'

'And this stone will help?' he asked.

'There's a word I really like. Psychogeology,' Aura said. 'It means the influence of geology on the mind.'

'So it won't help unless I believe it will?'

'Well, I like to think of crystals as tools. They won't do the job for you, but they'll make it a lot easier if you use them.'

Harry nodded. 'I like that.'

'You do?'

'We all need a little help sometimes, don't we?'

'Oh, yes,' she agreed.

'So, I keep it in my pocket?'

She nodded. 'You can bring it out or just touch it in your pocket – a touch stone, if you like, ready for whenever you need it.'

'What do I owe you?' he asked.

'Oh, no! It's a gift.'

Harry was touched by her kindness. 'Thank you.'

'Just let me know how you get on with it and if you'd...' She stopped.

'What?'

'I was just wondering if you'd like a treatment sometime. I mean, only if you think you'll benefit. If you think it might help you with your...' She paused and bit her lower lip.

'My general depletedness?' Harry suggested.

'I wasn't going to say that. But, if you'd like to have a session with me, we could go through a few relaxing techniques that you could count on whenever you're feeling stressed.'

Harry, who'd never in a million years thought he'd agree to such a thing, found he was nodding. 'I'd like that.'

'You would?'

'I really would.'

He turned to go, giving her a smile and taking one last smile of hers with him, and that's when he noticed something. She wasn't wearing any shoes and a pair of very pretty feet greeted his eyes, their nails painted a sparkly sky-blue.

CHAPTER FOUR

It was a warm May morning when Abi left Winfield for the short journey to see her sister. Ellen Fraser, her husband Douglas and their two daughters, Bethanne and Rosie, had recently sold their large townhouse and had moved into a semi-detached cottage in a small village. The idea was to simplify life – to cut down on bills and to enable Douglas to spend more time at home with his family rather than working long and stressful hours to pay their massive mortgage.

Abi hadn't seen the home yet even though they'd been in a whole month now.

'Not yet, not yet!' her sister would cry down the phone. 'It's a horrible mess!'

'It can't be any worse than Winfield was when I moved in,' Abi said, but Ellen wouldn't hear of it. She wanted her new home as perfect as she could get it before anyone saw it. What Ellen didn't know was that Bethanne had already given Abi a little tour using Ellen's phone. She'd laughed at her ten-year old niece's technical know-how.

Now, as she approached the village, she looked out for the brick and flint cottage on the country lane, parking her car a moment later in the little gravel driveway that was big enough for at least three cars. It was a pretty house with a red-tiled roof and a yellow-painted door but, as she got out and approached it, she noticed the door paint was flaking and there was some coming off the window frames too, and grass was growing out of the guttering.

'It's a lot more work than I imagined,' Ellen confessed as Abi entered the cottage a moment later. 'I'm not sure we should have taken it on.' Her fingers pinched the end of a piece of loose wallpaper, giving it an experimental tug. 'When we first moved in, the boiler kept stalling. We've spent a small fortune on that alone. Honestly, there's so much to do. I thought it would just be a bit of painting and decorating, but it's more than that apparently. You were so lucky having Edward and all those builders doing the work for you. You always were the lucky one.'

Abi sighed inwardly. There it was again. Ellen was forever saying that and it hurt Abi because, although she'd had a fair amount of luck in her professional life, she had nevertheless worked extremely hard in order to get that lucky. And as for her personal life, well that had been one big disaster with her relationship with Dante ending when she'd found out she was pregnant – something he hadn't been happy about. But it had been his reaction to her subsequent miscarriage which had been the real deal breaker for Abi.

'Ellen,' she said now, trying to keep calm, 'you have a beautiful home here. Yes, it's a little rough around the edges and needs some time and money spent on it, but you knew that. It's not like your old place that had every modern convenience you needed and a few more too. But you weren't happy there. You said it was putting too much financial pressure on you and Douglas.'

'I know.'

'Don't forget that, will you?'

'I haven't. It's just that this all seems so insurmountable!'

Abi rested a hand on her sister's shoulder. 'Things always do at first. You can't expect everything to be perfect right away. It's going to take time. But you'll get there especially with Douglas having more time at home now.'

Ellen didn't say anything and Abi couldn't help read the message in her silence.

'That's a good thing, right?' Abi prompted, noticing that Ellen hadn't mentioned Douglas herself.

'I'm not sure,' Ellen said with a sigh.

'What do you mean, you're not sure?'

'It's funny having him at home more.'

Abi frowned. 'Ellen, you were complaining that he was away all the time!'

'I know, I know. But the house was always – well – my domain, and now he's here more, it just feels odd.'

Abi sighed. There really was no pleasing her sister, was there? She walked through the kitchen, noting the old-style units and the cracked linoleum floor that had yet to be replaced. It wasn't a pretty sight, but she didn't dare draw any attention to it for fear of another round of complaints from Ellen. Instead, she looked out of the window onto the garden at the back of the property.

'The garden's wonderful,' Abi said. 'So lovely for the girls and Pugly.' She waved at her nieces who were playing out there with the dog. As they saw her, they picked Pugly up and came tearing back into the house.

'Aunt Abi!'

'Hi girls! How are you? How's my little dog nephew?'

They laughed. 'He's just pooped on a garden gnome!' Rosie said.

'You have a gnome?'

'The previous owners left it,' Ellen told her, 'which won't surprise you when you see it. It's hideous!'

'That's why Pugly pooped on it!' Bethanne declared. 'It was on its back staring up at the sky and Pugly went to the bathroom on its face.'

Abi laughed at the graphic description. 'Poor gnome! I'm sure he didn't deserve that.'

'Have you seen our bedrooms?' Rosie asked.

'Not yet!'

With that, Rosie grabbed Abi's hand and dragged her up the stairs at such a speed that she barely had time to notice the tired old floral stair carpet.

'This is my room!' Rosie declared with all the delight of a little girl who hadn't yet outgrown walls painted bubblegum pink.

'It's very cheerful,' Abi said.

'Come and see mine, Aunt Abi,' Bethanne said politely from the door. Abi followed her into a much more subdued room. The walls were grey, but it wasn't a pale warm grey nor was it a characterful steely-grey, but something in between that just looked a bit washed out.

'Mum said I can paint it whatever colour I want,' Bethanne said, trying to sound enthusiastic.

'And what will you choose?' Abi asked.

'Yellow, I think – like your sunflowers.'

Abi smiled, touching the silver locket she always wore which contained her very first sunflower sketch. 'That sounds perfect!'

'Aunt Abi!' Rosie called through from her bedroom. 'You can see the poopy gnome from my window. Come and see!'

Abi stayed for another hour, having a cup of tea and then playing with the girls and taking them for a walk with Pugly in the local woods. When they got back, Ellen was on her hands and knees scrubbing out one of the kitchen cupboards.

'Filthy beasts, the previous owners!' she complained.

Abi dared to look into the cupboard, but couldn't see anything worth cursing about.

'I don't suppose you've had any time to use the sewing machine?' Abi asked, remembering how she'd gone to get their mother's much-loved possession from their Aunt Claire's house.

'Hah! Time! Let me know where I can get some of that from.' She went on scrubbing, her arms going back and forth like angry pistons. Abi decided to leave her to it.

'I'd better be off.'

'Yes, go back to your immaculate manor where you have all the time in the world to do a bit of sketching!'

Abi didn't say anything even though she felt stung by the callous words. Perhaps she'd caught her sister at a bad time.

After hugging her nieces and squashing noisy kisses on to their cheeks, then giving Pugly an affectionate tickle, Abi left the cottage feeling very disgruntled. Her sister, she realised, was one of those people who was never happy in life and who seemed to thrive on that very fact.

Edward had just finished consulting with one of the builders when he saw Abi come into the hall. Unusually for her, she didn't look happy and Edward instinctively felt he should check on her.

'Hey, Abi!' he called as he came down the stairs.

'Edward – hi!' she said, her voice not as bright as he was used to hearing it.

'Just sorting out that leaky skylight,' he told her.

'Oh, good. It's such a lovely feature, isn't it?'

'It is, but we can't have it dripping all over the place,' he said. 'You okay?'

She nodded, but her eyes betrayed her. She looked as if she might have been crying.

'Really okay?' he asked and he saw her swallow.

'I've – erm – just been to see my sister.'

'Ellen, right? With the two girls?'

'Yes. They've just moved house and – well – you don't want to hear all about that.' She'd crossed to her door now, her hand in her bag to find the key.

'Of course I do.'

She turned around. 'You do?'

Edward checked his watch. 'Listen, it's a bit late, but I've not had any lunch yet. How about we go out for some? My treat.'

'Won't the pub have stopped serving food now?'

'We can go into Lewes. Plenty of places there.'

'Actually, I am quite hungry.'

'So your sister didn't feed you?'

Abi smiled. 'No, she didn't. Come to think of it, I didn't even get a biscuit with my cup of tea.'

Edward shook his head. 'Shameful.'

She laughed and Edward realised that it was a sound he really liked.

'Let's have lunch,' she said and the two of them left Winfield together.

They found a little place on the edge of town that served food all day, placed their order and chose a table by the window.

Suddenly, Edward felt awkward and wondered why he'd suggested this. He hadn't spent a lot of time with Abi and it still felt new and slightly strange. Other than their swimming, of course, but that was different somehow. He tried to identify how as they waited for their food. Perhaps being outdoors helped him relax more. Outside, they had the whole world to focus on and, when there were fields to look at and a river to plunge into, there wasn't this strange nervousness that came from just sitting at a table in somebody's eye-line.

He cleared his throat, determined to ease himself into something approaching normal conversation. He'd asked Abi out to lunch after seeing her looking so lost and hurt. Her sweet vulnerability had touched him and it was silly to get all tongue-tied now.

'So, tell me more about your family,' he said.

Abi looked up from the napkin she'd been fiddling with. 'My sister, you mean?'

'Yes. Did you have a fight or something?'

'No. Not really a fight. At least, I didn't fight with her, but perhaps she was fighting with me. That's what it felt like.' Abi shrugged. 'I don't know. I don't understand her sometimes. She's always...' she stopped and began fiddling with her napkin again.

'What?'

'She's always in a bad mood.'

'Ah, I see.'

'She's never happy, you know? She's one of those people who can be heaped with blessings and good things and yet find fault and feel hard done by.'

'That must be difficult to be around,' Edward said.

'It is. I feel I can't always be myself around her. If I talk about good things, for example, she'll say, "Oh aren't you the lucky one" and then go on a tirade about how very *un*lucky she's been. I got a bit of that again today. I honestly think she believes I've never worked a day in my life – that I just sit at a table and idly sketch and that the business I built just magically formed itself with no real sweat or toil involved at all.'

'She doesn't believe your business took real hard work to build?' Edward shook his head.

'I think she's one of those people who equates art with ease. Because my business was based on my art and because that's something I love and have always had in my life, I think she believes that I've never had to work very hard. Don't get me wrong – I adore my art and I love spending time sketching and coming up with ideas, but that will only get you so far. You can't run a company by just doodling.'

'No, of course not,' Edward said, feeling sympathy for Abi. 'Have you talked to her about how you feel?'

'Not so that she ever really understands.' She sighed. 'And sometimes – I don't know – I can't help feeling there's a subtext to what she's saying.'

'How do you mean?'

Abi glanced out of the window to the street beyond. There was a busker playing a guitar and she focused on him for a moment before returning her gaze to Edward.

'I'm not sure. Douglas – that's my brother-in-law – he said something recently – that there are things Ellen says about me. That I'm lucky. And I don't think she just means the money I've made or the house I'm living in.'

'Then what does she mean?' Edward asked.

'Well, that's it – I don't know! Douglas says she clams up whenever he asks and I've never had the courage to ask directly. Maybe it's nothing.' She shrugged.

'It doesn't sound like nothing.'

'No. I just try to believe it is and ignore it, hoping it will go away. Hoping she'll change.' Abi gave a little laugh, but it sounded hollow and without the merest hint of merriment. 'I thought this move would help her be happy, but it's just given her a different set of things to complain about.'

'Oh, dear!' Edward said. 'I'm sorry to hear that.'

'Thanks,' Abi said, chancing a smile. 'It hurts – seeing how very unhappy my sister is all the time. There just seems to be this cloud of negativity surrounding her. Bethanne feels it. I know she does.'

'Which one is she?'

'The eldest daughter.'

'The eldest normally takes the brunt,' Edward said, remembering his own position growing up in the Townsend household.

'And Bethanne is particularly sensitive. She's artistic. Like me!' Abi smiled. 'And, well, we do tend to feel things more, I think. We're sensitive souls.' She glanced out of the window again. 'I'm sorry. I don't want to bore you with all my problems.'

'You're not boring me.'

'It's just silly family stuff.'

'Not at all. But, if it's any consolation, I think it's a sibling's job to try us, isn't it?' Edward suggested.

'I wouldn't be a bit surprised,' Abi replied. 'Is it like that for you too. With Oscar?'

Edward flinched. Why had he gone and mentioned siblings? He should have known he was opening himself up for questions. After all, that's what a conversation was and, so far, Abi had done most of the talking. Luckily, it was then that their food arrived which made a wonderful distraction from intimacy. At least for a few minutes.

'So, tell me about Oscar,' Abi continued.

Edward tried not to visibly bristle at the mention of his brother. 'What's to tell?' he said in as light a manner as possible and then loaded his fork with as much salad as possible in the hope of halting the conversation.

'Well, seeing as I know very little about him, I'd say there's quite a lot,' Abi said with an encouraging smile. 'He's younger than you, isn't he?'

'Yes.'

'And you get on?'

'We...' Edward paused. He found it so hard to talk about his family. 'We don't exactly see eye to eye, I'm afraid.'

'Oh, I'm sorry,' Abi said, frowning. 'What does he do?'

'As little as possible,' Edward said. 'The last he told me, he was working in a warehouse, which is ridiculous as he's bright. He could do anything he set his mind to, but he just doesn't have it in him to apply himself. For him, work is a means to an end.'

'And what's his end?' Abi asked.

'Having a good time which usually means some sort of destructive behaviour.'

'Oh, I see. And you're not like that?' Abi asked, a naughty smile hovering over her lips.

'What do you think?' Edward said with a small laugh.

'It always amazes me how different siblings can be. You and Oscar. Me and Ellen. Bethanne and Rosie. Do you think losing your parents has affected Oscar's behaviour perhaps?'

'Pardon?'

'Losing both your parents,' Abi repeated.

Edward tried not to show his discomfort. 'I don't know. Maybe.'

'I think these things affect us. Perhaps in ways we're not

even conscious of. I often wonder that about Ellen – if she'd be different if our mother had lived. I think she took on a lot after Mum died. I was so much younger, you see. I don't think it affected me in the same way.'

'Do you remember her?'

'My mother? Little bits and pieces. I remember her tucking me in at night and calling me her little angel. And running through the park kicking autumn leaves together. She used to love having her hair brushed and I loved to do it for her. I'd brush it until it shone and then she'd do mine.' Abi's eyes took on a wistful look. 'So we're both without our parents, aren't we?' she suddenly said.

Edward swallowed hard. 'It certainly feels that way.'

'You miss them, don't you?'

Edward looked up from his plate, straight into the clear gaze of Abigail and found himself nodding.

'Who were you closest to?'

'My mother,' he said, finding it surprisingly easy to answer a question nobody had dared to ask him before. 'She was kind. Gentle. Maybe a bit too kind.'

'How do you mean?'

Edward's mind spiralled back to an evening when his father had come in drunk from the pub. A friend had dropped him home because he was too far gone to walk and he'd slumped into the hallway. Oscar had been in bed, but Edward was up and he'd watched as his mother had picked his father off the floor, ignoring the torrent of abuse she was getting from him.

'He's just had one too many,' she'd told Edward as he'd stared in horror at his the scene. 'You know how merry he gets.' Merry indeed.

But Edward couldn't tell Abi about that, could he?

'People would sometimes take advantage of her,' he said instead.

'That's rotten.'

'It is. It was.'

'And your dad?'

It was on the tip of Edward's tongue to say that his father had been the worst offender, but he didn't. He couldn't. There was something that shut off inside him whenever his father was mentioned.

'We weren't close,' he said. Well, that was true, wasn't it? They hadn't been close. Nor were they now. 'He was a worse version of my brother, I'm afraid.'

'Oh, Edward, I'm so sorry.'

'It's okay. It's all done.' That, at least, was something he kept telling himself even though he hadn't been able to completely sever ties with his father – like the most recent incident when Oscar had asked Edward to check up on the old man. Sometimes, Edward wondered if it had been a mistake buying Winfield Hall which was so close to his old family home where his father still lived.

Now, he lowered his gaze, aware that Abigail was looking at him and hoping that her questions about his family had ended.

'Families can be very trying, can't they?' she said. 'I think I've told you about my Aunt Claire? She's the one who brought me and Ellen up after our mother died. Only, she didn't really like children.'

'Not a good start.'

Abi smiled ruefully. 'It's hard to know what's normal and what isn't when you're growing up, isn't it? But we had the feeling that our childhood with Aunt Claire was a little odd. She took care of us in as much as we were fed and clothed, but that's where things ended with her. There was no... warmth. I remember going round to a friend's house once and seeing the way her mum buzzed around the place, making sure we were okay, giving us cookies and hugging my friend when she fell over in the garden. It was all so alien to me. My friend's mum even asked me questions and I'd never been asked questions before by an adult who wasn't a teacher. She asked me what my favourite sandwich was and then made it for me. Aunt Claire just used to give us whatever she was having only a slightly smaller portion. I still can't eat rice pudding to this day.'

Edward couldn't help smiling at that. 'Did you ever have friends round to yours?'

'Oh, no. That was strongly discouraged. What was it Aunt Claire used to say? "Children are noisy and messy and I haven't got time for either." The thing was, I never worked out what she did with all her time. She spent it alone downstairs while me and Ellen were upstairs. It was like cohabiting with a stranger because we never got to know her and she certainly was never interested in getting to know us and that's something that's hard to live with because you feel somehow that there might be something fundamentally wrong with you. Because a member of your own family really isn't that interested in you. That you don't matter.'

'But you know that's rubbish, don't you? You know we can't be responsible for other people's behaviour and that it certainly isn't a reflection of us as human beings,' Edward told her.

'I know. My mind tells me that, but my heart sometimes feels the ugliness of being rejected like that.' She sighed and then took a sip of her drink. 'But, hey! Then I remember all the good luck I've had in my life and the happiness I get from my work and the beautiful home I have at Winfield. And the new friends I've made.'

Edward nodded, seeing her smile. 'Oh, you mean me?' he said, suddenly realising.

'Well, of course I mean you, silly!'

He laughed, feeling flattered that this kind, sweet woman should think of him as a friend and not just somebody she shared a roof with.

They finished their meal and left the restaurant, arriving back at Winfield half an hour later.

'Thank you,' Abi said as they entered the hall. 'I really enjoyed that. It was good to talk.'

He nodded. 'My pleasure,' he said, and he meant it because something strange had happened – he'd talked. For the first time in a long time, Edward had opened up to another person and, while he might not have told the exact truth about everything, he'd certainly confessed a few things he'd never revealed to anybody before and that had felt good. He felt lighter somehow.

'We should do this again sometime,' she added, and then she did something that took him completely by surprise – she stood up on tiptoes and kissed his cheek. Edward felt so stunned that he didn't move for a few moments, but stood watching her walk towards her apartment door where she turned around and gave him a little wave.

CHAPTER FIVE

Harry Freeman's day hadn't been going well. His boss's nephew was on work placement for the week and Harry had the great honour of having the lad under his care. So far, he'd misfiled some important papers, lost two incoming calls and had spilt tea over the printer. Harry had then given the lad a pile of old magazines to go through, singling out any interesting adverts. Surely that was one job he couldn't mess up.

Working quietly in the peace of his office, Harry reached for the carnelian stone Aura had given him, feeling the comforting weight of it in the palm of his left hand. It was a pretty thing. So simple and yet it had the ability to capture the attention if you just gave yourself permission to look at it. He liked that. You could learn a lot from that, he thought, as he placed the stone on the corner of his desk where he could reach it.

There was a knock on his door and, before he had time to say come in, Letitia had waltzed inside.

'I've brought those files you wanted to see from Bernadette's team,' she said, placing them on his desk.

'Oh, thanks.'

'She wants them back later today.'

'I'll get to them right away,' he told her, waiting for her to leave, but she hesitated.

'What's this?' she asked, picking up the carnelian. 'Is it a crystal?'

'What? Oh, that! It's just a rock I'm using as a paperweight,' Harry said, watching as Letitia put it down.

'It's a pretty thing,' she said.

'I suppose,' Harry replied.

Letitia seemed to be studying him. 'I'll have it if you don't want it,' she said.

'Who said I didn't want it?'

She shrugged. 'You just don't seem that enamoured with it.'

It was then that a colleague's head popped round the door. 'Letitia – Joe from accounts is on the phone. Wants to have a word with you.'

'Oh, lord!' Letitia sighed. 'I'm afraid I have to go, darling.'

It was on the tip of Harry's tongue to say, "Don't let me stop you", but he thought that would just be rude so he nodded instead and watched in relief as she left. Then he closed his eyes, cursing himself.

A rock! Why had he said that? Why had he felt ashamed at having a crystal on his desk? He felt as if he'd somehow betrayed Aura by dismissing it as a mere rock whose only use was as a paperweight. She'd given him this gift and he'd accepted it too, graciously and gratefully, and yet he'd treated both her and it abominably. He picked up the carnelian now and shook his head as if in apology. Was it possible that these rocks could sense when you were misusing them? Did they harbour grudges? Could they curse you as well as bless you? Harry wasn't sure.

'Sorry,' he said to the stone now.

Gently, carefully, he placed the carnelian in the centre of his desk in a clear space all of its own where the light hit it in such a way that it turned a gloriously glossy red. There, he thought, it could never be mistaken for a paperweight.

When Harry got back to Winfield that evening, he paused in the hallway just by the stairs. His apartment was to the left, but Aura's was to the right. He took a deep breath, and crossed to her door, knocking a moment later. There was no telling if she was in of course, but he knew he wanted to see her again.

The door opened and there she stood, her long red hair loose around her shoulders and a tiny diamante sparkling in her nose. She was wearing a long turquoise dress and at least three bead necklaces which waterfalled down her slim body.

'Harry! How are you?' she asked with the best smile he'd seen all day, open and honest.

'I'm good. I just wanted to thank you.'

'Oh?'

'For the carnelian stone.'

'Has it worked its magic for you?'

'Yes! I've got it on my desk at work and I've been picking it up and holding it just like you said,' he told her, skilfully omitting how he had so casually dissed it in front of his work colleague.

'I'm so glad,' she said, that smile of hers radiating such warmth that Harry swore he could feel it in his belly.

'You mentioned teaching me,' he said hesitantly. 'About breathing, wasn't it?'

'That's right.'

'I'd like to book a session if I may.'

'Of course. When were you thinking of?'

'As soon as possible really,' he said with a sigh.

'There's one of those big sighs of yours,' she pointed out.

'Would you like a session this evening. Say eight o'clock? It's still lovely and light for a while. We could open the French doors and let some of that downland air in to help with our breathing.'

'Sounds great!' He grinned. There was something about being in Aura's presence that had him smiling like an idiot and it was a very pleasant feeling.

After taking a shower, changing clothes and making himself a light dinner, Harry sat watching the clock until he could venture across the hallway to Aura's.

She answered the door promptly and he could feel the evening breeze as he stepped inside and saw that she'd opened the French doors as promised. The room had been transformed since he'd seen it last with a large blue and green rug on the floor, making him feel as if he'd stepped into the sea. There was a large cream sofa over which was draped a colourful blanket in green and silver. There were mirrors on the walls, reflecting the light from the sash windows and, everywhere, there were little tables on which sat bowls full of crystals.

'Wow – it all looks amazing,' he said, trying to take it all in.

'Thank you. I wanted to try and create a calm environment.'

'You've succeeded.'

She smiled at that and he watched as she moved around the room, lighting candles everywhere.

'Do the candles help?' he asked.

'I find they do. I think it's important to get yourself into a sacred frame of mind and having a ritual – lighting candles, burning incense, helps with that.'

He nodded, more than willing to learn.

'Have you had a good day?' Aura asked.

'Not exactly.'

'Oh, dear. And is there anything in particular you'd like to work through tonight?'

'I'm not sure,' he said. 'To be honest, I've never done anything like this before, but it does kind of appeal to me – the idea of being able to sit and switch off.'

Aura nodded. 'Talking of sitting,' she motioned towards two large round cushions, one turquoise, one sea-green, which had been placed on the floor near the French doors. Harry sat on the green one.

'Before we begin, I just want us to loosen ourselves up a bit. Stretch your arms up in the air and then give your shoulders a roll. Maybe rock your head from side to side.'

'Oh, yeah!' Harry said a moment later when his neck cracked. 'So *that's* where I'm storing all my stress!'

Aura smiled. 'When you focus closely on your body, it will tell you all sorts of interesting things. It really is there to help you.'

They continued to do stretches for another minute.

'Okay, now find a position that's comfy,' Aura told him. 'One you can hold for a little while.'

Harry fidgeted a bit.

'We just want to settle ourselves first by getting comfortable and closing our eyes. By shutting off the sense of sight, we can focus on our other senses first and then, slowly, turn inward.'

Harry closed his eyes, slowly becoming aware of the breeze on his face from the downs, pure and refreshing after his day shut up in the office.

'And we want to start by taking some deep breaths just like we did in the garden. In through the nose, filling our lungs, and then sighing it out through the mouth.'

Harry breathed, filling his lungs with the glorious air and then sighing it out as he'd been told to. Why, after being on the planet for thirty-two years, had he only just discovered how to do this when it felt so good?

'When we breathe in,' Aura said, 'we're accepting all the good things that the world has to give to us and, when we breathe out, we're letting go of anything that is no longer needed. So think about what you no longer need in your life. Are there any problems you shouldn't be thinking about? Any issues you'd like to release? Take a big, deep breath and then, on the exhale, let all those problems go. Just let them go.'

Harry thought about the problems he'd had that day – all the little stresses and niggles that had mounted up and given him a headache. *Just let them go*, Aura was saying. Was it as simple as that? If it was, why hadn't someone told him before? It was like being handed a superpower. He was in control of his response to things.

'Just let them go,' she said again. And Harry did.

'And take another deep, refreshing breath in and, on the exhale, let it take away anything that is no longer serving you.'

Harry went on with the big, deep, lung-filling breaths, listening to Aura's gentle guidance, feeling the cool evening breeze on his skin and slowly letting his body relax as it hadn't relaxed in years.

'Now just let your breathing fall into a more natural pattern. Be aware of the movement in your body as you breathe. Be aware of it, but don't overthink it. We want to feel now, letting go of the hold that our thoughts have on us. Be mindful to be in the present moment. Don't think about the events of the day or what you might be doing tomorrow. That doesn't matter. All that matters, all that there is, is the present moment.'

Harry continued to focus on his breathing, waiting for the next thing Aura would tell him to do, but she didn't say anything for the longest time and so he opened his eyes. She was sitting opposite him, her eyes closed, her face calm. Just breathing. And he realised that that was part of it – the silence, the stillness. He was so used to filling every single minute, every single second of his life with noise and business, thoughts and productivity that he'd forgotten how to be silent and still. So he continued to sit and to breathe and to feel the sensations of his body without overthinking them. And, for a few blissful minutes, he truly forgot about the stresses of the day, the resentments he'd been holding on to, the pressure he'd been under to meet a deadline. It all drifted away somewhere outside of him.

'Notice any tension in your body,' Aura said after – well – Harry wasn't quite sure how long. 'Now take a deep breath, nice and full, breathing into that tense place. And, as you breathe out, let all that tension float away from your body. With every breath, feel yourself relaxing, becoming lighter, becoming your higher self.'

As well as his headache, Harry had had a crick in his neck, a niggle in his lower back and RSI in his right wrist for most of the day and he focused on those areas now, one at a time, patiently, giving each one its due attention, breathing into each of those spaces until he could feel them relaxing.

'We're looking for those spaces between thoughts,' Aura said gently at last. 'Those wondrous moments when we're not thinking at all. They can be elusive. Especially, if you've not meditated before. But they are there. Just let them come.'

Harry could feel that he was frowning. *The spaces between thoughts.* Did that mean you could stop thinking? The thought was revolutionary to him. So, he hadn't been doing that yet, obviously. He'd managed not to think about work and he hadn't been planning his day tomorrow as he'd been breathing, but he had been thinking about what he was doing – the breath he was taking in and releasing, how his body felt; he'd thought about the breeze whispering around his face and his mind had taken him on a little journey into the garden and he'd thought about how he'd met Aura sitting on the bench. He'd thought about how lucky he was to have found Winfield, and he'd been trying to work out how many of these sessions with Aura he could fit into and afford each week. So he hadn't really switched off. His mind had kept on chugging. Pleasant thoughts, they may have been, but thoughts nevertheless.

'If a thought pops into your head – which they will – just dismiss them. The stillness of your mind is the blue sky – it's always there, but it's sometimes obscured by thought clouds, but just let them drift by. Don't attach yourself to any one of them. Return to that high blue sky beyond thought.'

Harry concentrated. *Don't think. Don't think.* But then, thinking those thoughts *was* thinking, wasn't it? It was very confusing and a lot harder than he'd imagined. He wasn't sure what he'd been expecting – maybe he'd thought he'd just fall in to a pleasant, doze-like state and it would all be easy. A massage for the mind, perhaps. But this was hard.

'Don't beat yourself up if thoughts keep popping up,' Aura said as if reading his mind. 'Just acknowledge them and let them float by. You don't have to give them any power by holding on to them.'

He liked that. He must remember all this. Maybe he should write it down or get Aura to record it for him. Drat! He was thinking again, wasn't he? So he returned to his breath. In and out. In and out. Like waves on the shore. Never ending. Soothing. Life-giving. In and out.

'We're going to open our eyes in a moment but, before we do, we want to slowly come back into our bodies. Wiggle your toes, your fingers. Maybe rock your head from side to side. Just slowly. Take a couple of deep breaths again and then gently open your eyes.'

Harry wiggled and rocked and then opened his eyes, his gaze finding Aura who was sitting opposite him on her cushion, her long red hair blowing in the breeze. The sky had darkened a little and the air had cooled since they'd begun. And something else had changed too – him.

'How do you feel?' Aura asked.

'Like I'm about to float away!' he said with a laugh.

'Would you like to do some more grounding work? Make sure we've got you properly rooted to the earth before you stand up?'

'No, no. I feel wonderful just as I am!'

'Good. Well, just take a moment before you get up.'

He nodded. 'Can I ask you something?'

'Of course.'

'Is it good not to think? I mean, it felt good to switch off like that even if it was for just a few seconds at a time, but I also feel that it's not natural. I feel like – well – maybe I shouldn't be wasting time just sitting with my eyes closed.' He paused, realising what he'd said. 'Sorry – I shouldn't have said "wasting time". That's not a reflection on you – it's merely how I feel about sitting still and not working.'

'It's okay. It's perfectly natural to feel that way,' Aura assured him. 'It's because we've been conditioned to think all the time. It's our default setting if you like. Our minds rule us. Our thoughts govern us. It's called having a monkey mind.'

'*Monkey* mind?'

'Yes!' Aura said with a light laugh. 'You know – that endless chatter that we carry around inside our heads. We leap from one topic to the next like a naughty, playful monkey – sometimes not even finishing a thought. It can be exhausting.'

Harry nodded, knowing that feeling alright.

'So learning to control that, making time to switch that off, can only be a good thing. And it's not forever, is it? We can return to our thoughts and you may even find they become sharper and more focused if you take the time to meditate every once in a while.'

'So we're in control of our thoughts?' Harry asked, coming to terms with this idea.

'Oh, yes. It sometimes doesn't feel like it, I know, but we are. It's the one thing we are in control of. We can't always control what's happening around us, but we can control our response to it.'

'Wow!' Harry cried. 'This is all amazing. I never expected...' he stopped.

'Never expected...?'

'I never expected to make all these discoveries in a twenty minute session.'

Aura frowned. 'Twenty minutes? We were meditating for fifty.'

'*Fifty* minutes? No way!'

'Time takes on a new dimension, doesn't it?'

They smiled at one another.

'Listen, I'd love to book another session if I may.'

'Of course you may.' He watched as Aura walked across to a little table where a small salt lamp glowed and she opened a diary.

'There's a full moon's next week. Shall we book a full moon meditation? We could go out into the garden if the weather's warm.'

Harry grinned. 'Why not? And thank you for tonight. I'm so glad I did this.'

When Harry returned to his apartment, he made a conscious effort not to switch on the TV to watch the news or to pick up his phone or check his email. He wanted to guard that peaceful feeling he'd gained with Aura for a little longer. So he sat in the chair he'd placed by the large sash window and gazed at the darkening shapes of the downs and watched as the first stars silvered the sky.

And, that night, he had the best sleep of his life.

CHAPTER SIX

May was proving to be a glorious month and Abi didn't want to waste a minute of it. Most days, she got up early, pottered around the garden, planting seeds, digging beds and keeping the weeds down, and then she'd have breakfast before heading out into the hills with her sketchbook. She was working on a series of linocuts of the wildflowers she loved so much, using her new printing press and marvelling at the results. This was a new territory and what was wonderfully freeing was the fact that she was doing this just for her. There was no business plan. She didn't even have so much as an Etsy store – she was simply making art for art's sake. It really was going a long way to making her content and keeping her from brooding on the behaviour of her sister.

Abi still felt sore from her last encounter with Ellen and hadn't been in contact with her since. But she knew she'd cave in before too long. It was always the same pattern: Ellen would say or do something to hurt Abi. Abi would slink away and lick her wounds, hoping against hope that Ellen would call and apologise – which she wouldn't – and then Abi would be the one to reach out. So much for this house move providing the cure-all for her sister that Abi and Douglas had been hoping for. Abi guessed that it took more than that to change a personality.

But Abi wasn't going to think about her sister today. Today was for art and scenery and friendship for she was going to sketch, walk and pay her friend Ronnie a visit. For a moment, she thought about cycling to his village on the new bike she'd just bought. She'd taken it out for its first spin just yesterday and had loved the exhilarating feel of the wind in her hair but, today, she needed a more sedate pace.

As she followed the path she was beginning to know so well, Abi luxuriated in the warm air that seemed full of birdsong and the scents of spring. Days like these shouldn't be spent indoors, she determined, thinking of all the hours she'd spent in her previous role, running her company, and not even noticing if the sun was shining or not. Life choices so often meant making sacrifices, Abi knew that, and she knew how blessed she was now.

When she'd filled a few of her pages and taken some photos and then had the light lunch she'd brought out with her, she followed the path along the ridge. The sky was a vibrant blue, but there were some large clouds hanging low and, every now and again, Abi would walk through the shade they cast, marvelling at the warmth of the sun once she returned to it, knowing it was a gift not to be taken for granted.

As she descended into the village where Ronnie lived, she glanced at the time on her phone. It was just after two in the afternoon. It was quiet in the lane. A cat sat on a high red-brick wall watching the world go by and Abi could hear the distant sound of a lawn mower from a garden further along the lane.

Of course, Ronnie's garden was lush with late spring loveliness and she admired the indigo of the irises and the pink shock of roses that climbed the front of his house, half obscuring the front door which was wide open. She took a moment to take it all in, listening to a fat bumblebee as it made its drowsy way from flower to flower, and then she heard the happy sound of whistling coming from the depths of the garden.

'Ronnie?' she called.

'Is that you, Abi?' He emerged from behind an apple tree. 'What a lovely surprise.'

'I hope it's okay just to drop in unannounced?'

'That's the very best way to drop in,' he assured her. 'You walk, did you?'

'Of course!'

'Fancy a drink?'

'I'd love one.'

'Outside or in?'

'Outside please!'

'Good choice.'

She followed him inside as he made them both a cup of tea which they took out into the garden, sitting on a mossy bench in the orchard.

'Best blossom in years,' Ronnie said, gazing up into the pearly pink depths of the trees. 'Should be a good harvest come the autumn.'

'There's always something to look forward to when you garden, isn't there?'

'Oh, yes!'

They sat in companionable silence for a while and then Ronnie spoke. 'How are you, Abi?'

'I'm well.' She turned to look at him, knowing that he wasn't just asking after her physical health. 'I take each day one at a time. I look for the positives and I work. And walk.' She smiled.

'Good. Good.'

'There are tricky days,' she said, her voice a whisper.

Ronnie nodded. 'Always.'

'But the good ones outweigh them now.'

'And that's as it should be,' he told her. 'Life really does go on even though we sometimes leave a little piece of ourselves in the past.'

Abi felt tears prick at her eyes at his words. He was quite the poet.

'And that reminds me,' he said before she could dwell on sadness for a moment longer, 'I notice you always wear that silver locket.'

Abi's hands instinctively reached to touch it. 'I do. It's my lucky charm. Look.' With careful fingers, she opened it to reveal a tiny image of a sunflower. 'It's a miniature of the sketch that kind of launched my business.'

Ronnie chuckled. 'Did you know it would at the time?'

'No! I doodle a lot of things and this one – I don't know – there was just something about it. Right flower, right time?' She laughed. 'I think the world could always use more sunflowers.'

'Oh, yes,' Ronnie agreed. 'Come with me. I'd like to show you something.' He got up from the bench and beckoned her with one of his old, gnarled hands. She followed him back to the house where they put their cups down in the living room before Ronnie led her into the hall and climbed the stairs. Abi hadn't been upstairs in the little cottage and was fascinated to see it. There were photos hanging on the walls up the stairs – faces from the past. Relatives, she guessed, wearing clothes from another era but smiles that transcended all time. Reaching the landing, she saw that three rooms led off it: a bathroom and two bedrooms. It was the smaller of the two bedrooms that Ronnie led her into, home to a single bed, an old wardrobe and a dressing table.

'It's the guest room only I don't have a lot of guests,' he confessed. 'Still, I like to keep it ready just in case someone wants to visit.'

'It's lovely,' Abi said, noticing the wallpaper, faded and fragile, but still so pretty with its delicate repeat pattern of peonies. The sash window was open and Abi noticed great purple swags of wisteria dangling across it and the view out over the garden was beautiful. Any guest would be lucky to stay here, she thought.

It was then that Abi noticed a wooden photo frame on the dressing table and she approached it.

'That's my Emma,' Ronnie told her.

'What a beautiful picture,' Abi said. It was black and white and showed a young woman standing on a cliff overlooking the sea, her right hand holding onto a hat that was about to take flight otherwise. But it was her smile that was so mesmerising. It was so all-encompassing.

'Devon nineteen-seventy...,' he paused. 'Seventy something or other. Emma was always great with dates, but me – well – not so much. She could tell you the dates I had fillings put in and teeth pulled out.'

Abi watched as Ronnie opened a drawer in the dressing table and pulled out a wooden box inlaid with mother-of-pearl, placing it down gently and opening it.

'This is what I wanted to show you,' he said. 'Emma was a funny one. She didn't care much for diamonds or rubies, which was just as well as we never had money for such things.

Anyway, she was a gardener like me. A cook too. Splendid cook. Rings wouldn't have been much use to her. But there was something she was very keen on.'

He beckoned to Abi who came forward and peered into the box. There, inside the velvety depths were a collection of brooches. Abi's eyes took in the splendid sparkle of silver, gold, enamel and paste. There were stars and moons in clear paste and wild swirls and circles in deep blues and vibrant pinks. But it was a pretty gold filigree design that Ronnie picked up.

'Have a look at this,' he said and Abi took it from him, holding it up to the light and noticing the tiny harebell-like flowers in pink, blue and yellow which were entwined among the filigree.

'It's lovely. Such delicate workmanship,' she said. 'Do you know how old it is?'

'Ah, well, there's that thing with dates again,' Ronnie said, 'but I know Emma liked a few older pieces.'

'It looks old,' Abi said, turning it over to see the old catch.

'I don't suppose young women wear brooches much these days, but my Emma loved them. Always had one pinned to a blouse or cardigan.'

'I think they're wonderful. They should be more popular, shouldn't they?'

'Maybe you could bring them back into style?'

Abi looked down at the little brooch. 'That's not a bad idea.'

'Then I hope this might inspire you,' he said as she tried to hand it back to him. Instead of taking it, he covered her hand with his. 'It's yours now.'

Abi gasped. 'Oh, Ronnie! I can't take this! It's much too valuable.'

He shook his head. 'No, no. It's only a little bit of gold. The rest isn't anything special. A bit of enamel or some such thing.

And it needs to be loved. It needs a woman who'll appreciate it. I've got plenty more brooches to keep my Emma close to me, and I thought of you when I remembered this one.'

'Are you sure, Ronnie?'

He smiled softly and squeezed her hand that was holding the brooch. 'More than anything.'

'Then I shall treasure it always. Thank you.' She leaned forward and kissed his powder-soft cheek that smelt of the earth and of apple blossom and all good things from the garden.

He chuckled. 'It's been a long time since a pretty young woman kissed me!'

Abi carefully pinned the brooch onto her dress, delighted with how it looked and felt, and the two of them went back downstairs and out into the garden.

'You miss her, don't you?' she said and heard him sigh in response.

'Every day. I can't believe she's been gone two years now and I still haven't got used to it.'

Abi placed a hand on his shoulder. 'I'm so sorry. Life can be so mean sometimes to take our loved ones away.'

'It's the evenings that I find difficult. Not so much at this time of year when I can spend them out in the garden. But, when the nights start drawing in and there's all this silence inside the house. We used to talk all evening about our day, preparing our meal together. It was a simple ritual, but it was so much a part of us and that's gone now.' He gave a little sniff. 'I'm a bit of a spare part in my own home.'

'Oh, Ronnie!'

He gave another sniff – a little bigger this time. 'No, no! I mustn't go on. Plenty to be grateful for.'

Abi squeezed his shoulder. 'Well, I have *you* to be grateful for,' she told him.

'My dear,' he said. 'And I have you.'

One of the things Harry had promised to do when moving to Sussex was to spend more time with his parents only that hadn't actually happened yet other than at Christmas. The truth was, his new role was so all-encompassing and exhausting that the little time he had to himself was spent either catching up on things at home that he hadn't been able to do in office hours or desperately trying to do mundane jobs like shopping and cleaning. Other than his recent meditation with Aura, Harry hadn't really had any meaningful time to himself to relax. But, when his mother rang to invite him for lunch one weekend, he knew he couldn't put a visit off any longer. Maria Freeman, although generally sweet and mild-mannered, had an iron-like will when it came to certain things and she wasn't waiting another single day before seeing her son.

His parents' home was only a few miles away in a village that stretched its length along a river. The house was a detached barn conversion built around a courtyard with a garden at the back overlooking open countryside. It was all large windows and grand spaces, with endless beams. He'd never dreamed his parents would go for such a place. They were usually so conventional and he'd always expected to see them in a neat bungalow by the sea but, as his mother had pointed out, 'Why be predictable?'

He parked his car by the double garage and went round the back of the property towards a side door his mother preferred them to use. It led into a utility room.

'Hi Mum! I'm here!' Harry called as he opened the door that had been left unlocked for him.

'Darling!' she said brightly, putting down a tea towel and walking towards him, embracing him in a cloud of heavy perfume. 'How are you? Are you eating enough? You feel all boney.'

'I'm not all boney, Mum!' he said, used to her worrying ways.

'Well, it's a good job I'm cooking your favourite for you,' she told him. 'You're working too hard, aren't you?'

He sighed. There was never any hiding from her. She always went straight to the heart of things.

'It's been busy if that's what you mean. But that's normal. We're setting up a brand new office with new staff and new clients.'

'And new stresses,' she said, pushing his hair from out of his eyes as she used to do when he was a child. 'You need a haircut.'

He grinned. 'No doubt. Where's Dad?'

'In the courtyard, marching his boys up and down.' His mother said this with an absolutely straight face because marching was a serious business. 'The village hall is being reroofed so the club couldn't meet there and your father offered to take the boys here. Isn't that kind of him?'

'Yes,' Harry said through gritted teeth. 'I'll pop out and let him know I'm here. He's nearly done, isn't he?'

His mother glanced at the clock. 'Should be.'

Harry crossed the kitchen towards the sliding doors that led out to the courtyard. It could have been a beautiful space with its old brick walls. Instead, it had been turned into a place of misery. Harry counted three boys. The others, for there were surely more in the village's version of the Scouts, had obviously seen sense and made their excuses, but these poor three hadn't been so lucky, being forced by their parents to spend their Saturday mornings being marched by his father.

Harry watched as the three young lads paraded up and down.

'Left, left, left right left!' his father cried, his voice loud in the echoey space. Harry wondered if the neighbours could hear and, if so, what they made of it.

'And HALT!'

The three boys almost crashed into each other.

'No, no, no!' his father cried.

Harry watched as the boys corrected themselves before standing rigid, uncomfortable and with a bored look on their faces which clearly told Harry that they wished they were somewhere – *anywhere* – other than here. Harry closed his eyes and shook his head, feeling the pain of the young boys and remembering all too well the days when his father would have him marching up and down the garden. It might not have been so bad if Harry had had a sibling to accompany him. He often wondered what possessed parents to hand their boys over to his father, but perhaps they were unruly little lads and it was a relief to unload them if only for an hour or so a week.

The truth was, Leonard Freeman was a frustrated would-be army major, but he'd failed the medical – three times. Many conversations would begin with the phrase, 'If it wasn't for my feet...'

'And your ear, dear,' Harry's mother would invariably add.

'Yes, if it wasn't for my feet and my dodgy ear, I could have done great things, don't you know?'

So, instead of rising through the ranks of the British Army, Leonard Freeman had spent his life in a building society, sitting behind a desk shuffling papers.

'Hey, Dad!' Harry called now, doing his best to end the boys' torture.

His father turned around with a glare. 'I'm not quite

finished,' he said, returning his formidable stare towards the boys, his hands tucked neatly into the small of his back. 'Right, boys, at ease. Today wasn't perfect. Far from it. But an improvement. A definite improvement.' He cleared his throat, making the smaller boy on the right jump. 'That's it for today, but remember the three D's, boys. Dedication, determination and discipline! Dismissed!' he added, making it four D's.

Harry watched as the boys' shoulders relaxed before they quickly ran out of the courtyard, back towards freedom.

'Hey, Dad,' Harry said again, watching as his father's hands unfolded from behind his back.

'Harry!' he said. 'Too old to march around the courtyard?'

'Oh, yes. *Much* too old.'

His father nodded, the tiniest of smiles on his face. 'You were one of my best marchers,' he said.

Harry frowned. It was the first he'd heard of it. 'Really?'

'Not perfect, of course. Nobody's ever perfect. But pretty good.'

Harry couldn't help smiling. His father was full of surprises.

'Lunch ready yet?' his father asked.

'Mum's got it on.'

'Good!'

The two of them returned indoors and the smell of something savoury and delicious wafted through the open-plan space.

'He's working too hard!' his mother yelled across the vastness.

'What?' his father said.

'I'm not working too hard,' Harry said.

'No time for fun, I'm betting,' his mum went on as she took a pasta bake out of the oven. 'No time for seeing anybody, I'm imagining.'

Harry sighed. He might have known that was coming. It was only ever a matter of time before that particular subject came up again.

'What happened to that nice girl you were seeing?'

'What nice girl?' Harry asked.

'Well, I don't remember her name because you never brought her to meet us!' his mum said, her tone accusatory.

'Colette,' Harry said.

'That's right,' his mum said as if it had been on the tip of her tongue. 'What happened to her?'

'Nothing. We just drifted apart.'

She shook her head in despair. 'You let that happen, didn't you?'

'Mum, it wasn't working. I went one way and she another. It happens.'

'You should have made more of an effort,' she said as she set the long trestle table by the picture window which looked out over the valley.

'You can't make something work when it just isn't,' Harry said, picking up the cutlery and helping his mum lay the table.

'So are you seeing anyone now?' she continued as she passed him the thick linen napkins that had been wiping the Freemans' mouths for decades.

'No.'

'Anyone you like?' she persisted.

'Mum, you'll be the first to know, I promise you.'

She sighed. 'I'll be too old and creaky to pick up my grandchildren by the time you get yourself sorted.'

Harry could feel himself blushing. 'These grandchildren,' he said, 'if they're boys, you're not allowed to march them, Dad.'

'What?' his father said.

'No marching my future sons!'

Leonard harrumphed. 'Just make sure their mother's the right sort first,' he said.

Harry frowned. His parents often used phrases like 'right sort' or 'well to do'. Harry loathed them. The fact was that his parents were just a little bit snobby and he knew exactly the kind of woman they hoped Harry would bring home one day. She'd be tall but not as tall as Harry. Classically beautiful in a very conservative sort of way. She'd favour navy or grey clothes, well-tailored, well-fitted. She'd be a lawyer or a doctor. A teacher at a pinch, but only if she taught at a reputable school – ideally an all-girls' school or one of those that charged eye-watering fees each term. Her name would be conventional too: Catherine, Elizabeth, Anna or something like that, he thought as he carried the jug of iced water to the table.

'Just don't leave it too long,' his mother said as she brought a bowl of salad through.

'No, I've only got so many marching years left in me,' his father added and, for the life of him, Harry couldn't tell if he was joking. But he suspected he wasn't.

After lunch, Harry spent a few hours with his parents, helping his mother with some chores in the kitchen before going out into the garden for a spot of digging.

'Your mother wants a wildlife pond,' his father said and the two of them got to work. It felt good to do something physical. After another week spent hunched over his desk, Harry had forgotten the simple pleasure of moving his body and resolved to get back to his fitness regime as soon as possible. It was yet another thing that had been put on the back burner since his new post in Brighton.

By the time he got home, he was pleasantly tired and took a shower and then a nap, nodding off in the chair overlooking the downs. When he awoke, he felt wonderfully refreshed and noticed that the moon was just becoming visible. The full moon.

It was time to meditate.

CHAPTER SEVEN

Harry had been watching the moon from his apartment. It had risen whole and perfect to flood the grounds of Winfield Hall with its silvery light. He'd never really noticed it before. It had been one of those things he was aware of but, tonight, he'd been paying it special attention and he realised how very beautiful it was.

The moon continued to rise and the hands on the clock continued to turn and, finally, it was time to join Aura. He crossed the hallway between their apartments and knocked on her door. When she opened it, she greeted him with a bright smile. She was wearing a dress the colour of midnight, but it was threaded through with silver – reminding him of moonlight, and her long red hair was loose with a tiny diamante clip pinning a section back from her face.

'Hello,' she said. 'Come on in.'

'Hi Aura. How are you?'

'I'm good. How are you?'

'Yeah, okay. I've been watching the moon rise,' he confessed.

'Isn't it beautiful? We're lucky that it's a clear night. We've got an amazing view of it over the walled garden. Come and see.'

They walked towards the French doors which were open and he grinned as he saw that, although the sun had set a while ago, the garden was flooded with light. Moonlight.

'Isn't it magical?' Aura said, her voice breathy as if in awe. 'It amazes me every time I see it. It's something I never take for granted and I think it's all the more precious for only being a full moon once a month – or twice if we're very lucky.'

'I can't say it's something I've paid much attention to in the past,' Harry owned up.

'Perhaps you will after tonight.'

'Perhaps.' He smiled.

'Shall we take our shoes off and then go outside?'

He nodded and removed his shoes and socks. Of course, Aura was already barefoot, her toenails a sparkly pink. He then followed her out into the garden. It was a little cooler now, but refreshingly so. Aura had spread out a large rug in swirling blues and greens and two cushions had been placed onto it. That was all. She hadn't lit any candles tonight and he guessed that she didn't want to take any focus away from the light of the moon.

'You've done this before, haven't you?' he asked her as she motioned to the rug.

'A few times. Although my old flat didn't have any outdoor space. I'd have to wait until I could see the moon through my window which wasn't very often, I'm afraid.'

Harry sat down on the rug, getting himself comfortable on the cushion before gazing up into the inky sky where the moon sat cradled among the stars.

'Did you know the moon plays a central role in many

religions and belief systems?' Aura asked. 'It's thought to be a divine feminine energy as the sun is a masculine energy.'

'I didn't know.'

'And the full moon is especially revered. It has so many different names depending on the month and the faith. This one, for example, in May, is known as the Hare Moon because it's the time of year when you can easily see hares in the wild, and it's also known as the Willow Moon in the Celtic calendar.'

'I like that,' Harry said. 'I always find it interesting to hear something being given a new name.'

'The full moon's a pretty special time,' Aura went on. 'It's about being grateful and counting your blessings and of seeing how far you've come with any goals you've set. It's also to do with letting go if something hasn't worked out. Because that's important too. Sometimes, you have goals and projects that simply don't work out or your priorities change and it's important to acknowledge that and let things go. It's freeing and releasing. And that's important too when there's a full moon – releasing. Forgiving anything that needs forgiving.'

Harry nodded, wondering why he'd never thought about any of this stuff before.

'So, are you ready to begin?' she asked.

He rocked himself on his cushion and nodded. 'Ready.'

'We'll just spend a few moments connecting to our breath,' Aura began, a slight breeze lifting her hair away from her face as if the world was breathing alongside her. 'Gently close your eyes and take a deep breath, letting it go on the exhale. Then again. Deep breath in. Big breath out.'

Harry closed his eyes and breathed, feeling the cool night air entering his body and his own warm breath leaving it.

'Allow yourself to be completely present – mind, body, soul,' Aura went on. 'And take another deep breath in, letting go of all

your worries and fears on the exhale. Give them to the moon –
to Lady Light. You don't have to carry them any longer. Just let
them go.'

Harry was struck by the simplicity of Aura's words and yet
they had such a profound effect on him. Just as he'd
experienced in his first meditation with her, the feeling of being
handed power – being told that he could simply let things go –
was astonishing. And so he took a big deep breath in and, with
the exhale, he let it all go: his fears about his job and if he was
doing it well enough, and the anxiety his parents caused him
when they pressed him about his future. He let it go.

'So often, we carry around our anxieties in our bodies – our
physical bodies, our emotional bodies, our mental bodies. We
tense up. We have headaches, backache, stomach ache. So allow
yourself a complete release, giving anything that is not needed
to Lady Light. Allow your body to soften and loosen as you feel
all those stresses and strains leaving you. You are being blessed
by the gentle energy of the moon. She is shining right above
you, shining her light down upon you. Feel it enter you at the
crown of your head. The light is filling you up, travelling
through your heart space, your belly, your limbs. You are one
with the moon. You can feel her radiance becoming a part of
you. Sink into that feeling now. She is holding you, guiding you,
supporting you.'

With his eyes still closed, Harry listened to Aura's voice. It
sounded like it was coming from somewhere above him and he
had the strangest thought that she had somehow morphed into
the moon. He felt a smile tickling his lips and then banished it,
coming back to his breath. Focusing. But then another thought
popped into his mind. What would Aura make of his parents,
he wondered, and what would they make of her? For a moment,
he saw her bare feet walking across the immaculate wooden

floorboards of their barn conversion. What would his ever so conventional mother make of that?

'And come back to your breath,' Aura's sweet voice interrupted his naughty train of thought. 'Always come back to the breath. If you're distracted, if you're thinking, if you're anxious, you have your breath.'

Like before, Harry couldn't help wondering if Aura could actually read his mind and had known that he was thinking about her.

They sat like that for a while longer, the night-time sounds and scents of the garden enveloping them. He was sure he could smell honeysuckle or was it jasmine on the night breeze and, in the distance – somewhere beyond the walled garden – he could hear an owl calling. Sights and sounds he wouldn't have experienced if he'd stayed indoors.

'Now, slowly, we're going to come back into the garden,' Aura said at last. 'Just wiggle your fingers and toes, feeling that wonderful warmth and life.'

Harry wiggled.

'And, very gently, and only when you're ready, open your eyes.'

Harry continued to wiggle and then opened his eyes. He'd expected it to be dark, but his vision seemed flooded with moonlight. If anything, it appeared even brighter than before.

'Wow! This moon!' he said.

Aura smiled, her face pale in its light. 'It's pretty amazing, isn't it? Do you think it made a difference tonight?'

'I think it did. I could feel it, I'm sure.'

'Oh, yes.'

'I was aware of it. All the sounds too.'

'Did you hear the owl?' she asked.

'Yes! I could smell something really sweet too.'

'It's jasmine. Abi has it growing against the wall over there.' She nodded towards her landlady's apartment. 'So, how do you feel?'

'Good. Warm and relaxed. I think my bones might have melted.'

Aura laughed. 'Would you like to do a bit more breath work before we get up?'

'That would be good.'

Aura led him, taking the breaths gently this time. Nothing was forced. It all seemed natural, gentle, and Harry felt himself slowly coming back into his body so, when she next told him to open his eyes, he felt totally centred.

'That was amazing,' he told her as they got up off the rug.

'Good. I'm glad you enjoyed it.'

'Enjoyed seems such a little word. It was more than enjoyed. It was...' He shook his head. 'I'm actually at a loss to say exactly what it felt like and I work with words for a living. I can usually find the right one for the job.'

'It's okay. I don't actually need to hear a word from you because I was there too. I felt it.'

'You did?'

'Some things, some experiences go beyond words. Words are just a human convention – a rather unsatisfactory way to label something and not all things can be labelled. We shouldn't live in our heads so much. We forget our spirit if we do.'

Harry nodded. He wanted to say something wise in return, but he couldn't. Besides, he didn't need to. He just loved listening to Aura.

They walked back into her apartment through the French doors and Harry put his socks and shoes back on.

'Here, it's time I paid you,' he said to her, pushing some notes into her hand.

'Oh, Harry – this is too much!'

'No, no. I've got so much from my two sessions with you and don't forget the carnelian you gave me.'

'But that was a gift,' she protested.

'And this is my gift in return.'

'Well, thank you.'

'You're welcome. And I'm hoping we can continue with this – whatever this is – my spiritual journey, perhaps?'

'There you are trying to label things again.'

'Sorry!'

'It's okay. I'm just teasing you.' She smiled. 'We could do some grounding work if you like.'

'That sounds interesting.'

'I think you'd get a lot out of it,' she said, glancing down at his shoes. He glanced at them too, wondering what she was thinking.

'Shall I book that now?' he asked.

Aura nodded and walked to the little table where her diary sat open alongside a large clear quartz crystal and a lump of something pink. Aura saw where he was looking.

'Rose quartz,' she said, her hand stroking it. 'It reminds me to only make appointments which I will love.'

Harry stepped forward. 'Can I touch it?'

'Of course.'

He reached a hand out. It felt cold and rough but not unpleasant. 'What does it do?'

'It sits here,' she said with a little grin. 'You mean, what are its properties?'

'Is that what I mean?' He returned her smile.

'Rose quartz is the stone of love – romantic love, self-love, empathy and compassion. Just looking at it fills you with love, don't you think?'

Harry continued to look at the stone. Could meaning be given to a piece of rock? Mind you, could meaning be given to anything? Humans had a habit of suffusing objects with their own feelings, didn't they? Why should stones be any different? And surely it was all a question of belief. If you believed it, then it was so. The world was but a projection of your beliefs, that was what he was learning. And so he looked at the rose quartz more closely, taking in its sharp edges and its smooth ones, and marvelling at the translucency of it – how the light seemed to shine from its pink depths. Yes, he did indeed believe it could fill you with love.

'Aura?'

'Yes?'

'I've got a presentation coming up. It's pretty important and – well – I'm a bit nervous about it to be honest. I want to do well.' He paused.

'Okay.' She cocked her head to one side. 'Do you think a crystal might help?'

'Do you?' he asked. 'I mean, should I take the carnelian in with me?'

'It wouldn't hurt,' she told him. 'It would give you courage. But perhaps it's good luck you're looking for.'

'There's a stone for that?'

'Oh, there are many. Jade has long been held as a stone of prosperity and abundance. Then there's citrine – a type of yellow quartz known as the merchant's stone and often kept in the tills of shopkeepers. Pyrite – fool's gold – is believed to attract wealth. Here,' she said, 'I keep a little piece of that next to my laptop.'

Harry took the surprisingly heavy stone from her. It was a silvery-gold mass covered in tiny cubes.

'It's amazing!'

'Isn't it? I sometimes find myself just gazing at it.'

He handed it back to her and she placed it carefully on her desk.

'Garnet is good too, but I have something even better, I think.'

'What's that?'

She walked towards a set of drawers on which sat a bronze sleeping Buddha and a pair of tall candlesticks holding green candles. She opened the second drawer down and Harry could see it was full of crystals. Aura's eyes scanned the rows. Harry watched closely, wondering which one she had in mind for him. She didn't hesitate, she picked out a modest-looking green stone that was oval in shape and looked smooth to the touch.

'Here,' she said, handing it to him. 'How does it feel?'

Harry turned it over, marvelling at how pleasant it felt, his thumb fitting neatly into one side.

'Feels great! Like it was made for me.'

Aura looked pleased with that. 'It's a thumb stone. It's been cut and polished that way so you can keep it in your pocket or just hold it comfortably.'

'So what does it do?'

'Well, green stones are connected to the heart chakra and are great comforters and protectors. But green aventurine is more than that. The colour green has long been associated with harmony and growth as well as balance. And, perhaps more importantly for you, luck!' She smiled. 'It's a great stone for business decisions and new opportunities.'

'And do I have to – I don't know – activate it somehow?'

'You could say a few words and give it your intention.'

'How do I do that?'

'Hold the stone in your receiving hand. The one which you don't write with.'

Harry held the stone in his left hand, his thumb fitting naturally into its shape. 'Then what?'

'Before we ask for anything, I believe we should give thanks for what we already have,' Aura told him. She took a deep breath and sighed it out and Harry did the same. 'I give thanks for the prosperity in my life and I embrace more opportunities for prosperity and abundance.'

She said the words again slowly and Harry repeated them after her.

'How does that feel?' she asked a moment later.

'Like I'm going to totally nail this presentation,' he said with a grin.

'Good!'

'What do I owe you for the stone?'

Aura shook her head. 'You already paid me more than enough to cover the stone so look at it as my good luck gift to you. Being able to accept gifts plays a huge part in how we receive luck.'

'Okay,' he said graciously. 'Thank you.'

They stood for a moment looking at one another and Harry was loath to end the evening, but realised that Aura was probably waiting for him to leave.

'We didn't set a date for the grounding!' he suddenly cried.

'Oh, yes! We got a bit distracted by crystals!' Aura said, laughing. 'When would you like to pop by again?'

'What about mid-week? Wednesday?'

'I'll pencil it in – say eight o'clock? Does that suit you after work or would you like earlier?'

'No, that's fine.'

'We'll keep an eye on the weather. I'm sure you wouldn't want to do grounding work if it's cold and wet.'

'I'll be led by you,' Harry told her. 'Good night, then. And thank you again.'

'Good night, Harry.'

Returning to his apartment seemed strange after spending what had felt like a very intimate session with Aura. He switched a single lamp on and just sat for a few minutes, holding the green aventurine thumb stone. He was slowly becoming addicted to these sessions, but the question was what exactly was he drawn to? The lessons he was learning or the teacher who was teaching them?

It was a bright Sunday morning when Edward met up with his friend Stephen at the local pub for lunch. They had a couple of drinks in the pub garden and then went inside to eat.

'So, how's the lord of the manor doing then?' Stephen asked, crunching his way through a crisp salad.

Edward rolled his eyes at the nickname his friend had been teasing him with ever since he'd bought Winfield Hall.

'I'm doing all right.'

'Yeah? How's work?'

'Building slowly,' Edward said before taking a bite of his pasty.

'And how's that pretty neighbour of yours?' Stephen asked, eyebrows raised in mischief.

'We went out for a meal,' Edward told him matter-of-factly.

Stephen's mouth dropped open in shock. 'You did? Why didn't you tell me?'

'I'm telling you now.'

'When was this?'

'I don't know. Week before last? Abigail was looking a bit depressed so I offered to take her out to lunch.'

'And how did it go?'

'Good. We talked. Properly.'

'Really? *You* talked? What about?'

'About family mostly.'

'Really?'

'Yes,' Edward told him. 'Well, she told me a bit more than I told her perhaps.'

'Ah, I see,' Stephen said. 'So, you haven't told her about you and Oscar?'

Edward shook his head. 'She knows enough, I think. She can see that things are tricky between us.'

'Tricky? That's one way of putting it!'

They dropped the conversation for a few minutes and concentrated on eating.

'So, what exactly is going on with you two?' Stephen asked at last.

'Who? Me and Abi?'

'Well, of *course* you and Abi! Are you seeing each other now or what?'

'No!' Edward cried. 'We're just neighbours.' He could feel Stephen's eyes upon him. 'What?'

'Would you like to?'

'Like to what?'

'*See* her – you know – as more than a neighbour?'

Edward didn't answer at first. 'I'm not planning on getting involved with anyone at the moment.'

Stephen frowned. 'Not planning? What is this – a military operation? Love doesn't work like that!'

'Who said anything about love?'

His friend sighed. 'Okay, okay. Maybe it's a bit early to start talking about love, but what about fun and... and... *life*? Don't you want to live a little?'

'But I am living. I'm living in the most beautiful place in the world,' Edward told him, but he could see that wasn't what Stephen was getting at and so he added something else. 'We've been swimming together.'

'You and Abi? Where?'

'In the river.'

'Skinny-dipping?' Stephen's eyes widened.

'No!'

Stephen laughed. 'I'm just trying to picture that for a moment.'

'Yeah? Well, don't!'

'So tell me more – how did that come about?'

Edward shrugged. 'I saw her and asked if she wanted to come with me.'

'So you're swimming buddies?'

'We've been a few times now. Not this year yet.'

'Why not? It's been pretty warm, hasn't it?'

Stephen was right. The weather had been warming up for some time now and the evenings were long and light. Why hadn't he thought to start swimming again and asking Abi to go with him?

'You're right,' he told Stephen. 'I should start swimming again.'

'With Abi.'

Edward smiled. 'What is it with your obsession with me and Abi?'

'I'd just like to see you happy with someone,' Stephen said. 'It's been a while.'

'But what if it all goes wrong?'

'But what if it all goes *right*?' Stephen countered. 'Have you ever thought about that?'

'I daren't.'

Stephen gave a sympathetic smile. 'Look, I know you've had some bad experiences in the past. We all have. But you can't let your past determine your future. The way I look at it is that the more bad experiences you've clocked up in the past will surely increase your odds of it going better for you now.'

'I'm not sure it works like that,' Edward said.

'But just look at me and Becky,' Stephen continued undeterred. 'We're great together, but it's taken me all this time to find her. I had to go through Liz, Alexa, Carrie and – well – whatever that other one was called.'

'The one who was two-timing you with your manager?'

'That's the one!' he said. 'But I never gave up.'

'I haven't given up exactly. I've just been... taking a break.'

'A blooming long break if you ask me!'

'Yes, well, I'm not asking you.'

Stephen grinned. 'Seriously, though – you like her?'

Edward shifted a little on the oak bench he was sitting on. Of course he liked Abigail. He'd never have offered to sell half of Winfield Hall to someone unless he liked them, but that wasn't what Stephen meant and he knew it. And this was a question that Edward had been grappling with for a little while now. He liked Abi. He *really* liked Abi. And, ever since their recent lunch, he hadn't been able to get her out of his head. He'd lost count of the number of times he had replayed her kiss. It'd been such a simple gesture, kissing him lightly on the cheek like that. She'd probably never even thought twice about it and yet it had been so special to Edward. For him, it had marked a deciding moment in their developing relationship. They'd lost that early awkwardness between them and he didn't want to get ahead of himself, but he liked to think that they were at least friends now. If not more.

'What do I do?' he asked suddenly.

Stephen frowned. 'About Abi?'

'Yes. I don't want to mess this up.'

Stephen leaned slightly closer across the table. 'Why do you think you'll mess it up?'

'Because I always do!'

'Then acknowledge that and be determined not to mess it up this time.'

'Oh, it's as easy as making that decision, is it?'

'I don't see why not.'

Edward sighed. 'What if she says no? What if I just end up embarrassing myself and then there's this horrible awkwardness between us? We've got to live together, you know?'

'I know. I suppose you need to decide if you think dating Abi is worth the gamble – of risking that embarrassment if it doesn't work out.'

Edward took a sip of his drink. Stephen's words weren't the most reassuring, but he knew his friend was being honest.

'And don't delay it. Once you make your mind up with these things, it's best not to overthink your way out of them. Just do it. Go home, knock on her door and ask her out.'

'Today?' Edward was horrified.

Stephen laughed. 'Yes, today! And report back to me as soon as the deed's done.'

Edward left the pub feeling slightly disgruntled. He felt Stephen had set him some kind of primitive challenge and that put even more pressure on him to get things right. Mind you, if Stephen hadn't goaded him, would Edward seriously even be contemplating talking to Abi now? Probably not. Instead, he found himself standing outside her apartment as soon as he got back to Winfield. And that's when the meadow full of butterflies kicked in and he felt the way he had before his last job interview. Was this a bad idea? Was he building up to a lifetime of awkwardness? Would it ruin his enjoyment of living at Winfield if she turned him down or if she said yes and then things went horribly wrong between them later on? Would he be forever opening his door a crack, checking the hallway before leaving his apartment and dreading seeing her every time he took his rubbish out?

He sighed. He was overthinking things, wasn't he? What was it Stephen had said?

'Don't delay it.'

And so he ran a hand through his hair, took a deep breath and knocked on her door.

Abi answered a moment later. Her hair was pinned up and she had a smudge of what looked like blue ink on her left cheek.

'Hi Edward. I've not seen you in a while. I guess work's been busy?'

'Yes.'

'Did you want to come in? It's a bit of a mess, I'm afraid. I've been printing.'

He stepped inside and took in the large table in the centre of the room covered in papers and then he spotted something else.

'Is that a printing press?' Edward asked.

'An original Albion,' she told him. 'I'm surprised you didn't see it arriving. It was quite interesting getting it in here.'

'It's very impressive.'

'I'm totally in love with it although it's a little large for my studio so it's going to stay put in the living room, but I kind of like its companionship here.'

'And your pictures,' he said, motioning to the table. 'Were they done using the press?'

'No, I'm doing these by hand with the little rollers there.'

He walked towards the table and looked at the prints she'd made. 'These are lovely,' he said. 'May I?'

'Feel free.'

He picked up one of the pieces, the paper thick and creamy. 'It's our village church!'

'That's right,' Abi said. 'I was meant to be working on a series of flower prints, but then found myself doing this. I'm a bit all over the place at the moment. I really should discipline myself to working on one thing at a time, but I'm kind of enjoying this creative chaos.' She gave a little smile.

It was then that something caught Edward's eye on the wall. It was a picture of lemon yellow roses entwined with pale green vines. It was a delicate pattern, but very striking in its simple white frame.

'That's lovely too. Another of your designs?'

Abi laughed. 'Don't you recognise it?'

Edward frowned. 'Should I?'

'It's the wallpaper you were going to throw out.'

'Is it?' He stepped closer. 'Oh, yes!'

Abi joined him. 'Do you like it now?'

'I do.'

'Sometimes, you just need to frame things in the right way.'

He nodded and then cleared his throat. It was as if she knew why he'd come over to see her and that he was struggling.

'What was it you wanted to see me about?' she asked now. 'Is everything okay?

'Yes. Everything's fine. It's, well, I was wondering if...' he paused, knowing that this was the point of no return. Once he'd declared himself, once he'd let her know that he liked her, nothing would be the same again between them. He was crossing a line.

'What, Edward?' She smiled and the way it lit up her face made him feel even more nervous.

'I was wondering if you'd like to – well...' He stopped again. It was no good. He couldn't do it. The fear of rejection was too strong. 'Would you like to go swimming again?'

'In the river?'

'The river or the sea,' he said, his heart hammering as he endeavoured to sound normal and that this was the reason he'd called round.

'How about the sea then?' she suggested.

'Okay.'

'When were you thinking?'

Edward scrambled around for a mad moment. This shift in the direction of his proposal had caught him off guard. 'Well, the weather's meant to be good all week. Warm at least.'

'Shall we pencil in Wednesday then? If we don't do it while it's warm, I fear I'll back down.'

'I know what you mean,' Edward said, inwardly cursing himself for his cowardice at not having been able to ask Abi out properly.

CHAPTER EIGHT

No matter how many presentations Harry had given over the years, he still found himself getting nervous. But that was a good thing, wasn't it? He believed he was like an actor waiting to go on stage – there was that adrenalin rush which made one feel so anxious and yet, at the same time, drove the performance. In short, it was necessary. But today's presentation was going to be different, wasn't it? Because, today, he had an ally.

His hand dived into his jacket pocket and he brought out the green aventurine stone Aura had given him. He'd been reading up about it. It symbolised luck, prosperity and growing wealth. It was energising, full of vitality and also helped you maintain a positive outlook. He grinned. Could one simple stone really do all that?

It can if you believe it.

He could almost hear Aura's voice. He was even beginning to think like her now. What might she be telling him if she were here, he wondered? And he knew exactly what. He closed his eyes for a moment.

Take a few deep breaths and then feel what it will be like to win that account, and hold onto that feeling. Experience it as if it is happening to you. How do you feel in your mind and in your body? If you can believe it, you can achieve it. Belief is everything because dreams don't manifest into reality without it.

When he opened his eyes, he looked around his office as if he expected Aura to be there. Perhaps it was the power of the green aventurine, he thought, as he turned the stone over so that his left thumb fit snuggly into it.

A knock on his office door brought him back to himself and, before he could say "Come in", Letitia had entered.

'Hi Harry,' she said, walking right up to his desk and sitting on the corner of it. He really did wish she wouldn't do that. 'Ready for the big presentation?'

'Of course.'

'Not nervous, are you?' she said in that teasing way she had, like a bully in the schoolyard.

'Why should I be nervous?'

'Oh, I don't know,' she said, her red-painted mouth pouting slightly. 'Because you always are in that adorable way of yours. You get that little stammer. Don't tell me you hadn't noticed!'

Harry flinched. He wasn't sure if she was telling the truth or not. Did he stammer? Or was this just her way of undermining him because she was going to make a presentation tomorrow and didn't want anyone stealing the limelight from her.

'What's that?' she asked.

He cleared his throat, aware that he'd been absent-mindedly fiddling with the thumb stone as he'd been talking to her. But he wasn't going to dismiss the crystal this time.

'It's a green aventurine.'

'Let me see.'

Harry hesitated. There was something in Letitia's eyes that

made him not want to give the stone to her, but her hand was practically under his nose and so he relented.

'Another of your magic rocks, is it?' she asked, her left eyebrow raising in a sardonic expression.

'Maybe.'

'You don't really believe in all that mumbo jumbo, do you?'

'I'm coming round to it.'

'It's all New Age nonsense. Crystal healing and chakras and middle-aged people suddenly doing downward dog in the middle of the office. It's a lot of baloney.'

Harry couldn't hide a smile. He'd have to look up downward dog later and see if he was missing a trick.

'It's a little dull, isn't it?' she said, holding it up to the light.

'I don't think so.' He held his hand out, but she didn't return it to him immediately. Instead she turned it over, squinting at it as if she was trying to visibly find the magic inside.

'Come on,' he said, 'give it back.'

She sighed and got up off his desk, still holding the stone.

'Letitia!' he cried as she walked towards the door.

'Catch!' she said, turning around and throwing it towards him with a laugh. Harry caught it. 'If you do well in the presentation, I'll let you take me out for a drink after work to celebrate.'

'No can do,' he told her. 'I've got to be somewhere.' The truth was he had nowhere that he had to be, but he'd definitely rather be there than anywhere else with Letitia.

'Well, good luck, Harry,' she said and he was quite convinced that she was saying it through clenched teeth.

As she left the room, he looked at the stone, wondering if he should wash it or wipe it or something. Could a person's negative energy affect it, he wondered? Should he call Aura and ask? He shook his head, settling for a quick wipe with a tissue before popping the stone into his jacket pocket.

An hour later, Harry was standing at the front of the conference room, his presentation in full swing. His boss was there and most of his team. He made a good, strong start, capturing their attention immediately and it was all going pretty well until he forgot a key piece of data he'd discovered. He was quite sure he'd written it down somewhere prominent, but he couldn't find it now. He felt a surge of panic rising and did his best to bluff his way through as his hand dived into the pocket of his jacket, feeling for the green aventurine.

But it wasn't there.

He'd definitely put it in his pocket, hadn't he? And then he remembered. He'd taken his jacket off as he'd come into the conference room to set up all his things and, during that time, Letitia had come in. Had she taken it in that brief period before he put his jacket back on for the presentation? He glanced down the length of the table to where she was sitting and noticed that she was holding something. It was the green aventurine, suspended between her thumb and forefinger in such a way that nobody but Harry would see it and, on her face, was a fat smug smile.

Harry swallowed hard. She had wished him luck and had even wanted to go out for drinks with him if his presentation had gone well, so why do this to him?

You turned her down, a little voice inside him said.

Was that why she'd taken the stone? Was she trying to put him off his game? Did she believe that taking the stone would make her Delilah cutting Samson's hair and that Harry would lose all his confidence? Well, he had to admit to panicking for a second when he'd realised that the green stone wasn't there, but he quickly felt that just seeing it was enough to restore his confidence. Having it there in the room with him was like having a little piece of Aura's goodness there too, and that was something Letitia couldn't have imagined.

So Harry bluffed his way through the missing data, delivered his killer pitch for the product he'd been given to work on and received a round of applause at the end of it all.

'I suppose you'll be wanting this back,' Letitia said as they left the room together a few minutes later. She handed him the stone. He wanted to ask her why she'd taken it, but she stalked off and he watched as she linked arms with Rob, the new guy in the accounts department, and he couldn't help feeling relieved that her attention wasn't directed towards him anymore.

When Harry got home that evening, he went straight to Aura's door and knocked.

'Aura? Are you there?'

'Harry!' she said, answering a moment later. 'What is it? What's the matter?'

'I just had to tell you.'

'About what?'

'About the stone!'

'The green aventurine?'

'Yes! It worked.'

'Well, don't sound so surprised!'

He laughed and then he told her all about it – how Letitia had taken it and taunted him with it and how he'd lost his nerve for a few brief moments until he fixed his gaze on the stone.

'And that was enough,' he told Aura. 'I didn't need to hold it – just looking at it, seeing it there in the room with me, was enough. It reminded me of all the things you said and all the things I'd told myself – that I could do it. That I had confidence and that I was good enough.'

'Of *course* you're good enough,' she said and he smiled.

'Well, I wanted to thank you.'

'You don't need to thank me. It sounds like you did most of the hard work yourself.'

He smiled and it struck him how very happy he felt in Aura's presence. Ever since his first meeting with her, he'd felt a wonderful sense of calm around her, the like of which he'd never experienced before. It felt so very right. Perhaps it was particularly striking to him at that moment after having spent the day with Letitia and remembering how incredibly prickly he always felt around her. Where Letitia was akin to having a rash, Aura was like a balm.

'What is it?' she asked and he suddenly realised that he must be grinning like an idiot at the thoughts swirling around his head about rashes and balms.

'Come out with me to celebrate,' he found himself saying.

'What – now?'

'Unless you're busy of course. Sorry!' Harry said. 'I just want to say thank you in a slightly more meaningful way than knocking on your door.'

'Okay,' she told him. 'I'll just grab my bag.'

He watched as she disappeared into her apartment and he suddenly felt rather nervous because he'd only spoken to Aura in a professional capacity before – making appointments for sessions with her. But this was different. They were crossing into new territory, which was great, he acknowledged. They should get to know each other better as neighbours, shouldn't they?

Only, as he waited for Aura to get her bag, Harry realised that he was already thinking of Aura as more than a neighbour.

More even than a friend. He was beginning to fall in love with her.

Aura had had a good day. She'd seen two clients at Winfield and had done sessions with another online. Her business was, at last, beginning to take off and she'd never been happier. There was nothing she loved more than reaching people, offering them hope, peace and a moment of calm in a turbulent world. She got so much personal joy from giving to others and she couldn't wait to expand her business even more.

It was also nice to be earning some money too. The reduced rent at Winfield Hall had made such a difference to her and she had been able to save a little bit. That was one of the things in her line of work – many of her clients paid in cash and it was rather lovely to see it all adding up. She'd placed it in one of the drawers of her crystal cabinet along with a beautiful piece of citrine and a hefty chunk of pyrite – both good abundance stones. She was saving the money so she could buy a new computer. The one she was using at the moment was horribly slow and she'd had some problems conducting her meeting with a new client. So, as tempting as it was to spend some of the money she was making on crystals and some new clothes, she was going to be practical and put it towards her business needs.

Grabbing her handbag now and quickly checking her reflection in a mirror she'd decorated with seashells collected from trips to the beach, she paused, thinking about Harry. She liked him. He was sweet and awkward and wonderfully open to what she had to teach him. She'd had some clients in the past who'd reached out to her and then did nothing but ridicule her methods. Aura never made any pretence about

who she was or what she did and so it always surprised her
when people thought it was okay to debunk her beliefs. But
she accepted that it had nothing to do with her. She'd learned,
over the years, that people came to her for many reasons and,
although they were usually trying to fix a problem, sometimes
they just weren't ready to face it full on and would lash out.
Like the woman who'd once thrown a black tourmaline in
Aura's face.

'You and your stupid crystals!' she'd yelled before running
out of the door five minutes before the end of the session. Of
course, she hadn't paid either for the session or the tourmaline
which had chipped when it landed on the floor. Aura had often
wondered if the client had gained some kind of healing from
that anger being released.

At least Harry was benefitting from his sessions, she
thought. It was always heartening to see that she was able to
make a real difference in somebody's life, even if that was only
by giving them some time in which to think of nothing else but
the passage of their breath. But Harry really seemed to be
responding to the power of crystals, using them to give himself
confidence in moments when he needed just that little extra
boost.

'Okay, I'm ready,' she said, joining him in the hallway.

'There's a pub I know on the river,' he said. 'Fancy that?
They have a beautiful garden and we can sit outside.'

'Sounds lovely.'

They left Winfield in Harry's car and, being the perfect
gentleman, he'd opened the passenger door for her to get in and
out and took her drink order so she wouldn't have to stand at
the bar.

'Would you like something to eat?' he asked as he brought
their drinks out.

'No, thank you. I don't usually eat much in the evenings. But don't let me stop you.'

He shook his head. 'I'm still wound up after today. Got too much nervous energy to digest properly.'

Aura giggled.

'Sorry!' he said. 'That was way too much information.'

'It's okay. It's good to be honest about how we feel.'

'Yeah?'

'Yes.'

'You know, that goes against everything I've ever been taught.'

'By whom?'

He shrugged. 'My parents. Family. Society.'

Aura sighed. 'It's this thing called adulthood – it gets in the way of being a real person.'

'What do you mean?'

'I mean, when we're children, we have this natural ability to express ourselves, don't we? When we're sad, we cry. When we're happy, we laugh. When we're mad, well, we cry again or shout. Our emotions just leap out of us,' she told him. 'But then, somewhere, at some time, we're told that we must regulate those emotions. We shouldn't show them. It's weak to show our vulnerabilities. Or else it's embarrassing to those around us. So we lock everything away – sometimes so deep inside us that it becomes a part of our DNA and we carry it around for the rest of our lives and it gets heavier and heavier until we sink under the weight.'

'Bloody hell!'

'Sorry,' she said, 'now it's me giving too much information.'

'No – no – it's all fascinating. You know, I learn so much from you. The way you think and talk and... behave.'

'Behave?'

'Yes. You're not like anyone else I've ever met. You're uninhibited.'

Aura bit her lower lip. 'Is that a good thing?'

'I'd say it is.'

'It's got me into trouble.'

'How?'

She sighed. 'Just being me. Not everyone understands, you know, if I start talking about meditation or the phase the moon's in or the power of crystals.'

'How do you handle that?'

'Well, mostly, I'm just careful about who I talk to. You can often tell who's going to be receptive to what you believe in. There are always surprises, mind. I was recently at a friend's dinner party and was sitting next to this...' she paused.

'What?'

'I was going to say "stuffed shirt", but that sounds rude.' She could feel herself blushing. 'Rude, but true. He spent most of the evening talking to the person the other side of him and, as I was at the end of the table next to the wall, I was left out of things somewhat. Anyway, he finally turned towards me and gave me this funny sort of sweep with his eyes as though I was some alien creature. I could feel my skin prickling with resistance because I thought I knew what was coming. I thought he was going to ask what I did and I'd tell him and he'd make some crass comment that would leave me feeling ghastly for the rest of the evening, but, instead, when I told him, he seemed really interested and told me how fascinated he was with the moon. Ever since he'd been a little boy, he'd watch its progress across the sky each night, making time just to look at it.' Aura smiled at the memory. 'And we talked. We really talked and, at the end of the evening, I gave him a business card because he actually asked me for one.'

'And did you hear from him again?'

She smiled. 'Not yet. But I sometimes think of him when I look up at the moon. I wonder if he's out there somewhere, looking at it too. Of course, not everybody surprises me in that kind of way. There are plenty of people who openly say that I'm completely woo-woo and belittle my practices. They seem to get some sort of perverse pleasure from being mean about it. I'm the first to get that people might be resistant to what I do, but I can never understand how people can be so mean about it. I'd never do that to someone. Just imagine if you told somebody about what you do for a living and they spent the next ten minutes ridiculing you.'

Harry shook his head. 'Who can fathom people?' He took a sip of his drink. 'So where do I fall in your opinion? I hope I've never upset you with silly questions.'

She smiled. 'No. Never. You're wonderfully open and curious – the best combination.'

'Yeah?'

'Absolutely,' she said.

'Well, I have a good teacher,' he told her, watching in delight as she blushed.

CHAPTER NINE

Abi wasn't entirely sure if she was looking forward to Wednesday or not. She and Edward hadn't swum since September when a warm and gloriously golden day had enticed them down to the river, and she was anxious that she'd now lost her nerve for swimming in the wild. Just how warm was sea water? It had been years since she'd taken a dip in the sea. She hoped she wasn't going to make a fool of herself. But she had committed to going and she didn't want to let Edward down.

Edward.

She thought about that moment when he'd asked her to go with him. There had been a few seconds when Abi had thought he'd been about to ask her out. He'd had a nervous sort of look about him and the way he'd been gazing at her made her wonder. But perhaps she'd imagined it.

How would it have made her feel though? And what would she have said? Abi wasn't sure she was ready for a relationship yet and having one with the co-owner of Winfield might not be such a great idea. Anyway, there was no point stressing over something that hadn't happened. She'd obviously misinterpreted things. Edward was only interested in her as a swimming companion and that suited her just fine.

It was a half hour drive to the beach. On the way, Abi and Edward talked about Winfield – the progress on the next apartment Edward was going to rent out and how he was getting on furnishing his own.

'Just buy a big old printing press and you won't have to worry about furniture,' Abi had joked. 'It will fill the space for you more than adequately.'

Abi thought back to something her sister had once said.

'You could fill the Albert Hall with all your art stuff if you were given the chance.' *Art stuff.* The term had been used as a kind of insult. Ellen had always seen it as messy and Abi knew that Ellen dreaded her daughters getting their felt tips and paintboxes out for the mess it would make. But that was creation for you – it was often very messy and Abi liked that. She liked the jostle of materials and the little collections she would amass around her home.

'Do you collect anything?' she asked as Edward parked the car.

'Collect?'

'Yes – antiques, paintings, piggy banks...' She smiled.

'Erm, no.'

'Nothing at all?'

'No. Is that a failing?'

'Not exactly. It just seems a shame. I mean, if you're struggling to fill your apartment and make it feel more homely.'

'I'm not trying to fill it. I just need a few more pieces – a nice armchair, perhaps, a coffee table. I don't want it stuffed full of anything. I kind of like having all this space after my pokey flat.'

'Oh, I see.'

'I rather prefer space to – well – *stuff*.'

Abi nodded. She couldn't help wondering what he thought of her own apartment now, stuffed to the brim with – well – *stuff*.

'I've been reading about the poet Edward Thomas. You know him?' Edward asked.

'I've heard of him.'

'He wrote a lot about Sussex. He lived here with his wife. Anyway, she wrote something that really resonated with me. She said, "I wanted less furniture in my bedroom and more air." Isn't that interesting?'

'It is. I like it.'

'I do too. Anyway, I'm trying to keep that in mind at Winfield. My London flat had too much stuff. I kind of collected gadgets.'

'So you *did* collect something?'

'Not intentionally. It was a way to treat myself, I suppose – you know, after a tough month at work or as a way to celebrate something. I would buy the latest phone or a bigger television or a piece of exercise equipment that would subsequently stare at me accusingly from the corner of the room.'

'Have you got all those things at Winfield?'

He shook his head. 'I donated most of them. Sold a few. Gave some away. I didn't want them. I wanted to come to Winfield and start afresh. All those big white walls kind of inspired me to create more space in my life, in my environment.'

'Gosh, you must think my apartment's a tip!' she dared to say at last.

'No! Not at all.'

'Are you sure?'

'It's – well, it's you, isn't it?'

'I do try to be tidy, but I'm afraid creativity sometimes spills over the edges of life.'

'And that's what makes it so you. You exude creativity. You mustn't try and hide that or pack it away in a cupboard. That wouldn't be right.'

She smiled. 'I'll try and remember that the next time I trip over a can of paint.'

They got out of the car and Edward reached for his bag on the back seat. 'You've got your costume on already, haven't you?'

'Oh, yes.'

'Good. I'm afraid there isn't anywhere private to change here. Not like our secret river.'

They left the car park and headed towards the beach. The air was cooler on the coast and Abi's nerves began to resurface. It was as they reached the sand that she noticed he was limping slightly. She'd seen it before, but had never asked him about it, but he was visibly wincing now.

'Are you okay?' she asked, nodding to his left leg.

'Yes.'

'What's the matter?'

'It's nothing. Just an old injury.'

'It looks painful.'

'The sea will do it some good. It's one of the reasons I like wild swimming – the cold water helps with the pain both when I'm swimming and for some time after. Come on!' He put his bag down on the sand and Abi placed her towel next to it. They then took their things off, ready for the sea, and walked to where the waves were frothing lace against the beach.

Tentatively, Abi dipped a toe. It was icy cold.

'I don't know if I can get in,' she told him, thinking she might just sit this one out on the beach. Maybe she could sketch while Edward swam. She'd brought a pad and pencil with her as always.

'But you got in the river,' he said with a frown.

'That was easier somehow,' Abi said. 'You had to plop in from the bank. But here you have to walk in.'

'Don't think – just do!' Edward advised. 'It'll do you so much good. It gets the heart pumping and your breathing will deepen and you'll feel amazing afterwards.'

But Abi wasn't thinking of afterwards as she waded in a little further, following Edward as he strode in with a confidence she wasn't feeling at all. She was all too mindful of the present discomfort with the cold waves splashing against her thighs. It was agony. There was no way she was going to be able to...

'I'm doing it!' she suddenly cried, forcing her knees to bend so that the whole of her body was swallowed up by the water. 'Oh, god, oh, god!'

Edward laughed. 'Well done. Now, keep moving. You'll soon acclimatise.'

Abi was quite sure he was lying, but she kicked for all she was worth and, pretty soon, the water started to feel a little more comfortable. Luckily, the sun was shining and that made all the difference. Abi watched as Edward swam out a little further than she wanted to venture. He looked so at home in the sea, so at peace. Would she feel like that if she stayed in long enough? She was already eyeing up the beach and thinking about how wonderfully warm she'd feel when she got out of the water and felt the sun on her limbs.

She did a few strokes and then rolled onto her back so that she was floating and there was a wonderful moment of buoyancy, when her body became one with the water and the grand swell of the sea rocked her so that she had to fight to keep her place within it.

Gazing up into the high blue sky, Abi could see why Edward was so drawn to wild swimming. There was a freedom in it which felt different from just walking through a landscape. Swimming meant you were fully immersed in the wild – you were truly a part of it. She'd felt it in the river swims she'd done with him, but there was something special about the sea because it was just so big and powerful. It made you realise how very small you were and that wasn't necessarily a bad thing. It was nature gently putting you back in your rightful place.

There was also something a little unworldly about it which appealed to Abi's artistic eye – it was the different perspective of seeing the land from the sea. She'd stepped out of her normal land-based existence and was able to see the curve of the Sussex coast, the great white cliffs, and the strange experience of her toes touching seaweed, shells and stones. It was challenging and it filled one's mind with sensations so that it was impossible to actually think of any issues you might be carrying with you. All problems were parked firmly on the shore.

Another thing you lost was your sense of time. Abi had no idea how long they'd been in the water. Edward was still swimming up and down, keeping parallel to the coast but just edging a little further out. She quickly came to the realisation that it didn't matter what the time was. The sun was high now so it was probably midday, but did that matter? Did she have anywhere she'd rather be than here?

She floated for a while longer and then swam for a bit and, when Edward joined her, they had a little water fight, sending droplets of sea water falling over their heads, their laughter dancing with the cries of the gulls high above them.

'We should go,' Edward said at last. 'We'll turn into salty prunes if we stay much longer.'

For one who hadn't wanted to venture in to the sea, it surprised Abi how reluctant she was to leave it, but she had to admit that the sun felt good on her skin as she dried herself a moment later.

'How's your leg?' she asked Edward.

'Like it isn't there,' he said and then he smiled at himself. 'I mean the pain. Oh, you know what I mean! How do you feel?' he asked.

'Surprisingly good actually.'

'There's nothing surprising about it. Cold water is energising. It does us all sorts of good. I try and take a cold shower as often as I can.'

'Oh, now I draw the line there!'

'You should try it. Really. Start warm and then gently turn the dial round to cold.'

Abi shook her head. 'I like my showers hot!'

He grinned. 'And you weren't going to get into the sea before, remember?'

'Well, thank you for pushing me.'

'Want me to coach you with cold showers?' he asked.

Abi's mouth dropped open in surprise.

'Sorry!' Edward said. 'That came out wrong. I meant...'

Abi stifled a giggle. 'It's okay.'

'Sorry,' he said, turning his attention to drying himself and quickly putting his clothes on. Abi did the same and then the two of them walked back towards the car.

The drive home was pretty much in silence, but it was a friendly sort of silence, Abi felt, and not an embarrassed one, she hoped. A couple of times, she glanced at Edward and, sensing her attention, he glanced back and smiled.

When they arrived home, Abi got the impression he was about to say something. Perhaps he was still embarrassed by the shower comment, she thought. His brow was furrowed as if in consternation.

'It's all right, you know,' she told him.

Edward's frown deepened.

'The shower thing.'

'Oh. Good.' He nodded.

Abi watched him closely. Had she misread him? Perhaps he hadn't still been anxious about the shower thing. He looked confused somehow, though.

'What is it, Edward?' she asked him gently.

He looked at her with something in his eyes that she couldn't quite read.

'Thank you,' he said simply.

'For what?'

'For today. For coming with me.'

'But I should thank you. It was *your* idea.'

'So you enjoyed it?'

'I loved it – eventually. Once I'd got over hating it.'

There it was again – that strange pause between them when she was sure Edward was on the brink of saying something. Only, he didn't. Instead, they got out of the car in silence.

'I guess I'll see you later,' he said.

'For another swim perhaps?'

'Yes. Let's do that sometime,' he agreed, and she watched as he walked ahead of her, entering the hall a moment later.

Abi turned around and looked up at the sunny flank of the

down. It had been good to have a trip out, but it was always wonderful to come back to Winfield.

It was as she was combing her hair after showering and dressing when something made her start. Someone was knocking on her door and it wasn't her front door, but the French doors at the side of the house.

Putting her comb down, Abi walked through to the living room and did a double take when she saw who was standing outside peering into her apartment.

'Oscar?' She opened the French doors.

'Hey!'

'What are you doing?'

'Hiding from Edward! Can I come in?'

Abi couldn't hide her bafflement. 'I suppose. How did you get here?'

'I drove.'

'I didn't see your car in the drive.'

'It's in the village, tucked away behind the church.'

'Oh, Oscar – why can't you sort things out with Edward?'

'Because he doesn't want them sorted out.'

'Now, that can't be true.'

Oscar scratched his head. 'I'm afraid it is. I'm a hopeless case, Abi!' He laughed. 'Hey! Your hair's all corkscrewy.'

Abi's hands flew to her hair. 'Yes, it gets very curly when it's wet.'

'It's pretty.' He threw her a smile so casually that Abi caught it and returned it before thinking and it was only then something occurred to her.

'Oscar? Why are you here if you've no intention of speaking to Edward?'

He took a deep breath, puffing his cheeks out and then looked directly at her. 'I wanted to see you.'

'Me? Why?'

He grinned and Abi wished that she didn't find him quite so attractive when he did that.

'Because I like you?' It was said as a question, but the directness of his gaze told her he was in earnest. 'I thought it would be fun to spend some time together. We could go out somewhere.'

Abi laughed. She couldn't help it.

'What?' he said.

'You're so – I don't know – up front.'

'Why waste time?' he asked, giving her a wink. 'I like you! I want to get to know you better.'

Abi could feel she was blushing.

'Is that a yes then?' he asked, his head cocked to one side as he tried to catch her eye.

'I don't know. I'll have to think about it, okay?'

'Okay.' She watched as he reached inside his jacket pocket and brought out a card. 'Don't ring that number. I don't work there anymore. But my mobile's on there. It's on all the time.'

He left through the French doors and then turned to look back at her. 'Listen – don't tell Edward you've seen me, okay? And give me a call – soon!'

Abi watched him go. He didn't leave via the driveway, but cut through a hedge to the side of the property. Abi frowned. She hadn't realised there was a way out there, but it obviously led down to the village where Oscar was parked. She shook her head. Everything about the way he spoke and the way he behaved was sending warning signals, but she couldn't help being curious. There was a definite something about him.

She looked down at the card he'd given her, debating whether she would ring him or not. Then she put the card down and got on with making some lunch. But the card sat there, quietly taunting her.

After lunch, she did some printing and then spent a bit of time in the garden. When she came back in, the card was still there and she sighed, finally picking up the phone.

'Hello? Yes, it's Abi. I'm good. Can I come and see you? I was thinking right now? Is that okay? Lovely. I'll see you soon.'

CHAPTER TEN

Abi arrived at Ronnie's ten minutes later and, ten minutes after that, they were sitting in the garden, each with a glass of freshly-squeezed lemonade, chinking with ice cubes.

'So, let me get this straight,' Ronnie said. 'You like Edward and you think he likes you, but he hasn't actually made a move on you?'

Abi grinned at Ronnie's phrasing. 'That's right.'

'And you think you like Oscar and you know he likes you because he's asked you out?'

'Yes.'

'Okay then,' Ronnie said, taking a long draught of his lemonade as he contemplated things. 'Here's a revolutionary thought – why don't you ask Edward out? I mean, women can do that these days.'

'I know they can,' Abi said, 'but I'm not sure if he wants me to. I don't know. I just keep having these odd feelings around him – like perhaps he's trying to ask me out. But what if I'm wrong?'

'But what if you're right? What if he is trying and failing

miserably, although heaven knows why. I mean, how hard can it be to ask a lovely lady like you out?'

'I don't want to push him if he isn't – you know – interested. Can you imagine how unbearably embarrassing that would be?'

'So go out with Oscar then. You like him, don't you?'

Abi nodded. 'But won't that be a signal to Edward that I'm not interested in him? I mean, if he is interested in me?'

'I can see that might make things tricky if he is trying to pluck up the courage to ask you out, yes.'

Abi sighed. 'I really don't know what to do.'

'Sit here and drink lemonade with me for a bit. That's the answer to everything I reckon.'

Abi couldn't help smiling. 'This is the very last thing I expected to happen when I moved to Winfield. I thought life would be quieter here. Less complicated.'

'Ah, but life has a way of seeking you out no matter where you are. And that's as it should be. None of us should live in a safe little bubble. Where would the fun be in that, eh?'

Abi agreed in principle, but it was a little harder to put it into practice.

'How can two brothers be so different?' she asked Ronnie after finishing her lemonade. 'Edward can barely say two words to me without seeming awkward whereas Oscar just blurted out his feelings to me as if he didn't have any kind of filter at all.'

'And which do you prefer – the shy one or the bold one?'

'I don't know,' she said honestly. 'I've known Edward longer although, when I say I've known him, I realise that we don't really know much about each other. We've spent a little time together, but we've always been doing something else like swimming or eating. And that's okay. I like that quiet sort of friendship.'

'Can I hear a "but" approaching?' Ronnie asked.

Abi sighed. 'But things are just so easy with Oscar. He wants to talk to me. He tells me he likes me. He doesn't hide his feelings and that's rather refreshing, isn't it?'

'Well, it's certainly good not to waste time,' Ronnie said.

'But there's something going on between Edward and Oscar. Do I really want to get in the middle of that?'

'Maybe you should ask Edward's opinion.'

Abi winced. 'I don't like the idea of that!'

'He's bound to find out sooner or later – if you do go out with Oscar, that is.'

'I don't like the idea of that either.'

Ronnie put his empty glass down on the grass and scratched his head. 'So, let me get this straight. You're absolutely no clearer on what you should do?'

Abi placed her glass on the grass too and looked at Ronnie. 'I'm afraid it very much looks that way.'

'Another lemonade?' he suggested.

'You think it will help?'

'It can't hurt to try!'

Harry was very excited arriving home after work on Wednesday evening because he was going to spend it with Aura. It was the night he was going to be grounded – in the best possible way. Grounding, he'd discovered, had nothing to do with being punished.

He took a shower and got changed. It wouldn't do to turn up at Aura's in his stiff work shirt which he was quite sure smelt of stress. Instead, he changed into a forest-green T-shirt and a pair of grey jogging trousers. It was amazing how good these loose clothes felt against his body after the stifling office clothes he'd been wearing all day. He felt as if his body could breathe again and that was a wonderful feeling.

Aura was wearing another of her long, loose dresses that evening. It was midnight-blue shot through with turquoise waves. Her red hair was tied back with a bright silver clasp and she was wearing large silver hooped earrings threaded through with blue beads.

'Hello Harry.'

'Hi Aura. You look...' he paused, 'amazing!'

She looked down at her dress. 'I do?'

'You always do.'

She smiled shyly.

'I don't know anyone who dresses the way you do.'

'No?'

He shook his head, trying to imagine Aura drifting around his work place. No. She was much too much of a free spirit to be anchored to a nine to five job, stuck in an office. It would be like putting a rare orchid in a dark cupboard and expecting it to thrive. No, the office was okay for people like him, but not for souls like Aura.

'So, what are we doing tonight?' he asked.

'We're going outside,' she told him, 'and you might want to take your shoes and socks off.'

'Oh, of course,' he said, quickly removing them, noticing that Aura was barefoot again and suspecting that she had been all day.

'Grounding is all about bare feet and their contact with the earth. *Skin to earth*, I call it.' She led the way through the open doors into the walled garden where there were candles in pretty glass lanterns, lighting the space as the sun slowly set and making a circle for them to sit inside.

'We'll start with some breath work to get ourselves centred

and just to calm everything down after our long day,' she said, sitting down on the grass.

'Am I sitting right?' Harry was fidgeting like a toddler at playgroup.

'Just get comfy.'

'Do I have to cross my legs in that weird guru way?'

Aura shook her head. 'Not at all. Whatever's right for you.'

'Oh, should I have brought one of my crystals?' he asked as he noticed she was holding one.

'No. I like to hold one because it helps me to focus,' she confessed. 'It's a bit of a habit.'

'What is it?'

'A smoky quartz.' She opened her palm to show him the dark crystal held within.

'Beautiful. Should I have one too, do you think? Would it help me to focus?'

Aura seemed to think about this for a moment and then she gently placed the crystal on the grass between them.

'Shall we share it?' she asked.

He smiled.

'Okay, let's begin. If you remember from last time, we're looking for the spaces between thoughts,' she said.

'Right,' Harry said. 'Are you absolutely *sure* that they exist?'

'Oh, yes, but they can be hard to find if you're not used to seeking them out. But you've got to allow yourself the time to seek.'

'Well, that's why I'm here,' he said happily.

'All you have to do is listen to your true self. Give yourself time and space to go deep within yourself, okay?' She glanced across at him in the darkening evening. 'Let's start by focusing on our breath. Take a deep settling breath in and then let it go. Feel your chest rise and your body expand as you breathe in the gift of air. Then, on the exhale, give it back to the universe. Feel the circle, the cycle of give and take. Be grateful for our exchange with the world.'

Harry breathed, listening to the sound of it. Why hadn't he noticed how hypnotising it was? It reminded him of the sea upon the shore. In and out in a never ending rhythm.

Finally, after a few moments, Aura ended the breath work and Harry looked at her. He'd had his gaze on the quartz crystal and only now became aware of the fact.

'You okay?' Aura asked.

'Yeah,' he said. 'I had the strangest feeling for a minute there. I felt like I was almost dissolving into the crystal. Is that crazy?'

'Not at all. It gave you something to focus on. Like the flame of a candle or firelight. I think crystals have the same effect. We can gaze right into the heart of them and lose ourselves.'

'Maybe I could buy some more from you. You did say they were tools, didn't you? And tools make things easier, don't they?'

'They do. They can help you with whatever you need them to,' Aura said. 'If you think of chopping a tree for example. You wouldn't do it with your bare hands – you'd use an axe or a chainsaw. But those tools won't chop the tree down on their own. We have to work with them. Well, it's the same with crystals. They're our allies. They're there to help us.'

'So why did you choose this one for tonight?'

Aura bent forward and picked up the smoky quartz. It winked darkly in the candlelight.

'Smoky quartz is a very good grounding crystal. It reminds us of the earth and is used for the earth chakra as well as being a root chakra stone.'

Harry frowned. 'I'm not sure about all this chakra stuff.'

'No?' Aura nodded. 'That's okay. It's quite a normal

reaction, but just think of it in different terminology. For example, the chakras are merely energy centres, and I think we're all familiar with some of those.'

'For instance?'

Aura got up and came and sat next to Harry. She then lifted his right hand, placing it on his belly a moment later.

'Just a little lower,' she said, letting him move his own hand. 'There. Isn't this the area where you get butterflies when you're nervous?'

'Yes,' he said.

'That's your sacral chakra. An area of emotion. And here,' she said, holding her own hand to her throat. 'The throat chakra. Ever get that dried up feeling when you can't speak? When you're unable to express your thoughts clearly?'

'Oh, yes!'

'It's all different kinds of energy. That's all the chakras are really. Don't let a bit of terminology put you off.'

'So grounding's about the chakras?'

'It's good for our root chakra which is…' Aura positioned her hand somewhere below her belly button. Somewhere private.

'Oh, right!' Harry said with a laugh and Aura smiled.

'I like to think about the earth chakra too – it's a transpersonal chakra – it's beyond our own bodies – and it helps to focus our attention on our connection with the ground beneath our feet. So, our feet are what we're going to focus on now. Shall we stand up?'

Harry nodded. 'If my boss could see me now! Barefoot in the moonlight!' He laughed as he looked up at the piece of moon that was peeping out from behind a cloud.

'Should you be thinking about your boss right now?' Aura asked with a tiny smile.

'Probably not.' Harry admitted and, suitably chastised, he did his best to focus on what he was supposed to be doing.

Aura picked up the smoky quartz crystal, holding it in her left hand, and then she led the way out of the candlelit circle and Harry felt the cool grass under his feet. He paused. It actually felt really good – cold and a little damp, but strangely refreshing on his bare skin. It made him wonder why he hadn't tried this before, this barefootedness.

Aura didn't speak for a while. Instead, she led the way silently and slowly through the darkening garden, her head inclined down.

Live in the moment, Harry told himself, trying to remember the things that Aura had taught him. Focus on the senses. Breathe. Feel. Ground. For a moment, he got the feeling that he was breathing through his feet. Was that an outrageous thought?

'Aura?' he asked. 'Can you actually breathe through your feet?'

She turned back to face him. 'You breathe through all your skin.'

Harry nodded, suddenly feeling silly for asking. It was just one of those things he hadn't spent any time thinking about. Feet were just feet. They got you from one place to another. You covered them up first thing in the morning and only saw them for brief glimpses in the shower or getting in and out of bed. In short, he had never really thought about his feet before.

'Remember to breathe as you walk,' Aura reminded him as they wended their way back and forth across the lawned area of the walled garden. 'Feel the gentle energy of your breath as it enters your body and as it leaves it. Let go of any fears or stress or anxiety you may be feeling at this time. Anything that's unresolved. Just let it go. Release it all down into the earth beneath your feet. You don't have to carry it.'

They walked for a little while in silence. Harry's eyes were becoming accustomed to the dark now and he began to notice things he hadn't seen before like flowers and vegetables that Abi was growing in the raised beds. He hadn't noticed them in the daylight because he rarely had time to spend in the garden and, when he did, his head was so full of things that he didn't always see what was right in front of him. It had taken Aura to literally bring him back to his senses.

By the time they returned to the candlelit circle and sat down opposite each other, Harry was feeling totally relaxed and yet strangely energised.

'So, what did you think?' Aura asked him, her face almost luminous in the glow of the candles.

'I loved it!'

'You did?'

'I really did. I felt so *alive!* I was noticing things all around the garden that I hadn't seen before and I felt – I don't know – more connected.'

'Grounding will do that for you. It's so good for you. You're plugging yourself into the earth, re-establishing your physical roots.'

'I've got roots in my feet?' Harry asked with a laugh.

'Many people visualise that,' Aura told him. 'If you practice yoga or other forms of movement, it can benefit you to visualise yourself rooting into the ground. It helps with your balance. Anyway, it just feels good, doesn't it?'

'It really does,' Harry said, wiggling his toes. 'Blimey, my feet are pale. They look anaemic. They're practically glowing in the dark!'

'They need the sunshine just as much as our faces and arms do.'

'Yours are really cute,' he said and then felt himself blush.

'If you saw the soles of my feet, you'd take that back.'

'What's wrong with them?'

'Well, they're not as soft and supple as they could be. I go barefoot a lot and it kind of takes it out of the soles.'

'So grounding is good for the *soul* but bad for the *soles*?'

Aura laughed. 'I hadn't thought about it like that before.'

They sat still for a moment, listening to the sounds of the garden and then Aura stood up. Harry watched as she blew the candles out and a part of him wished that he could stay a little longer. But he had to remind himself that he was a customer and not a friend, and his session was over.

They went back inside and it felt odd to be indoors.

'I'd love to know what's next,' Harry said after paying her.

'I've been thinking about that,' Aura said. 'The summer solstice is approaching. We could do something that evening if you like.'

'Great!' Harry said. 'Will that be outdoors again?'

'I hope so.'

'I like being outdoors.'

She smiled at him. 'You can work on tanning your feet.'

He laughed. 'Not much chance of that with the hours I work.'

'That's a shame,' she said. Oh, I was going to ask you what the product was?'

'Product?'

'That you were doing the presentation for? The one the green aventurine helped with.'

'Oh, it was a new deodorant.'

'Right. Like the world needs yet another one.'

'I know, but still they come,' Harry said.

'Well, I hope it's all environmentally-friendly and not tested on animals. I hate it when they make things that harm the world. There's absolutely no need for it.'

Harry frowned. He didn't actually know the answer to that, but he told her the name of the company.

'Oh,' she said, her face creasing up into a frown.

'What?'

'They make that nasty weed killer, don't they?'

'I don't know about their other products.'

'It doesn't just kill weeds – it kills everything else too like insects.'

'I didn't know.'

'Don't tell Abi – she'll get you evicted if she knows you're working for them. She's into everything being organic and natural in the garden.'

'Right,' Harry said, feeling as if some of the peace he'd found in the session ebbing away from him now. Aura seemed to pick up on this.

'Oh, Harry – I'm sorry. That was insensitive of me. It's your work and I shouldn't make judgements.'

'No, no – you're right. You care about things. It's my fault. I didn't know and I guess that sounds like an appalling excuse, but it's the only one I've got. I was given this account and I didn't think to look into the company. Not ethically, anyway. Is that awful? It sounds awful to me now.' He scratched the back of his neck. 'I'll tell you what. I promise to do better in the future, okay? I'll find out what it is I'm helping to sell. How does that sound?'

'That sounds great.' She gave him a big bright smile and, before he could think, Harry had leaned forward and kissed her cheek.

'You're remarkable,' he said, watching as her face flamed red to clash with her hair.

'I don't know about that.' She lowered her head and then looked up at him in a shy, soft way that captured his heart so completely that he felt quite giddy.

'I'd better be off,' he said. 'Oh, my shoes! I was feeling so comfortable being barefoot, I almost forgot.'

'You'll find it's quite addictive,' Aura warned him.

'I'll try and incorporate it more into my life although it might be tricky at work,' he promised as he hid his pale feet back in his socks and shoes again.

'Yes, it's easier if you work from home,' Aura said, wriggling her own bare toes.

Harry did his best not to stare at them. They were so very cute.

'Thanks again,' he said quickly, diverting his attention. 'It was a really amazing evening.'

'I'm so glad you enjoyed it.'

'Goodnight then.'

'Night Harry.'

He left her apartment and walked across the hallway to his own and, as he sat down at his coffee table and reached for his laptop, he did a search for the company whose deodorant he'd helped advertise. Aura had made him think of something that had never occurred to him before. He'd been passionate about working on the project, playing with words and coming up with the slogan, but he realised that he hadn't really looked into the product itself nor its manufacturer. He did that now and he didn't like what he found.

The company was a large one. It had created all sorts of lines from cosmetics to health-care products, from pet food to paper towels. And, yes, Aura was right – they did produce a weed killer. And their reputation wasn't a good one. Although there was some positive debate online about the ethics of the company, it appeared that some of their products were, indeed, tested on animals.

Harry's heart sank and then he got mad at himself. Why hadn't he asked questions like this before? Why had it taken Aura to alert him to it? Was he so shallow that he just looked at his own interest in a product and not its wider reach? What on earth had he helped to promote, he wondered now? And was it too late for him to change?

CHAPTER ELEVEN

Abi had been staring at a blank piece of paper for a good ten minutes now and she wasn't contemplating anything artistic. She was thinking of Oscar, remembering that cheeky grin of his, and the sunshine on his face as he'd left her apartment. She remembered how vital he'd made her feel by giving her a simple compliment and by asking her to call him. She'd never got that feeling from Edward during all the time they'd spent together so perhaps they were destined to just be friends and that was fine. She liked the friendship that they were developing, albeit ever so slowly. But this thing with Oscar felt different. He wasn't just interested in her as a neighbour or a co-owner; he was interested in her as a woman, and that was something Abi hadn't experienced for a while and she had to admit that it felt rather wonderful.

So she rang him. He sounded delighted to hear from her although not altogether surprised, which made her smile.

'How did you know I'd call you?' she'd asked before hanging up.

He'd laughed. 'The way your eyes sparkled when I said goodbye to you at Winfield.'

Abi had hung up and looked at herself in the mirror. Did her eyes really sparkle or was that just a cheesy chat-up line? And had they been sparkling at Oscar? She bit her lip. Well, if they had been, she wasn't going to try and deny it. After all, everyone needed a little bit of sparkle in their lives, didn't they?

They'd arranged to meet at a farm shop café which Abi had discovered and loved. It was just far enough away from Winfield that Edward would be unlikely to see the two of them together. It felt awfully clandestine and Abi wondered if she'd made a huge mistake in starting something she might later regret.

She checked her watch. Oscar was late. Ten minutes and counting, which was strange as he wasn't far away and he'd been at home when she'd called. She looked up and down the road and then went into the farm shop, admiring the fruit and vegetables which looked so much bigger and juicier than those she had managed to grow so far in the walled garden. But she reminded herself that it was early days and she shouldn't be comparing herself to those who'd had a good head start when it came to food production.

Five minutes later, she heard the brakes of a car and watched as Oscar parked and got out of the rather beaten-up vehicle. Abi walked outside to meet him and couldn't help noticing that there were scratches along the driver's side and a ding in the front bumper, but she forgot those as soon as Oscar waved at her, that irrepressible smile of his lighting up his face.

'Hi Abi!'

'Hello.' She waited for him to apologise or give an explanation as to why he was late, but he didn't. Had he not noticed? He gave the impression that he hadn't and so they went into the farm shop together, making their way to the little café in the corner of the converted barn. It was pretty with its exposed beams and view out to the valley beyond where cows were grazing and they ordered a coffee each, with Abi also choosing a croissant and Oscar an iced bun. Abi had to smile at the delight with which he ate it. He was like a big kid.

'Didn't have any breakfast this morning,' he said. 'Not that I need an excuse.'

'One should never make an excuse for a treat,' Abi said. 'I can't remember the last time I had a croissant.'

They smiled across the table at one another as if sharing a delicious secret and she noticed that he looked very handsome in a white shirt that, although it wasn't as crisp as the ones Edward wore, did look clean and cute.

'Listen,' Abi said, deciding to address the issue that had been worrying her, 'before we go anywhere or do or say anything, I need to know what's going on with you and Edward.'

'Okay,' Oscar said, sounding very casual about it all. 'What do you want to know?'

Abi leaned across the table towards him. 'Why is Edward so – well...' she stopped, not quite knowing which words to use.

'Uptight?'

'No!'

'Miserable?'

'Oscar!' she chided. 'Don't be so mean.'

Oscar sighed 'The thing with Edward,' he began, 'is that he just doesn't know how to live. Don't get me wrong – he's a decent person. You won't find better. But he's – well – he's a bit stiff around the edges, don't you think?'

It was a leading question and one that Abi certainly didn't want to be led into.

'He finds it hard to relax – that's the root of it all.'

'And you don't?' Abi said.

'Does it look like I do?'

'No. It doesn't.'

'We might be brothers, but we're not exactly kindred spirits, I'm afraid, and that's fine. I've made my peace with that.'

'But he seems so uncomfortable even talking about you.'

Oscar took a sip of his drink. 'It's bizarre, isn't it? I try to reach out to him, but he's just not open to having any kind of friendship with me.'

'That's so sad.'

'It is, isn't it? But, believe me, I'm constantly reaching out to him and he just bats me away like an annoying fly.' He shrugged his shoulders and blew a raspberry as if to make light of something that could easily weigh him down.

'How long does this go back?' Abi dared to ask. 'Was there an event or something specific that happened between you?'

Again, Oscar shrugged. 'Beats me. I've tried to work it out, but I think it just comes down to us being different people, you know?'

Abi mulled this over. Was it as simple as that? Maybe it was. Maybe that's what was at the heart of her problems with her own sister too. They were just too different. Abi sometimes wondered if they would be friends at all if they weren't related, but the thought upset her too much to dwell on frequently. Maybe it was that way for Oscar and Edward.

Perhaps it was best if they didn't talk about it, she decided. After all, she wouldn't have liked to be grilled about her relationship with her sister, would she? It was one thing to offer up such information, but quite another to be asked for it.

'So, are you working at the moment?' she asked him.

He rolled his eyes. 'What a dull question!'

'Sorry!' she said quickly.

'It's so adult, isn't it?'

'I suppose. But it's what one asks, isn't it?'

'But it's so limiting, don't you think? To judge somebody in terms of their work.'

'Well, I've never thought about it before.'

He grinned. 'That's because you're an artist. You have a gift. But most of us don't, I'm afraid, and it's embarrassing to assume that what we do to make ends meet is who we truly are.'

Abi nodded. 'So, does that mean you *aren't* working?'

Oscar took another bite of his bun before looking at her. Abi swallowed hard, fearing that she might have offended him, but she hadn't been able to resist asking. He took a moment before answering her and he did so with a grin that stretched from ear to ear before he laughed out loud.

'You are funny!' he said, jabbing the end of his bun towards her. 'Edward didn't tell me you were so funny!'

'What has he said about me?'

'Nothing.'

'Oh.'

'Don't worry about it. He only talks to me if I really get in his face.'

'I'll try not to be offended then,' Abi said. 'Anyway, you've just danced rather skilfully out of answering my question.'

Oscar narrowed his eyes at her as he finished his bun. 'You really want to know?'

'I want to get to know you.'

'Okay. If you insist. I'm currently working nights at a restaurant in Brighton. It's not a very nice restaurant actually and I only got the job because the guy hiring is an old mate from school and didn't ask to see any references.'

'You don't have references?'

'Ah, not good ones. The last restaurant I worked at didn't work out so well.'

'I'm sorry.'

'Don't be. There was a stuck up customer who insisted I got his order wrong so I told him he could put his lemon sole where the sun doesn't shine.'

'Oh, Oscar!'

He shrugged. 'I needed to get out of there anyway. The pay was rubbish. But this new place isn't much better.'

'Why don't you look for something else?'

'I will. I hate working in the evenings. It means I can't go out myself.'

'And you like going out?' Abi asked.

He nodded. 'I do when I have a beautiful companion.' He fixed his gaze on her and she could feel her cheeks heating up in response. 'So, what's that told you about me? Not shown me in a very good light, has it? I'm a man who can't hold a job down because I'm rude to people.'

'Perhaps you're too honest.'

'You think? That's a very nice way of looking at things.'

She smiled at him. 'Maybe you just haven't found your niche.'

'Niche? I like that. Well, let me know if you find it before I do.'

'I'll keep a look out for you.'

'Thanks.' He looked uneasy for a moment.

'You okay?'

'Yep. Sure. Just, I hope that hasn't put you off me. I know you're smart and creative and successful and everything and, well, I'm not.'

'I'm not here with you now because I thought you had a fancy job, Oscar,' Abi told him sincerely. 'I'm here because I like you. You make me smile and laugh and feel happy and you can never get enough of that in your life, can you?'

'But I'm not your usual type, right?'

Abi frowned. Did she have a type? If she did, it had clearly been the wrong type to date because she was still very much alone and happy about it too. But she couldn't help recalling Dante for a moment. Dante the intellectual, the arty, the smarty. She had loved how very knowledgeable he was, how cultured and passionate about the arts. She doubted if Oscar had ever set foot in an art gallery, let alone knew his Rubens from his Rembrandt. But did that matter? Did you always have to have the same interests as your chosen partner? Perhaps she was attracted to Oscar because he seemed to be the polar opposite of Dante.

'I don't like to think I have a type,' Abi told him. 'Like friends – it seems awful to set boundaries up. I don't think you can do that. You *shouldn't* do it because it's too limiting.'

'I agree.'

She smiled. 'I bet I'm not your usual type.'

'So you think *I* have a type, do you?'

'I don't know. Do you?'

He seemed to consider this before answering. 'I've had a few girlfriends and they've all had something in common, it's true.'

'What?'

'Me! They all liked me.'

Abi laughed.

'Of course, they all left me too,' he added.

'Ah!'

'But they all had something unique about them – some spark, some appeal that made me take notice. I don't know. It's hard to define, isn't it?'

'And perhaps we shouldn't try to. Some things just *feel* right, don't they?'

'Like us? Do you think *we* feel right?'

'Yes. Right here and right now, this feels right,' Abi confessed, surprised by how very forward she was sounding and how comfortable it felt.

'Want another coffee and croissant?' he asked. 'I could murder another bun!'

She laughed and nodded and Oscar got up to place their order.

When Abi got back to Winfield she spotted Edward walking round from the garden.

'Hello,' he said. 'Just had a delivery of guttering for that last section at the back.'

'Oh, good,' she said.

'You okay? Been out, have you?'

It seemed like quite an intrusive question coming from Edward and Abi felt the full weight of it. Perhaps he knew what she'd been up to. Perhaps he'd sussed out what Oscar was doing behind his back.

'Yes – just – you know. A spot of shopping.' She lifted up her canvas bag which, luckily, was a good alibi as it was filled with fresh produce from the farm shop.

Edward nodded. 'You look...,' he paused and Abi's hand flew to her hair, wondering if it was looking a little wind torn or something.

'What?'

'Happy. You look happy,' he said.

'Do I?'

'Have you worked things out with your sister?'

'No.'

'Oh. Sorry.'

'It's okay. Don't worry about it. It'll work its own way out.'

Edward gave her a sympathetic smile. 'I hope it will.'

They held each other's gaze and there was that thing – that palpable thing –between them again: a place where Abi felt words should exist, but where none were forthcoming. It was kind of awkward – a moment of anticipation, where something felt like it was missing. And then it was over with a single glance away and a shuffle of feet.

'I'd better get going,' Edward said.

'Yes.'

'I'll see you later.'

'Okay.' She watched as he walked round the side of Winfield to enter the hall through the French doors into his apartment and she couldn't help wondering, once again, what he'd been thinking and if he'd wanted to say more to her than he actually had.

Harry raked a hand through his hair and sighed. It was a little too hot in the office today after the air conditioning had stalled, and he'd just come off the phone with a client who was not happy with the preliminary sketches Harry's team had sent through even though the team had, to Harry's mind, implemented everything the client had asked for and in a unique and streamlined way. Some people were very hard to please, weren't they? And the way he'd expressed himself too. Really, there was no need for language like that on a Tuesday afternoon.

Harry thought of Aura. What would she do in such a situation? Pick up a crystal? Meditate for a while? Focus on the breathing? Harry mused on these things for a moment and then he could have sworn he heard Aura's voice clear next to him.

'Take your shoes off,' she told him.

Harry smiled. A part of him wanted to reply aloud, 'I'm at work, Aura. One doesn't just take one's shoes off.' But that's what the old Harry would have said and he wasn't the old Harry anymore, was he? He was changing, evolving. He was open to new experiences and so he pushed his chair away from his desk and bent to take his shoes off followed by his socks which he tucked neatly inside his shoes before pushing them under his desk.

He grimaced at the horrible whiteness of his feet. They were pretty ugly things, his feet, he decided. But he had to admit that releasing them from their woolly, leathery prison and being barefoot felt good, even on the modest office carpet. He experimented by curling his toes up, feeling the warm, slightly rough texture of the carpet on his skin. Then he got braver, standing up and walking around a bit. It was a good job he had his own office, he thought. He couldn't have got away with that in an open-plan space, which was silly really. Perhaps employees would benefit from a bit of barefoot time. Never mind a coffee break, how about a barefoot break with folks freeing themselves of their footwear and marching up and down for a bit, reconnecting, reinvigorating.

It was then that there was a knock on his door. Harry scooted back behind his desk just as one of his team entered.

'I've got the draft contract for you,' he said, placing the papers on Harry's desk.

'With the new clause?'

'Yes,' his colleague said. 'You okay? You look a bit red?'

'No, I'm fine,' Harry told him, clearing his throat. 'Never better.'

His colleague stood there for a moment, examining Harry and his desk as if trying to work out a puzzle, but mercifully, he then shook his head and left the office. Harry breathed a sigh of relief and got on with vetting the contract, his bare feet tucked safely under his desk. It was rather a naughty, illicit feeling to be barefoot in the office. It wasn't as if he was completely naked or anything and yet there was still that naughty thrill of having broken with conventional behaviour.

After a while, Harry quite forgot he was barefoot, making his way through the new contract before ringing another client and sorting through his email. And then it happened. The fire alarm went off. Harry groaned. He was just getting somewhere with his work, but he got up, quickly leaving his desk.

It wasn't until he was in the middle of the main office that he remembered and, by then, it was too late. He was completely surrounded by work colleagues, jostling at the top of the stairs as they made their way out of the building. A couple of women glanced at him in undisguised amusement, looked at one another and then burst out laughing and Harry swallowed hard, feeling quite helpless, with his pale feet exposed to the whole office.

'Hey – what happened to your shoes?' someone else blurted out.

'Up to no good in his office,' someone else said.

Oh, heavens, Harry thought. He only hoped his boss didn't see him. He'd have to come up with some excuse. Like he was testing out a new product or experimenting with a theory about something for an amazing tagline he was working on.

The office stairs felt cold and uncomfortable as he made his way down them. No wonder the world had been forced to invent shoes, he mused. Bare feet were all very well when it was lush grass or comfortable carpet underneath them, but the urban landscape didn't lend itself to the whole earthing experience.

The tarmac of the office car park felt hot and rough and he wished he could swap it for the damp, moonlit grass of Winfield Hall. To take his mind off his discomfort, he thought again of the night he'd shared those special moments with Aura. He wondered if he should message her, taking a photo of his bare feet and saying, 'See the trouble you've got me into!' He wondered what she'd say. She'd probably say that he shouldn't be worrying about what others thought of him; he should only be focused on what felt good to him. And she'd be right, of course, and so Harry tuned out the voices around him and the jokes being made about his naked feet and focused on his breath and, slowly, the harsh sound of the fire alarm faded into the background and he was no longer anxious about the voices around him. He was safe and happy in his own space.

Aura would have been proud of him.

CHAPTER TWELVE

Aura adored her clients. Since moving to Winfield Hall, she'd never been happier in her work. It was a real privilege to be able to conduct some of her sessions from her home, not only from the point of view of convenience, but because the setting really added something magical to them. All of her clients who'd seen her there had commented on it, falling under the spell of Aura's spacious room filled with her colourful throws and cushions and the gentle presence of the crystals. And, of course, they adored the walled garden – a sanctuary of peace and tranquillity.

In the last couple of weeks, Aura had been working with a woman who'd just got out of a difficult relationship and had had her confidence completely broken. She seemed afraid of everything – of being stuck where she was or of starting anything new, of giving up on her dreams or of daring to have any at all. Aura hoped she had provided a safe place and that her sessions had been encouraging and inspiring. It was a true privilege, she felt, to meet people when they were so vulnerable and to watch their progress back towards strength and confidence.

But something had struck her recently. So many of her clients were people who were simply stressed by the modern world. Take Harry for instance. She often thought of how his job, his lifestyle, had robbed him of the most important thing we had as humans: our breath. He had simply forgotten how to breathe. His days were so busy and his nights so full of the stress that carried over into them that he never had time to focus on the one thing that could make such a difference. It was something which came up time and time again: people no longer had time to breathe.

What kind of a world was it when our minds raced twenty-four seven to the detriment to our bodies? A world where it was deemed right to be working around the clock, to always be seen as being busy and productive. It seemed to Aura that humans had moved so far away from the natural state they were meant to live in: one of peace and harmony with nature, of having the time to take care of oneself both physically, mentally and spiritually. Something very vital had been lost and she, in her small way, hoped that she could reintroduce those who came to her to the pleasures and great benefits of taking time out from the rush and the stress of it all, of sitting down barefoot in the grass, closing one's eyes and focusing on the breath.

Aura had just finished a session with a client online as the light was fading from the early June sky. She loved these longer, lighter evenings and she was about to venture out into the garden with a cup of tea when her buzzer went. She walked towards the intercom to answer it.

'Hello?'

'Sis?'

Aura froze. 'Johnny?'

'Of course, Johnny! You gonna let me in?'

Aura hesitated. Johnny was at Winfield. How had that

happened? When had he got out of prison? And why was he here?

Oh, god! The letter! In a moment of big sister stupidity, she'd let him have her address in case of emergencies and now here he was and there was no hiding from him.

'Sis?' he called again.

'Yes – just a minute.'

She left her apartment and walked to the front door, waiting a moment, gathering all the inner strength she needed to deal with the hurricane that was her little brother. And then she opened the door.

'Johnny!' she cried. 'What are you doing here? Why didn't you tell me you were out?'

'I wanted to surprise you.'

'Well, you have!'

'Good surprise?' he said, that cheeky, slightly scary grin of his daring her to contradict him.

'Of *course* good!' Aura stepped forward and hugged him, trying not to grimace at the strange odour that hung around him. He smelt of an institution.

'Wow, Sis, you've certainly landed on your feet. This is some place you've got here.'

'I don't own the whole thing, you know.'

'I know.'

'Just a little bit. And it's rented. The landlady let me have it for a special price. She likes arty types.'

Johnny grinned. 'Really?'

It was on the tip of her tongue to tell him that he couldn't stay, but perhaps he didn't have that in mind at all and she was worrying about nothing.

'Can I come in, then?'

'Of course.'

'I want to see this place of yours.'

She led the way inside, noticing how Johnny gazed up at the stairs in awe.

'Blimey! It's like a cathedral or something.'

'Isn't it beautiful?'

'How did you get so lucky?'

Aura gave a nervous laugh. 'Right place, right time.'

'Ah,' Johnny said. 'That's where you and I differ, see. I'm always in the wrong place at the wrong time!'

'Johnny! You don't need to be, you know. You can change all that so easily.'

'Yeah, yeah. Don't start with a lecture.'

'Sorry, but I do worry about you.'

'I know you do.' He reached out and ruffled her hair. It was something he'd always done which she didn't wholly like, but she put up with it as a sign of his affection for her.

They crossed the hall towards her apartment and Aura couldn't help thinking this was the point of no return. Once she let Johnny over the threshold, she knew her life could change forever. But wasn't she pleased to see him? Wasn't she glad he was out of prison at last? Of course she was. And he was looking fit and happy, wasn't he? She glanced at him as she hesitated at her door.

'Come on!' he said, 'I'm dying to see where my big sis is holing up these days.'

She smiled nervously, anxious that he would think she was earning a lot more money than she was.

'I couldn't believe it when I found this place and the rent was so low. The landlady hardly charges me anything.'

'Yeah, you said that already.'

'I did?'

Johnny's arm came up and she flinched slightly, unsure of what he was about to do, but he merely pushed the door open, gently easing Aura inside.

'Jeez, Sis!' he said with a long low whistle. 'This is pretty cool.'

'Isn't it?'

'Look at the ceiling!'

'I know.'

'And all the space.'

'I'm very spoiled after my horrible little flat. Remember?'

'The one where all the neighbours' smells came in through the vents?'

'Smells, noise, everything!'

'Still, better than where I've been.' For a moment, he looked like a little boy, standing lost in the middle of her palatial apartment, and her big sister genes kicked in and she found herself hugging him close.

'I missed you!'

'You did?'

'Of course I did! And you never wrote back to me.'

'Hey, you know what my spelling's like.'

'You should read more, Johnny.'

'Read? I don't have time to read!'

'No? Not even in prison?' He shook his head. Aura was confused. The image she had of prison was of inmates with nothing *but* time on their hands. And weren't there libraries and classes and things? 'But reading's so good for the brain!'

Johnny laughed. 'I love that you think I have a brain.'

'But you do. You're smart, Johnny.' He pulled a face at her words. 'You *are!*'

'Let's agree that you got the beauty and the brains in our family, okay? I got the big nose and bad luck.'

'Oh, Johnny!'

He walked over to the French doors and looked outside. 'This yours too?'

'Well, this part's Abi's. She's the owner, but she's happy for me to share it.'

'Sure beats the outside space we had to use.'

Aura frowned. She couldn't imagine what Johnny had been through. Eighteen months locked away from the world and that had been reduced from his initial sentence of three years. Aura hated to think about it. She'd have gone mad if it had been her. But, then again, she hadn't been caught burgling the local bank manager's home, had she? That's what the sentence had been for. Of course, she knew Johnny had been stealing for years. He'd fallen in with some dubious types back in secondary school – the sort that were always daring one another to do crazy things. It had been a laugh, Johnny had always told her. They hadn't meant any harm. But things usually escalated and, like a lot of things that were bad for you, it proved highly addictive.

But they didn't talk about any of that. Aura usually found out what Johnny was up to via the local newspaper. She'd lost count now of all the shoplifting and burglaries. She could only hope that this stint in prison – his longest yet – had helped him rethink things and that he was starting anew now.

She looked at him as he gazed out into the garden. His dark hair was short and neat. Unlike her, he hadn't inherited their mother's red hair, but there were little glimpses of it if he grew a beard. He was clean shaven now and, despite the nose he always made fun of which wasn't really big at all, he was handsome. He looked like he could quite easily hold down a decent job if he put his mind to it. It was just a shame that that mind of his always chose a different route.

'How many bedrooms?' he asked, spinning round from the door.

'Just one.'

'Why do people make apartments with just one bedroom?'

'Well, I don't know if they're all like that, but this one is.'

'Stupid.'

Aura swallowed hard. 'You can't stay here, Johnny.'

He frowned, his whole face colouring with anger and Aura suddenly remembered how he could be sometimes if he didn't get his own way.

'But I've got nowhere else to go,' he told her, his voice a flat and rather menacing monotone.

'How can that be? Surely you've got lots of friends.'

He gave a hollow laugh. 'Yeah, right – *friends!* I'm sure you'd love to meet some of my friends sometime.'

'Oh, Johnny!'

'Trust me, Sis, you wouldn't want me sleeping on their sofas.'

'I don't think my landlady allows guests.'

'She won't know. And I don't take up much room. I'll kip on the sofa. I don't need no special treatment.'

'Any.'

'What?'

'You don't need *any* special treatment,' Aura said. She couldn't help correcting his grammar.

'That's what I said, dumb dumb! Just get me a duvet or a blanket.'

Aura tried not to flinch. The thought of Johnny kipping on her pretty cream sofa was most unsavoury, but it conflicted horribly with the big sister in her who knew she could at least keep an eye on him if he was under her roof.

'I work from home,' she told him, feeling helpless now.

'I can make myself scarce when I need to. I've got some errands to run anyway.'

Aura dreaded to think what they might be, but she didn't say anything. She didn't want to bait him.

'Honest, you won't know I'm here,' he told her, the charmer in him coming out again as he gave her a crooked smile.

'I'm sorry, but I don't think it's a good idea. My landlady...'

He took a step towards her. 'You sure it's your landlady that's the problem here?'

'What do you mean?'

'You sure it isn't you who doesn't want me kicking around? Sis has got her nice shiny new apartment. She doesn't want her nasty criminal of a brother messing things up.'

'It's not that at all.'

'No?' Suddenly, he grabbed hold of her ponytail and yanked it – hard.

'Ow! Johnny! What are you doing?'

'Hey – you don't want your hair pulled, don't wear it like that!'

She glared at him and slapped his hands away from her. 'We're not kids anymore.' But that was the problem with Johnny. He'd never really grown up, had he? 'Look, you can stay for a couple of nights, okay?'

He gave a vague nod and Aura knew that he wasn't really listening to what she was saying. 'A couple' to him meant as long as he needed. Not that he required her consent at all. He'd made his mind up to stay and she watched in undisguised horror as he left her apartment and came back a moment later with a big bag which he plonked down on her pretty sofa.

'Cup of tea, Sis?' he asked as he got a little tin out of the bag and started rolling up a cigarette on her coffee table, casually pushing one of her favourite amethyst clusters out of his way.

She nodded and made her way into the kitchen and, as she reached for a blue mug with a gold crescent moon on it, she realised that she shouldn't be at all surprised that her thief of a brother had so casually come into her home and robbed her of her life.

Abigail was blissfully unaware of what was going on in the apartment next to hers. As far as she was concerned, Aura was the perfect tenant. She was kind and sweet and appreciated all the beauty of Winfield and, perhaps most importantly, she was quiet. That was something Abi couldn't compromise on and it was a joy to know that Aura also appreciated the peace that the hall and its surroundings bestowed on its inhabitants.

She was just pouring herself a glass of white wine after a long but very satisfying day working with her printing press when her phone rang.

'Abi?'

It was her sister. 'Hi Ellen. How are you?'

'Flustered!' came the reply. Typically, Ellen then launched straight into how all the woes of the world had managed to find their way to her doorstop without taking one minute to apologise to Abi for her behaviour at their last meeting nor to ask how Abi was herself.

'I haven't heard from Cassie for years and then, all of a sudden, I get this email inviting me to her wedding this weekend. An email! Can you imagine? I can only think that a guest has pulled out and she wants me to plug the hole.

Anyway, I'd still like to go and see some of the old gang even if I am a last minute add-on.'

Abi listened patiently as Ellen complained about having nothing suitable to wear and the price of train tickets and hotels these days.

'I'll have to buy a gift too. I don't suppose you've got any of those oven gloves with the cute little ducks on them kicking around, have you? I mean, they're too kitsch for my taste, but Cassie will love them.'

Abi bristled. Her duck oven gloves had been hugely popular and were a personal favourite of her designs. 'I don't have any, no,' she told Ellen.

'Oh. I suppose I'll have to fork out and buy a real gift then.'

Abi felt herself heating up like a furnace with rage and was on the verge of hanging up when Ellen got to the heart of the matter.

'So can you babysit the girls? You'll need to come over at lunchtime on Saturday and stay the night because Douglas is away too.'

She sighed, annoyed that Ellen always assumed she was doing nothing. 'Of course.'

'They'll need feeding and putting to bed,' Ellen said as if she were still talking about ducks rather than children.

'I know.'

'And they might have some homework left over from Friday if I don't have time to check with them. Make sure they do it before they watch *any* TV and you'll have to feed Pugly too. Bethanne knows the drill.'

There was a pause.

'Abi?'

'Yes?'

'You went all quiet.'

'You noticed?'

Ellen sighed. 'Look, you don't have to do this if you don't want to.'

'Well of course I want to. I always want to see my nieces.'

'It's no biggie. I can pay a stranger to babysit the girls and run riot in our home.'

'Don't be silly, Ellen.'

'What is it then?'

'It's just...' Abi closed her eyes as if that might help her search for the right words, but it didn't.

'What?'

'Nothing.'

'Then you'll be here for twelve on Saturday when Douglas has to leave?'

'Of course.'

'He'll be back around mid-afternoon on Sunday and I should be back shortly after that.'

'Okay.'

Her sister hung up.

It was one evening after work when the June air was still warm and the sky was turning from blue to pink just above the horizon that Harry took himself off for a walk. It was a revolutionary idea, he couldn't help thinking: to walk without purpose – he wasn't going to any particular destination, he didn't have something to achieve – he was simply walking because he wanted to. He quickly found that he liked it too. It felt good to get outside and breathe in the downland air. He was mindful to do that, hearing Aura's sweet voice reminding him of the importance of coming back to your breath.

'Your exchange with the universe,' she would say. He loved that.

And he was mindful to be aware of his senses too – not just the sights he was seeing, but the sounds and the feel of the air on his skin when he rolled his sleeves up, the smell of the gorse which was surprisingly like coconut, and the roughness of the chalk path under his boots.

It was good to just walk, to breathe and to look, especially after the day he'd had. It hadn't been particularly difficult or trying; it had just been one of those monotonous days where he felt like he'd done everything a thousand times before. There was no real challenge and no pleasure to be found and that was unusual as far as Harry was concerned because he used to thrive at work. So what had changed? Why wasn't he enjoying it now?

As his feet found a rhythm, he thought about his job. Since Aura had asked about the product he'd been advertising, Harry had felt dissatisfied with what he was doing. He'd looked back through his portfolio at some of the products he'd helped to advertise in the past and he'd started asking questions. Did the world really need yet another pair of trainers? Another brand of toothpaste? What was he actually contributing to the world? Was he making a difference or just passing the time? He used to enjoy coming up with slogans, finding new ways to rebrand old products. It had stimulated a part of his brain that liked being tested. But he had never really thought about the wider picture until meeting Aura.

He stopped at the top of a hill and took a deep breath, letting go of the stress with his exhale as he looked at the deepening colours of the sky and how the coppery pinks slowly wound their way into tangerine.

When he got back to Winfield, he hesitated in the hallway.

The temptation to knock on Aura's door was strong and, although it was late, he couldn't help himself.

'Hey!' he said a moment later when she opened the door.

'Harry!'

Was it his imagination or did she look flustered?

'You okay?'

She nodded. 'You?'

'Just been out walking. Amazing sky tonight. I remembered all your tips about breathing and focusing on my senses.'

'That's great.' She gave him a smile, but it was a little less joyous than normal, he thought. Maybe she was tired. And then he noticed the odd way she was standing in the doorway, almost as if she was blocking him from entering which wasn't like her at all. In fact, he was a little disappointed that she hadn't invited him in. He knew it was late and he hadn't booked an official appointment or anything, but he had been kind of hoping to spend a little time with her and maybe sit out in the garden as the last of the colours faded gently from the sky.

'Is everything okay?' he asked.

She nodded again and gave him a weak smile.

'Oh, listen,' Harry said. 'I had an idea as I was out walking just now. You know we were going to do something for the summer solstice?'

'That's right.'

'I was wondering if – well, rather than it being a meditation session – you know, with you guiding me, could we make it something less structured?'

'You find my sessions too structured?'

'No, no! Not at all. I *love* them just as they are. But, oh dear – I'm not making a very good job of this,' Harry said, scratching his head. 'I want to take you out. A picnic up on the downs.'

Aura smiled. 'You do?'

'Yes. Will you come with me? For a summer solstice picnic?' he asked, aware of the thump thump of his heart as he waited for her reply.

She nodded. 'Yes.' And there was that smile again. Harry felt like he'd been given a gift, a rare and precious gift that lit him up and made him feel almost buoyant.

'I'll call for you, then? On the solstice – seven o'clock okay?'

'I look forward to it.'

He watched as she closed the door and, although he was feeling like the happiest man on earth, he couldn't help thinking there was something not quite right with Aura.

When Aura closed the door on Harry, she was aware that Johnny was sitting forward on the sofa.

'Who the hell was that?' he asked.

'Just a neighbour.'

'He sounded very friendly. You're not seeing him, are you?'

Aura had forgotten how possessive her brother could be. It was funny. He could go months without seeing her or calling her but, as soon as he was back in her life, he thought he had a right to control it.

'No, I'm not seeing him.'

'So that wasn't a date he was asking you on?'

'He's a client, Johnny,' Aura said. Well, that was the truth, wasn't it? 'Anyway, I can see who I like. You can't come here and start running my life.'

Johnny stood up, a dark scowl on his face and Aura wished she hadn't said something quite so provocative.

'I'm just looking out for you,' he said, his words kind, but his manner menacing.

'But you don't need to,' she told him. 'I can take care of myself. I always have.' Aura walked through her living room, trying not to wince at the mess her sofa had become with Johnny's bedding, and sought sanctuary in the kitchen where she stood for a few moments at the sink, thinking about the two men who had come into her life and how she was struggling and juggling oh so many different feelings towards them both.

CHAPTER THIRTEEN

When Saturday arrived, Abi packed a little overnight bag which she threw on the back seat of her car together with some of her art materials for the girls. With Ellen away, they could all make as much artistic mess as they liked – as long as they cleaned up after themselves and didn't leave so much as a speck of paint anywhere.

She was still feeling a little confused after her evening with Oscar. Since their outing to the farm shop, she'd seen him twice – once in Lewes where they'd had a pizza and browsed a couple of antique shops together. It had been a lovely way to get to know each other. He was easy to talk to and showed an interest in everything around him even though she got the feeling that antiques really weren't his sort of thing.

But then there'd been the night in the pub. He'd got himself a little drunk, she had to admit that. Abi had watched as he'd ordered drink after drink. At one point, she'd reached across the table and touched his hand.

'Don't you think you've had enough?'

'What? No! I can hold my drink,' he'd told her with a gleeful smile.

'Yes, but you won't be able to drive.'

'Who says?'

Abi had looked at him aghast. 'The law.'

'You'll be safe with me,' he'd told her and Abi had decided that it would be best to end the night and call a taxi for them. Oscar was forced to leave his car at the pub.

He'd called her this morning sounding dreadful, but contrite, apologising over and over again and saying how stressful the day had been and how very easy it was relaxing in Abi's company. But relaxing to the point of inebriation was a little odd in Abi's eyes. Still, when the bunch of flowers arrived an hour later with a note from Oscar and two kisses, she'd forgiven him. Perhaps he'd just had an awful day and hadn't meant to get quite so drunk.

Abi looked at the flowers now. She had a garden full of blooms, but there was something special about receiving a big bunch from a florist, tied beautifully with ribbon and ready to pop into a vase. Oscar really was sweet to have thought of that. She wondered whether to take them with her to Ellen's, but thought it might be too much trouble in the car. They'd last the weekend, she told herself, and perhaps she could paint them when she got back.

There were a few changes to Ellen's cottage since her last visit. The living room carpet had been replaced and there was a new kitchen sink. Bethanne had had her room painted in the softest of yellows and the wallpaper had been taken off in the hallway, leaving a blank canvas of possibilities. Ellen, however, hadn't changed. She was buzzing around the place like an angry bluebottle.

'Where's my handbag?' she cried.

'Here, Mummy,' Rosie said, holding it up for her.

'Don't hold it like that, Rosie. It'll lose its shape!'

Rosie's face creased up and Abi thought she was going to cry so she swooped in. 'Your mummy buys very silly little handbags, doesn't she? You can't even fit a lipstick inside them let alone anything useful like a sketchbook.' She nudged her niece and received a smile in return.

'Or a puppy!' Rosie said.

'Exactly! You couldn't fit Pugly in there, could you?'

'Why on earth would I want to put Pugly in my handbag?' Ellen asked.

'Little dogs in handbags are a thing,' Abi told her. 'Or they were. They probably still are.'

'Well, that sounds very silly.'

'I *like* silly things,' Rosie said.

'Me too,' Abi agreed and the two of them giggled.

Ellen rolled her eyes at the pair of them and continued to buzz around the house, grabbing things.

'Okay,' she said at last, 'I'm ready.' Bethanne came forward to kiss her mother goodbye and Rosie followed. 'Be good, you two. Make sure you don't make a mess with your Aunt Abi. I know what she's like!'

'Thanks!' Abi said.

Ellen walked to the door with her handbag and small suitcase. Abi followed.

'You know what you're doing?' Ellen asked her.

'Of course I do,' Abi said with a laugh. 'Stop worrying and go and have a good time.'

Ellen took a deep breath. 'Thanks.'

Abi watched as she got into the waiting taxi and left. She waved until the car had disappeared around a corner in the lane and then she went back inside, closing the door and walking into the kitchen.

'Right, girls! Shall we get all the paints out?'

It was a wonderful weekend at the cottage. Abi and the girls cooked together, walked Pugly in the fields around the village and made a lot of mess with the paints. Most of all, they laughed, and Abi got the feeling that was something that the girls didn't do enough of. Bethanne in particular. Rosie was a little laugh machine – anything could set her off, but Bethanne still hid her emotions deep within that tiny frame of hers and needed them to be coaxed out of her.

But the atmosphere in the house felt so very different from when Ellen was there. There wasn't that awful tension that came from her sister simply moving from room to room with all the negative energy she carried around with her. Abi could sense that the girls felt it. Their body language had changed. They were running more. It might seem like such a silly thing to observe, Abi thought, but the difference between a child running into a room rather than tiptoeing was quite pronounced.

Abi wished that she could stay longer, but Ellen and Douglas were both back after lunch on Sunday and, after spending some time together with Ellen detailing how awful the food at the wedding had been and how the music had also shown the happy couple's very bad taste, it was time for Abi to go.

Douglas walked her to her car.

'How's life up at the big house?' he asked.

'It's good. We have two tenants now and we'll be letting more apartments soon.'

'Maybe I can rent one.' He grinned, but there was a little slice of pain that hinted he might not be completely joking.

'Are things okay with you guys, Douglas?'

He shrugged. 'I think Ellen might have actually been happier when I was working away from home.'

'Oh, dear!'

'She seems to resent me in the house even though I'm fixing it up whenever I can.'

'Maybe it'll get easier once you've got it all looking just as she wants it.'

'It'll never be just as she wants it.'

Abi closed the space between them and gave him a big hug. 'You are a saint. You do know that, don't you?'

He laughed. 'At least one person on the planet knows that.'

'I believe, and I know it sounds a bit like wishful thinking, but I truly believe that one day Ellen's going to wake up and suddenly realise just how very lucky she is to have you and Bethanne and Rosie, and this lovely house and this beautiful life!'

'And her kind and forgiving sister?' Douglas suggested.

'Perhaps. If we're *very* lucky!'

They hugged again and Abi got in the car for the short drive back home.

When she got back to Winfield, she crossed the hall towards her apartment and saw Edward walking towards her.

'Hello.'

'Been away?' he asked.

'At my sister's for the night, taking care of my nieces while she and her husband were away.'

He nodded, but didn't really seem to be listening. 'You had a caller last night.'

'I did?'

'Oscar.'

'Oh.' Abi felt confused. She'd definitely told Oscar that she was babysitting over the weekend, but he'd obviously forgotten or else not actually heard her properly which was very likely considering all the alcohol he'd had on Friday night. But that wasn't the worst thing because Edward now knew what was going on.

'Listen, Abi, Oscar told me that he's seeing you.'

'Right.'

'It's none of my business, I know, but I feel I should warn you about him.'

'It's okay, Edward. I know he's a little wild around the edges.'

He shook his head. 'It's more than that. He can't be trusted.'

'What do you mean?'

'I mean, you shouldn't trust him – not with anything. Your time, your money... your heart.'

Abi didn't know what to say and she could see Edward was struggling too.

'And don't, for god's sake, get in a car with him.'

Abi recalled the old vehicle Oscar drove and the scratches and dents she'd seen on it, and the fact that he'd thought himself perfectly capable of driving her home even though he'd been roaring drunk.

'I know how to take care of myself,' she told Edward, touched by his concern, but slightly annoyed that he didn't trust her to make good decisions herself.

'I'd hate for you to – well – you know, get hurt,' he added in a voice barely above a whisper.

'That's not going to happen,' Abi assured him. 'We're just having a bit of fun, that's all.' She bit her lip. She didn't like how that had come out. It made her sound far more frivolous than she was because she wasn't the kind of woman who just had flings.

'Okay,' Edward said. 'I just wanted to make sure you knew what you were doing.' He sighed. 'That sounds condescending. Sorry.' He pulled a face that looked so full of anguish that Abi took pity on him.

'It's all right, Edward. I'll look out for myself, okay?'

He gave a tight smile and nodded before turning to go.

'You're still going to invite me to go swimming with you, I hope?'

He turned to face her and there was a dreadful pause before he answered. 'I don't think that would be a good idea. Not now. Not with Oscar on the scene.'

Abi watched, feeling thoroughly miserable, as Edward walked away from her.

By late Sunday afternoon, Aura had just about lost her patience with Johnny. He'd slept in until midday which meant that the whole of her living room looked a mess and he'd been smoking again. She'd asked him to go outside, but he just ignored her.

'Well, you'll have to go out by five at the latest, Johnny. I've got someone coming over for a session.'

'Can't I stay and watch?'

'No. She's a client and the last thing she'll want is an audience. And can you please stop smoking in here? It smells horrible!' She walked towards the French doors and flung them wide open before lighting one of her burners, hoping the smell of orange and sandalwood might disguise Johnny's roll-ups.

She watched in horror as he moved across to a bookcase and picked up one of her crystals – a large rose quartz she was particularly fond of.

'You really into all this stuff?' he teased.

'Please be careful with that. Don't drop it.'

Johnny laughed and then casually threw the piece in the air, catching it a second later.

'Johnny! I mean it!'

He placed it back down on the shelf. 'My witchy sister.'

'I'm not a witch.'

'Sure you are,' he said. 'I mean, just look at all this stuff. What even is this?' he asked, picking something up and giving it a sniff. 'It's a dead plant.'

'It's sage.'

'What's it used for?'

'Purifying.'

'Oh, right. I could sure use some of that.' He made a few quick circles with it around his body. 'Am I pure now?'

'Probably not,' Aura said and she couldn't resist a smile. He really was a chump.

'So, can you do spells?'

'That's not what I do.'

'But you could, couldn't you? I could really use some money right now. Maybe just do a quick spell – one of those abundance things I've heard about. That's all the rage, isn't it?'

'Abundance is about more than money, Johnny.'

'Is it?' He looked confused by that notion.

'It's about having a good and healthy life with relationships we value and peace in our hearts and work we find fulfilling.'

'Yeah, and money!' he said. 'Look, just a little spell for a hundred quid or so would get me started.' It was then that he spotted something. Aura flinched because she knew what was coming. 'What's this?'

She sighed. 'It's a business card.'

'Whose?' he asked, but she had a feeling he knew exactly whose it was.

'Mine.'

'But it says "Aurora Arden" on here.'

'I know. It's my name now.'

'Your name?'

'Yes. Like a stage name.'

'What's wrong with your real name?'

Aura felt all fidgety, like she'd been caught out, which was silly really because she'd made peace with her name change a long time ago. It was nothing to feel guilty about. If you were born with a name that didn't suit you, why be stuck with it forever? Why not give yourself the gift of a name that fit you perfectly?

'My real name doesn't work for me now. Not in my business or my personal life.'

Johnny made a kind of snorting noise.

'I tend to shorten it to Aura,' she told him.

'That's even worse!' He put the business card down in disgust. 'Do you think I should have a stage name?'

'I'm sure you did – in prison.'

He sucked his teeth in. 'Is that you having a dig at me?'

'It might be.'

They stared at each other. Johnny backed down first, obviously out of boredom. 'I'm going down the pub.'

'Don't come back until at least seven o'clock okay?'

'Yeah, yeah, whatever.'

Aura watched him leave, relief surging through her at having her little home back to herself if only for a few hours.

That evening, Abi called Oscar.

'You're back! Where have you been?' he asked.

'I told you, I was staying at my sister's.'

'You didn't tell me that.'

'I did, Oscar!'

'I came over to see you.'

'Yes, I know. Edward told me.'

'Right. Yes, well, he wasn't that pleased to see me. I think I might have been a bit merry.'

'Oh, Oscar! Why do you do it?'

'Well, it was the weekend, wasn't it? And I wanted to see you.'

'You got "merry" on Friday night. Did you really need to on Saturday too?' she asked him.

'You mad at me?'

'A little.'

She heard him sigh. 'Did you get my flowers?'

'Yes. They're lovely. Thank you.'

'And the card? With the kisses?'

'Yes.'

'To remind you of our first kiss,' Oscar added, quite unnecessarily because Abi was already thinking about it. It had been in one of the antique centres. Oscar had been messing about, trying on a top hat and doing a few silly dance steps like a deranged Fred Astaire when he'd spotted a chandelier.

'Hey!' he'd said, pointing up towards it. 'Isn't that mistletoe?'

Abi had taken a closer look. 'It's meant to be ivy. Enamel, I think.'

'Well, I think it's mistletoe,' Oscar had said, locking eyes with her and leaning in to steal a kiss.

Abi blushed as she remembered it again – that wonderful tingly sensation of being kissed. She'd forgotten how heady it could make you feel.

'So, can I come and see you?' he asked.

'I'm not sure,' she said. 'I'm a very busy woman, you know.'

'Oh, really?'

She giggled, suddenly feeling very coy which was something she definitely hadn't felt for a long time.

'Too busy to see somebody who adores you?' he pressed.

'*Adores?*'

'That's right!'

Abi fiddled with a lock of her hair, twisting it around her fingers in a flirtatious manner. 'Well, maybe a little meet up wouldn't hurt.'

'I'll be right over.'

She hung up, her skin fairly buzzing with excitement, and she couldn't sit still after that. He was coming over – the man who adored her. Gosh, she felt like a teenager all giddy with that first flush of a new romance. Catching sight of her reflection in a mirror, she saw the blush on her cheeks and the brightness of her eyes. She looked obscenely radiant and... happy.

And then something occurred to her. What on earth would Edward think?

CHAPTER FOURTEEN

Edward was still furious. As he left Abi's apartment, he thought back to Saturday night. It had been a quiet evening and he'd had the doors open into the garden and a light breeze had stirred the newspaper he'd been reading. All was well in his world. And then he'd heard a car pulling up outside Winfield Hall. He didn't think much of it. After all, there were four people living there now; he had to get used to a certain amount of coming and going. But when he heard the raised voice from outside, he knew that it wasn't one of his neighbours.

'Abi!' Oscar was shouting.

Edward frowned. What did Oscar want with Abi? The truth was he didn't want to see his brother, but if Oscar was about to annoy Abi, he would make sure he put a stop to that. He got up from his comfy armchair and put his newspaper down.

He went out into the hallway. Knowing Oscar, if he wanted to see Abi, he would do his best to avoid Edward so that meant he'd probably go round the side of the hall and knock on Abi's French doors rather than risk coming face to face with Edward's wrath if he rang the front doorbell. So Edward hesitated. The truth was, there was nothing he could do if Abi had invited Oscar round, but why would she have done that?

As he was pondering all this, the doorbell rang.

'Abi? Are you there?' It was Oscar and he sounded drunk.

Fuming, Edward strode towards the door.

'What are you doing here?' he asked, as his brother stumbled into him.

'What's it to you?' Oscar asked.

'It's something to me when you ring the front door and shout the house down. Come with me,' Edward said sternly, leading the way. A moment later, Oscar almost fell into Edward's living room. 'Why were you calling on Abi?'

'What do you mean, *why?*' Oscar hiccupped.

'Somebody like you shouldn't be seeing somebody like Abi.'

Oscar blinked and shook his head in an exaggerated way, like a basset hound with waterlogged ears. 'I'm sorry! *Someone like me?*'

'Yes, someone like you! Just look at the state you're in. You're a disgrace.'

Oscar looked as if he might explode, but the moment passed and he simply laughed.

'Will you listen to you? Mister high and mighty! Who put you in charge of relationships. I mean, it's not like you've tonnes of experience. Remind me, when was the last time you went out with a woman, huh? I don't think you're capable. You're married to your work and this – this bloody draughty old house.' He started laughing again, amused by what he obviously perceived as his biting wit.

'I'm warning you–'

'Oh, you're warning me, are you? I'm shaking in my shoes.'

Oscar stumbled forward, crashing into a chair before sitting down on it.

'I'm warning you to keep away from Abigail. She's... she's sensitive.' Edward grimaced at his own choice of words. Abi would probably hate him for calling her that, but Oscar needed to know he couldn't just hurtle into any relationship he wanted to.

Oscar frowned and a moment of brief lucidity passed across his face.

'Oh, my god! You like her, don't you?' Oscar said with a grin.

'Don't be ridiculous.'

'No, no! You do! I can see it in your face,' he said, swivelling around in the chair to follow Edward as he moved across the room. 'But you haven't told her, have you? That's it, isn't it?' Oscar was practically jumping up and down in the chair. 'You didn't have the courage to say anything and I've nipped in ahead of you!' He laughed again. To Edward's ears, it sounded like an evil cackle.

'You'd better leave,' he told his brother. 'I take it you're in a taxi?'

Oscar looked blank for a moment.

'Tell me there's a taxi outside and that you're not driving.'

'Huh? Oh, yes. A taxi.'

Edward nodded. 'Then please leave.'

Slowly, and with considerable effort, Oscar got up from the chair, tipping forward slightly before righting himself.

'I'm going. But I'll be back. Not to see you, mind. To see Abi.'

'Please don't!'

'It might come as a shock to you, big brother, but Abi likes me. She thinks I'm funny. She thinks I'm cute. And guess what?

We get on. We have a laugh together. It's killing you, isn't it? That Abi actually likes me?'

'She likes you because she doesn't know you, that's why.'

'She knows enough.'

'Yes, well I might tell her some more.'

Oscar turned around, a murderous look on his face. Then he grinned. 'No you won't. You won't say a word because that's just your way. You're a closed book, Edward. You never share anything. That's how we're different, see. I'm as open as can be. I don't hide anything and that's what Abi's responding to.'

Edward could feel the anger rising up inside him, but he didn't react. The truth was, it wasn't worth it. You couldn't argue with someone who didn't really understand you and who certainly didn't listen to you. And so he watched as his brother left his flat, stumbling across the hall and crashing into the waiting taxi outside. He watched, making sure he was off the premises and then returned to his apartment, closing the door behind him. And that's when something occurred to him. He couldn't help thinking that Oscar was going to focus even more on Abi now that he knew his big brother was interested in her. But he couldn't tell Abi that. It would sound awful and Abi probably wouldn't believe him anyway. He tried to imagine it.

'Abi? You shouldn't go out with Oscar because he's just trying to get one over on me.'

He grimaced and yet he didn't believe for a single moment that Oscar was genuinely interested in Abi. Of course, she was beautiful and sweet and kind. Who wouldn't respond to that? But Oscar didn't normally go for women like Abi. She didn't seem to fit the mould of the fun-seeking, spontaneous soul that Oscar generally seemed to gravitate towards. She was altogether much gentler, quieter, refined.

Edward sighed. What did he know, though? Oscar had

been right when he'd said that Edward never opened up to anyone. In all the months he'd known Abi, he had confided so little in her so who was he to stand in judgement now and pronounce that she wasn't Oscar's type? He didn't know her – not really. He should just stand aside and let them both get on with it. They were grown adults and he had no right to interfere.

Still, as much as he told himself all this, his heart ached because he couldn't help feeling that this was going to end badly.

It was on a warm evening in June, just a couple of days before the summer solstice, when Harry called round to Aura's. He hadn't seen her for a while and wanted to touch base about their upcoming picnic, checking on the foods she liked and if there was anything special she wanted. Harry had already visited his parents and borrowed a beautiful wicker hamper and a travel rug. His mother's eyebrows had raised.

'Planning anything I should know about?' she asked.

Harry had cleared his throat. 'Just going somewhere.'

'With someone in particular?' The look on her face was priceless and Harry caved in.

'Yes. Someone very particular.'

His mother had smiled. 'Do we get to meet her at some point?'

It was something Harry hadn't thought of until his mother asked the question. It was also something Harry would really love to avoid if he possibly could.

'I don't know, Mum. We'll see.'

She'd looked a little disgruntled, but she hadn't pushed him and Harry was grateful for that, leaving with the hamper and blanket and a bottle of wine his mother gave him.

'For good luck!' she told him with a kiss. Harry sincerely hoped she wasn't going to get her knitting out as soon as he left in preparation for grandchildren, but he wouldn't put it past her.

Now, as he stood outside Aura's apartment, he couldn't help feeling anxious because he knew she was just the sort of girl his parents would disapprove of and that would surely lead to somebody getting hurt. But he was getting way ahead of himself, wasn't he? It was just a picnic.

With that thought, he knocked on the door.

When it opened, Harry was surprised to see a dark-haired man.

'Yeah?' the man said with a sniff.

'Erm, is Aura there?'

'No.'

Harry regarded the skinny fellow with the dark stubble and a tattoo of a gecko on his upper arm.

'Can you tell her I called? I'm Harry. I live across the hall.'

'Do you now?'

Harry regarded him for a moment. He didn't look like a client and couldn't be if Aura wasn't actually there.

'And you are?' Harry decided to ask.

'I'm a what?'

'Who are you?'

'Aura's brother.'

'Oh.'

'Yeah. Only I'm not really *Aura's* brother.'

Harry frowned. 'What do you mean?'

The man wiped his nose with the back of his hand. 'You don't know, do you?'

'Know what?'

'Aura's not her real name.' With that, he shut the door and Harry could hear him laughing on the other side.

For a moment, he was tempted to knock again and demand to know what the man meant, but he thought better of it. But what was he doing in Aura's flat? Harry got his phone out and texted her.

You okay? He wrote.

Good thanks. In Brighton stocking up on crystals!

Harry smiled and sent another message.

I'm looking forward to our picnic. Any foods you like/don't like?

Did I tell you I'm vegan?

No problem.

Got to go, Harry. Another customer's just clapped eyes on a crystal I want!

Harry laughed as he put his phone in his pocket and then took it out a moment later. He'd need to look up what on earth it was vegans ate.

Abi was sitting at her table, her latest prints scattered in front of her like so many autumn leaves. But she wasn't looking at them. She was still smarting from Edward telling her that they couldn't be friends if she was going out with Oscar. It had hurt her more than she could have imagined and she couldn't help but curse herself. As she'd told Ronnie, it hadn't been an easy decision. So had she made the wrong one? There was a part of her that was upset and annoyed with Edward for being all high and mighty and making her feel like she had somehow failed their friendship. He'd put her in an unfair position, she believed, denying her freedom of choice. Why couldn't she be friends with them both? It really was very silly, she thought.

Just that morning, she'd been coming down the hill when she'd seen Edward leaving the hall, his swimming bag in his hand. He'd spotted her and, out of instinct, she'd waved at him, but he hadn't waved back. He'd simply frozen and then continued to his car, driving off a moment later. He was going swimming. Without her. Abi had felt something approaching grief filling her chest. She'd made her choice, hadn't she? If she was seeing Oscar, she couldn't have a friendship with Edward. Or at least, not the friendship they had been enjoying with wild swims and the occasional meal out. And she missed those quiet, thoughtful talks with him, and those cold, invigorating swims. She couldn't imagine Oscar deriving pleasure from a walk across a field to jump into a freezing river. He was far more of a social person, happy in the buzz of a pub or a restaurant, surrounded by other people and noise, and Abi had been enjoying that with him, but she couldn't help missing the peace of her relationship with Edward.

As she picked up one of her prints, her phone beeped. She looked at the screen. It was a text from Oscar.

What are you doing?

She paused before replying. She wanted to text back, *Mourning for the loss of your brother's friendship*, but she didn't think that would go down well.

Just some printing.

Want some lunch?

You not working?

Not today.

Abi paused. Oscar never seemed to be working.

Okay. Usual pub?

I'll meet you there.

Yes, Abi thought. It was probably best that he didn't show his face at Winfield.

Oscar wasn't there when Abi arrived at the pub for lunch. She ordered a drink at the bar and took it outside so she could see when he arrived. He was fifteen minutes late this time, pulling up in his wreck of a car and startling a couple sitting at a picnic table when he screeched to a halt. Abi winced.

He saw her as soon as he got out, waving across to her.

'Abi! Did you get me a drink?'

She shook her head, embarrassed when everyone turned to look at her.

'I'll get one, then!'

He was back a couple of minutes later, a pint in his hand.

'Should you be drinking?' she asked in concern as he'd driven there.

'The food will soak it up.'

Abi grimaced, glad that she'd made her own way there.

'So, what have you been up to today?' she asked him after a waitress had taken their order.

'Oh, you know.' He gave a light shrug.

'No, I don't! Tell me.'

'A bit of this. A bit of that. Actually, I went to look at a new car. Not a *new* new one. A newer old one.'

'That's good.'

'Yeah. Bit expensive though. I'm trying to get it part deal, part cash.'

'What's the deal?'

'Ah, you know. A bit of work.'

Abi nodded, none the wiser.

'So, what has the most beautiful artist in Sussex been up to? Made any more masterpieces?'

Abi laughed. 'I fear not. But I'm working towards an interesting project.'

'With that strange iron thing in your front room?'

'The printing press? Yes!'

'It's like an instrument of torture!'

'It is a bit except it helps make the most beautiful art.'

'You're amazing.'

Abi smiled. 'I'm not, but it's nice to be told that I am.'

Lunch arrived and Abi stared at the size of Oscar's steak.

'You must be hungry,' she couldn't help commenting.

'Ravenous! That's why I thought it would be good to eat out. Got nothing in at my place anyway.'

Abi looked down at her modest jacket potato and salad. 'I like eating out. You don't have to do the dishes.'

Oscar laughed. 'Plenty of them at my house. Weird. No food, but plenty of dishes.'

Abi tried not to blanch at the visual Oscar was painting of his place.

'Listen, I was thinking, there's a band playing at club I know. It's a bit of a dive really, but I used to go to school with the drummer. It's good music. Should be fun. I wondered if you wanted to come.'

'When?'

'Friday night.'

'That's the summer solstice.'

'The what?'

'The longest day of the year.'

'Oh, right. You're not into all that pagan stuff, are you? I mean, you're not heading to Stonehenge to dance around a beanpole or something?'

Abi laughed. 'Don't you mean a Maypole and that's a whole different celebration!'

'Is it? Anyway, the offer's there. I've got a couple of free tickets.'

'I'd love to go.'

'Yeah? Great.'

They continued to eat, chatting easily about their favourite music with Oscar ribbing Abi gently for her pedestrian taste.

'You've got to get out more,' he told her. 'Festivals, gigs.'

'I know.'

'Maybe I could introduce you to some bands and you could introduce me to some...' he paused.

'What?'

'Art and stuff.'

She smiled. 'Maybe we could visit some museums,' she suggested.

He pulled a face. 'Sounds too much like a school trip. Would you give me a worksheet to complete?'

'Of course not! And don't be put off by memories from school. It's quite a different experience when you go as an adult and there are so many wonderful museums and art galleries.' Oscar didn't look convinced. 'Don't worry – we don't have to go to any if you don't want to.'

'No, I'd like to. I think.'

Abi took pity on him. He really was like a little child sometimes. 'How about I break you in gently with a very small local one first?'

'Yeah? Where's that?'

'Eastbourne. Have you heard of the Towner Art Gallery?'

'I think so. We might actually have had a trip there with school,' he said, nodding. 'Only me and a mate skipped out and went to a chippie.'

'Oh, Oscar!'

He laughed at her horror. 'Honestly, Abs, it was dead boring. Not that it'll be boring with you. But you know what teachers are like making you look at things for far longer than is comfortable. So me and Dean did a runner.'

'Did you get into trouble?'

'Nah! We met up with everyone when they were milling about the gift shop. Nobody knew we'd gone because there was another school party there and everyone was all mixed up.' It was then that Oscar got his wallet out, pulling a card from it. 'Ah,' he said. 'I'd better not use this one.' He put his wallet away and patted his pockets, cursing under his breath.

'It's okay,' Abi told him. 'I've got this.'

'Yeah? Great!' He grinned, getting up from the table. 'Listen, I've got to run now, but I'll call you about Saturday, okay?'

'Okay,' she said, watching as he rushed off towards his car. A moment later, he screeched out of the car park, leaving Abi in a cloud of dust and with the bill to settle.

CHAPTER FIFTEEN

Harry was glad that it was Aura who answered the door to her apartment when he called on the evening of the summer solstice and not the skinny fellow with the tattoo.

Aura was wearing a dress in soft swirling pinks and yellows that reminded Harry of a summer sunset and she carried a blue denim jacket. Her hair was partially up with diamante hair slides pinning it away from her face, and a pair of silver earrings shaped like crescent moons dangled from her ears. Harry had chosen to wear a sky-blue shirt and a new pair of beige trousers. He always felt slightly out of place in casual clothes. He was so used to spending most of his time in a suit for work. Now, that was a sorry state of affairs, he couldn't help thinking.

'You look lovely,' he told Aura.

'So do you.'

He smiled and held up the hamper he was carrying. 'Your picnic awaits,' he said and the two of them left the hall together, climbing the track that led away from Winfield, and feeling the breeze from the downs on their faces. Harry led the way. He'd been up on the downs the day before, searching for the perfect picnic spot and, when they reached it, he put the hamper down and laid the blanket out on the ground.

'Harry – this is lovely!' Aura said, sitting down on the blanket and surveying the view. They could see Winfield Hall in the distance, sitting in its valley like a golden crown, but there was also a tantalising glimpse of the sea from between the hills looking south. It was a splendid wraparound view and the sun, which was still gifting its warmth to the countryside, was fully visible.

'I'm surprised there aren't more people around,' Harry said as he began unpacking the hamper with the sandwiches and salad he'd made.

'I can see some walkers down there,' Aura said, motioning to the footpath which wound its way towards the next village. 'And a horse – look!'

Harry followed her gaze and saw a rider on a grey horse. They were far enough away not to bother them, he couldn't help noticing, and for that he was grateful for he wanted to talk to Aura about something very particular. But, before that, he got out the rest of the food, all neatly packed in plastic containers. He'd brought real dinner plates, though, and cutlery too, and had carefully wrapped two wine glasses in linen napkins, borrowed from his mum.

'You are spoiling me!' Aura said as he poured her a glass of wine a moment later.

'What shall we drink to?' he asked.

Aura took a deep breath and looked up into the sky. 'To the summer solstice.'

'Yes, cheers to the summer solstice and to spending the longest day – or at least the best part of it – with you.' He could feel that he was blushing as he chinked his wine glass to hers, but her smile gave him confidence. She was happy to be there with him, wasn't she? She wouldn't have trekked all the way up here if she didn't like him.

Together, they shared the food out and ate under the great dome of sky.

'Why does food taste so much better outdoors?' Harry asked.

'I think fresh air makes you hungry.'

'I'm so used to eating at my desk at work, surrounded by screens and papers. Isn't that a grim confession?'

'You should vow to have more picnics then.'

'Yes. I hereby declare that I, Harry Freeman, vow to become king of the picnic!'

Aura laughed. 'Well, you have made an excellent one here. Thank you.'

'You don't have to thank me. This picnic is *me* thanking *you*.'

'Well, it's lovely. All of it.'

'All vegan too,' Harry boasted.

'I loved the salad and this fruit tart is delicious.'

Harry beamed. He'd spent a careful few hours checking vegan recipes online and gathering ingredients. He was really quite impressed by his accomplishment and was especially pleased with the fruit tart he'd made.

'Maybe I should retrain and go into catering,' he said with a laugh.

'Sign me up as a customer!'

Slowly, the sun began its golden descent towards the horizon, the colours of the sky deepening and casting their rosy glow on Harry and Aura's faces.

'Aura?' Harry said after they'd finished eating and he'd tidied the things away, placing them carefully in the hamper.

'Yes?'

'There's something I wanted to ask you.'

'Oh?'

'I called round at yours the other day when you were out.' He watched as Aura's eyes widened ever so slightly. He guessed she knew what was coming.

'You met Johnny, didn't you?'

'Is that his name? He didn't tell me. He said he was your brother.'

'Yes.'

'What's he doing at Winfield? Is he staying with you?'

She nodded. 'He's got nowhere else to go.'

'How come?'

Aura looked out across the downs as if trying to avoid answering. 'He doesn't have a place of his own.'

'Right.'

Aura turned towards him now. 'He's just got out of prison.'

Harry blinked. 'Really?'

'Please don't tell Abi. I'm not sure she'd be happy with me having someone staying who's just out of prison.'

Harry nodded in understanding.

'What about you? Are you okay with him being here?'

'He's my brother.'

'That's not what I asked you,' Harry said and then cursed himself. 'Sorry. Look, it's none of my business. It's just – well – he seems so different from you.'

She gave a light laugh. 'Yes.'

'And, there was something else. Something he said.'

'What did he say?'

Harry shifted on the picnic rug, suddenly feeling awkward – as if he might be straying into territory he had no business in.

'He said that Aura wasn't your real name.'

A look of shock passed across Aura's face. 'What did he say?'

'Just that. Nothing else.'

Aura bit her lower lip.

'Why didn't you tell me that Aura wasn't your real name?' Harry dared to ask.

'I don't know. I guess I just think of myself as Aura now.'

'Well, it does suit you.'

'Thank you.'

'So, can I ask?' He leaned forward, trying to catch her eye.

She gave a shy smile. 'You want to know my real name?'

'Unless it's a real stinker and you'd rather I didn't know.'

She laughed at that. 'It's not a real stinker. It's Anna Blake.'

Harry nodded. 'I like it.'

'You do?'

'Yes. Why did you change it?'

'I guess I didn't feel like an Anna Blake anymore. It didn't fit. And I'm not saying it's a horrible name or anything. But it just seemed a little ordinary – for what I wanted to be. I mean, would you rather book a crystal healing session with an Anna Blake or an Aura Arden?'

'I wouldn't mind what you were called,' he said. 'As long as it was you.'

'That's very sweet of you, but I'm afraid people do make judgements and I wanted something that sounded right.'

'So how did you come up with Aura?'

'Well, it's really Aurora. I first came across it when I found out about the Aurora Borealis.'

'The northern lights?'

'That's right. I used to watch as many online videos as I could. I was mesmerised by the colours – all those greens and blues and purples. It was pure magic to me. Then I discovered that the crystal, labradorite, is thought by the Inuit people to be a piece of Aurora Borealis fallen to earth. If you look at a piece, it really does look as if all that light and colour is trapped inside the stone.'

'Do you have one on you?' Harry asked, keen to see.

'No. But I have plenty at home.'

'So, what crystal do you have with you tonight?'

'What makes you think I've got a crystal with me?' Aura asked, a little smile tickling the corners of her mouth.

'Come on,' Harry said lightly, 'would you really leave home without one?'

Aura giggled. 'No.'

'Show me then!'

Aura reached into her jacket pocket and pulled out a crystal which was about the length of the palm of her hand. It was a light yellow with a smoky quality to it, almost the colour of tea in places, and it had a beautiful point at one end. Harry reached out to take it, holding it up to the light.

'It's a citrine. I thought it was a good crystal for the summer solstice. It seems like crystallised sunlight, doesn't it?'

'It really does,' Harry said, marvelling at its beauty.

'Just looking at it fills me with warmth and happiness.'

'It's beautiful,' Harry said, handing it back to her. For a few minutes, the two of them sat in silence, watching the colours of the sky change.

'Oh, look! There's the moon,' Aura said. Harry followed her gaze. 'Waxing gibbous. It'll be full in a few days.'

'It's a funny shape at the moment, isn't it? More than half, but not quite whole.'

'It's known as the Rose Moon or Dyad Moon. Dyad means two parts, you see, echoing how the longest day is equal light and dark,' Aura told him.

They gazed at it a little longer and then Harry realised that it was beginning to get dark.

'I suppose we should head back while we can still see.'

'There should be enough light by the moon once the sun says goodnight.'

'I wouldn't want you tripping over,' Harry said, standing up and holding his hand out to help her. She took it and made to stand, but her legs buckled and she almost fell backwards. 'I've got you!' Harry cried.

'Thank you!' Aura said. 'I've been sitting down too long perhaps.'

'You're moonstruck or sunstruck or something,' Harry teased, suddenly realising how very close they were to one another and that he still had hold of her hand. And before he could think about it or talk himself out of it, he leaned forward and kissed her fully on her petal-pink mouth, feeling the warmth of her against him and hearing her soft sigh of delight as the kiss lengthened.

And it was the most magical kiss of his life, Harry thought. Under the setting sun and the rising moon, on the longest day of the year.

Abi's summer solstice evening wasn't quite as magical as Harry and Aura's. Oscar had been right – the venue the band was playing was a dive. Abi did her best not to touch anything. Even in the semi-darkness, everything looked dirty. It wasn't the kind of place she normally visited and she was finding it a stressful assault on all her senses. For a start, there were far too many people all crammed into a relatively small space and there weren't enough places to sit either. The bar was a heaving mass of folk and the dance floor was completely packed. Then there was the lighting or rather lack of it. It was so dim that it would be easy to lose Oscar in the scrum and she really didn't want to lose him because she didn't know anybody else and wouldn't have the courage to stay if she lost him.

Then there was the volume – not only of people shouting to be heard over one another, but also over the music that was being pumped out across the room. But that was nothing compared to the loudness of the band which, when they started, Abi felt not only in her ears but in her chest. Her body was actually vibrating with the sound and it wasn't pleasant.

'Isn't it great?' Oscar yelled at her between songs.

Abi nodded. Oscar was so obviously in his element that she didn't feel she could disagree, but she felt like she was drowning. There was no air in the place, no natural light. She wished with all her heart that she could magic herself away to the walled garden at Winfield where she could feel the gentle breeze from the downs on her skin and hear nothing but the last song of the blackbird before the sun set.

The music continued and Abi felt quite sure that her eardrums would soon be bleeding. She looked at the people surrounding her. They were all having a good time, their bodies moving to the beat of the music. Abi was an oddity, she knew that. She shouldn't have come, but she had wanted to please Oscar, and wasn't a relationship about exploring new things and finding out about each other? Well, she'd certainly learned a lot about Oscar tonight and realised that their interests were oceans apart.

She turned around to look at him, but he was no longer standing behind her. She panicked. Where was he?

'Oscar?' she called, but she quickly realised there was no use shouting for him. The noise of the band and the crowd would simply drown out any sound she was able to make. So she pushed her way through the throng, making her way to the bar, guessing that's where Oscar was. And she was right. She saw the back of him, his sandy hair bright under a light as he laughed, a pint in his right hand and his left hand on a woman's shoulder. Abi frowned. Who was she? Had Oscar forgotten that he'd come out with her tonight?

'Oscar?' she called, but he couldn't hear her. She pushed through the people who were between her and him, finally reaching the bar. 'Oscar!'

'Abi!' he turned round, looking surprised to see her.

'What are you doing?'

'What do you mean?' he asked, his hand still on the other woman's shoulder.

'Who's she?' Abi nodded towards the woman with the pink hair tied back in a ponytail.

It was only then that Oscar removed his hand and motioned towards the exit.

'I couldn't hear a thing in there!' he said once they were both outside, the throbbing of the music still audible out in the street.

'Oscar, what were you doing with that woman?'

'Huh?' he looked confused. Had he been drinking again?

'The woman at the bar. You must have noticed her – she had a pink ponytail!' Abi said, a touch sarcastic because she was feeling annoyed with him.

'Oh, that wasn't a woman – that was Chrissie.' Abi frowned. 'A mate from work.'

'You disappeared, Oscar.'

'No I didn't. I was at the bar. You saw me.'

'I had to find you. You left me in the middle of the dance floor. I didn't know where you were.'

'You can look after yourself,' he said, his right foot slipping off the kerb so that he stumbled into the gutter. Abi pulled him out of the road just before a taxi sped by.

'I don't know what to say,' she told him.

'You like the band?'

'You're not listening to me, Oscar!'

'You *didn't* like the band?'

'I didn't like being left by you. I thought we were on a date together.'

He looked at her as if she was crazy. 'We are! Come on, let's go back in. We're missing the music.' He made a grab for her, but she dodged out of the way.

'I'm not going back in.'

'Why not?'

'I'm going home.'

'Oh, Abs! Don't be boring. Come on – I'll get you another drink and we can have a dance.'

Abi stood by the side of the road and waved down another passing taxi. It pulled up by the kerb and she got in.

'I'll call you!' Oscar cried as she closed the door and she watched as he stumbled back into the club.

It was after ten o'clock on Sunday morning and Harry had just got out of the shower and was getting dressed when his phone rang.

'Harry?'

'Mum. Hi.'

'Well?'

'Well what?'

'How did it go? The picnic!'

Harry shook his head. His mother had probably been pacing up and down hoping he'd have rung her and given a full report by nine o'clock sharp.

'It went well. Thank you for the hamper. I'll return it soon.'

'Never mind the hamper – who was your date?'

There was no getting out of this one.

'You don't know her.'

'Well, whose fault is that?' she said.

Harry groaned. He'd walked right into that one. 'She lives here at Winfield.'

'So a business woman?'

'Yes,' Harry said, imagining his mother's interpretation of that as being a high-flyer in a suit cut from expensive material rather than a crystal healer in a floaty dress.

'Bring her over,' his mother blurted.

'What?'

'Next Sunday. I'm making a little birthday lunch for Uncle Arthur.'

'Who's coming?'

'It's just us and your uncle, but I thought it would be nice if you brought... a date.'

He heard the awkwardness in his mother's voice and her hesitancy to use the word "girlfriend".

'I'll see.'

'You will? I mean, do try.'

'Mum!'

She gave a laugh which did nothing to hide how very seriously she was taking this matter.

When Harry hung up, he sighed. His feeling was that it was much too early to take Aura round to meet his parents. They'd only just shared their first kiss the night before and, although it had been the loveliest, most romantic kiss of his life which whispered sweetly of the future, he didn't want to get ahead of himself. More importantly, he didn't want to spook Aura because he knew that his parents were perfectly capable of doing that very quickly indeed.

Harry's mother was just so needy and his father could come across as abrupt and judgemental. It wasn't a good pairing, and yet there was a part of Harry that just wanted to get it over and done with because he adored Aura and he knew he wanted to be with her and that he wouldn't be able to avoid the scrutiny of his parents forever. Still, he knew she wasn't what his mother was expecting. She probably had somebody very different in her mind when picturing who'd been sitting on her picnic blanket with her son.

And then it occurred to him that Aura might not actually want to meet his parents. He might be getting all worked up for nothing. There was only one way to find out and that was to ask her.

He opened the door of his apartment and crossed the hallway, standing outside her door a moment later. He could hear voices from inside and assumed it was Aura and her brother and he wondered if he should come back later. Aura sounded distressed about something, but he couldn't quite hear what she was saying. He hesitated. If Aura was distressed, his calling round could put an end to that, couldn't it?

He knocked. The voices stopped.

A moment later, Aura appeared, her hair slightly damp and dishevelled as if she'd just stepped out of the shower.

'Hey,' he said, trying desperately not to look at her mouth as he remembered their shared kiss.

'Hey,' she said back, glancing behind her into the room.

'Are you busy?' he asked.

'No, I'm not busy.'

'Fancy a walk around the garden? There's something I want to ask you.'

'Okay.' She glanced back again. 'I'm just popping out, Johnny, okay?'

'Don't be long,' the voice came back. Harry frowned. Was Johnny her keeper now? He looked at Aura and she didn't appear too happy.

'Let's get out,' she whispered.

It was lovely being outside with Aura again. It was funny, Harry mused, whenever he thought of Aura, she was always outside, and he was taking delight in the fact that he was spending so much time outdoors since having met her. Now, as they walked into the walled garden, he was aware of the painfully sweet awkwardness between them after having shared that perfect sunset-moonrise kiss just a few hours before. He wondered if she was thinking about it too.

'You okay?' he asked.

She nodded, but didn't say anything.

'How are things with your brother?' he dared to ask.

'Tense.'

'Right.'

'He's – erm – staying longer than I hoped.'

'And he's nowhere else to go?'

'Not that I know of.' She sighed. 'It's just awkward because he's in my space. My home – it's my workspace too, you see.'

'Yes, I know.'

'And it's special. It's this calm, quiet sanctuary that I've spent a lot of time creating and it just doesn't feel like that anymore.'

'But it won't be forever, right?' he said, attempting to keep her spirits up.

'I hope not.'

'Maybe you could give him some meditation sessions?'

'Johnny? You're kidding! He thinks I'm a crank!'

'Say he has to do two a day, then. That would get rid of him, wouldn't it?'

Aura laughed and reached out to touch his shoulder. 'You are funny.'

Harry smiled. 'Listen,' he said as they reached a bench and sat down next to one another. 'I had a call from my mum. She's arranging a little party for my Uncle Arthur. Nothing big. Just me and my parents really. He's on his own, you see, and he's a bit of a recluse. If it wasn't for my mum, he'd never get out at all let alone celebrate his birthday. Anyway, she asked if I wanted to bring anyone.' Harry paused, taking a deep breath. 'And I said yes. You.'

'You want me to go with you?'

'It's just at my parents' house. It won't be anything fancy. Just a bit of lunch and some cake.'

'Sounds lovely.'

'Yeah?'

'I'd love to go.'

Harry smiled, but then the worry kicked in again. 'Listen, I'll be honest. My parents aren't easy people to please. They can be... judgemental.'

'Oh. You mean the way I am?' Aura said. 'What I do for a living?'

He nodded. He didn't dare mention her clothes because he adored them, but he knew that his mother wouldn't be a fan of the floaty look.

'And what do you think?' Aura asked.

'Of what?'

'Of what I do? Do you approve?' Her forehead had creased into a look of concern that touched Harry's heart deeply.

'Aura – I *love* what you do! I'd defend it to the ends of the earth – to the moon and back! You know how I feel about the time we've spent together. I've loved every minute of it.'

'Then that's all that matters surely?'

He nodded. She was right. Of course she was. 'Look, I'm probably making a fuss about nothing. They're going to love you because,' he paused. It would have been so easy for him to say that he loved her at that point but, once again, he didn't want to scare her off. 'Because you're so lovable,' he said instead and she smiled.

'Harry, it's okay to be anxious where family is concerned. I understand completely and thank you for warning me. It's very sweet of you. But don't worry – I can defend myself and what I do. You have to get used to it in my profession.'

'Yes, I'm sure you do.'

Aura placed a hand on top of his. 'You worry too much, Harry.'

'I know.'

'And I'm delighted that you want to take me to your uncle's birthday lunch. Thank you for thinking of me.'

A gentle breath of downland air blew her hair back from her face and Harry leaned in to claim a kiss.

'That was nice,' he said a moment later.

'Like last night,' she whispered.

'I haven't been able to think about anything else,' he confessed.

They kissed again and it was only when Harry opened his eyes that he noticed Aura's bare feet and, as much as he loved them with their sparkly blue nail polish, he suddenly heard the voice of his mother.

'Doesn't she own any shoes?'

CHAPTER SIXTEEN

Abi woke on Sunday morning to a splitting headache which wasn't surprising really because she felt as if she was still carrying the weight of noise from the nightclub in her head. Groaning, she swung her legs out of bed, grimacing at the bright sunlight that was streaming through the white muslin curtains. She normally rejoiced in such a scene, but not today. Today, anything light or bright was to be avoided.

With slow and unsteady steps, she hit the shower and then made herself a cup of strong coffee and ate a couple of custard creams and took some painkillers. Not exactly the breakfast of champs – more like the breakfast of chumps, she couldn't help thinking. Why, oh why, had she agreed to go the club with Oscar? She'd known it wouldn't be her sort of thing and yet there'd been that little seed of pleasure in doing something new with somebody she was trying to get closer to. Well, that had been a mistake.

After downing a second cup of coffee and feeling slightly less blurry-eyed, Abi reached for her phone. It was after eleven in the morning and she had two texts – both from Oscar.

Where did you go last night?

Abi stared at the message. Was he serious? Did he not remember her leaving? Had he been so drunk that he didn't recall them going outside after the pink ponytail incident? She sighed and read the second text.

I'll call you. Oz x

'Oh, no! Please don't,' she said with a sigh, turning her phone off quickly.

She opened the French doors and breathed in the calming air of the garden and then she turned round to the table covered with her recent prints. They weren't quite right, she thought. They were missing a layer, a colour, and she instinctively knew how to fix it.

Abi felt very lucky that she could lose herself to the medium of art. It was such a wonderful release and distraction from the world around her. But it couldn't stop somebody entering her home through the French doors she'd left open.

'Abi!'

'Oscar!' She jumped. 'What are you doing here?'

'I came to see you. You weren't answering your phone. I was worried about you after you disappeared last night.'

'I didn't disappear. You saw me getting into a taxi.'

'What?'

'We left the club together to talk away from the noise, remember?'

He shook his head. 'No.'

'And I left. You went back inside.'

'Really?'

'Yes!' Abi couldn't hide her frustration. 'You were all cosy with that woman with the pink ponytail.'

'What woman with a pink ponytail?' Oscar looked incredulous.

'You don't remember?'

'No!'

Abi put her hands on her hips. 'Oscar, what *do* you remember from last night?'

'I remember the band was good. Wasn't it?' He didn't sound too sure now.

'Anything else?'

'I remember turning around and you were gone.'

Abi sighed as she looked at his face, all wounded and – yes – handsome.

'Oh, Oscar!'

'Are we having our first fight?'

Abi didn't like to tell him that they'd already had several only he hadn't noticed.

He came over to her and wrapped his arms around her, burying his head in her shoulders. 'I'm sorry, Abs! Did I neglect you last night? I hope I didn't. If I did, if I flirted with a pink-haired woman, if I missed you leaving, I'm sorry. Really! I'm a beast, aren't I? A no-good rat of a man. I don't deserve you. You should shoot me. Right now! Do you have a gun around here?'

'Don't be silly!' She pushed him away from her.

'No, really – I deserve it. You shouldn't have to put up with me.'

'Oscar, are you pouting? Seriously?'

He grinned. 'I've been told I'm cute when I pout.'

Abi laughed. She couldn't help it. He was very cute, but he was also ridiculously annoying. 'You know, I was actually working before you barged in.'

'Oh, let's see.' He approached the table and peered down at the prints. 'Wow, Abs! You're so talented.' He picked up one of the prints. It was of the downs, looking across the next valley towards a church.

'I'm thinking of adding another layer of green. Slightly darker.'

He nodded. 'It would make a nice birthday card.'

Abi bit her lip. It was the kind of comment you got from someone who didn't know what else to say about a piece of art.

'Thank you,' she said graciously.

'Look, I know I don't know much about this sort of thing, but I'd like to learn. When are you going to take me round this gallery, then?'

Abi frowned. She'd been hoping he might have forgotten about that but, looking at him now, all sweet and contrite, she didn't want to let him down. And maybe, just maybe, he genuinely couldn't remember his behaviour of the night before and it wouldn't happen again. Maybe Abi would be a good influence on Oscar. She'd teach him about art, introducing him to some of her influences, telling him about movements she admired and how artists used colour and light and texture.

'How about Friday?' she found herself saying.

'Sounds good.'

'You're not working?'

'Nah! Not on Friday.'

Abi didn't probe. 'I told you about the Towner Art Gallery, didn't I?'

'In Eastbourne, yes.'

'The one you ran away from on a school trip!'

'You remember my story?' he said and Abi nodded. 'I'd better meet you there.'

'Okay. For lunch? Say noon?'

'Great.'

'They have a lovely café. I can meet you in the foyer, okay?' Abi told him.

'You got it.'

He put the print down and moved towards her, cupping her face in his hands and kissing her tenderly.

'I'll see you on Friday,' he told her and then he disappeared out of the French doors.

Harry was fiddling with his green aventurine thumbstone when his boss walked into his office on Monday morning. Quickly pocketing the stone, he glanced up to gauge the mood Anthony was in. He seemed pretty calm, but you never could quite tell. He was under a lot of pressure from head office in London and he wanted to make the new Brighton office a big success.

'Hi Harry. Can I have a word?'

'Of course.'

'We were all really pleased with your work on the deodorant.'

'Oh, thanks.'

'In fact, the client was so impressed that they've requested you for their next job.'

'Really?'

'It's a tricky one and not everyone would want to take it on, but I know you'll be up for the challenge.'

'Okay,' Harry said guardedly.

Anthony leaned across the table and handed him some papers detailing the product.

'A weed killer?' Harry said.

'Yup! It's one of their biggest sellers. Or rather, it used to be, but this whole new green movement is losing them sales.'

'I'm not surprised,' Harry said.

'Yes, it's a problem. That's why they want to rebrand.'

'How? Have they changed the product then?'

'Not exactly. It's the packaging they want to change. The sales pitch. They want to make it seem more green.'

'But it's still the same product?'

'You got it!' Anthony gave a smile.

'A green weed killer?' Harry said. 'Isn't that called a hoe?'

His boss laughed. 'You a gardener?'

'Not exactly,' Harry thought, his mind drifting to the beautiful walled garden at Winfield Hall and the thought of the damage this weed killer could do to the vulnerable ecosystem there.

'I don't know, Anthony,' Harry said, shaking his head.

'Sure you do. This could do all sorts of things for your career. You get this right and I'll make sure your job here's secure.'

Harry frowned. Was Anthony threatening him? But, before he could question him, he'd left the room.

Harry looked up the weed killer online and it was just as Aura had told him. It did all sorts of harm to both flora and fauna.

There were also claims that it could cause kidney and liver damage and even cancer. In short, it was a nasty piece of work and Harry felt guilty for even having the sample in his office. Of course, the company defended their product, but the information Harry managed to find in just a quick search online seemed pretty damning, particularly the effect it had on the honeybee population. He could just imagine Aura's response if he told her this was the latest product he was advertising. She'd be appalled and he wouldn't blame her. But this was his job, wasn't it? It's what he was paid to do and, if he didn't do it, how would that impact his career? Anthony seemed to be suggesting something vague like redundancy would happen if Harry didn't take the product on, but could he really do that? There were other people in the company who could work on this. Did it really have to be him?

But, even if he did manage to pass the job on to someone else, was that good enough? Wasn't he still part of the team, part of the company that took this sort of work on? A company that took money in exchange for helping to promote a product that did untold damage to the environment and heaven only knew what to humans.

Harry cursed. He was having a professional melt-down. His job, his reason for getting out of bed every morning, was slowly slipping away from him. It was morphing into something else – something he wasn't at all sure he wanted anymore. And where did that leave him? If he didn't want to do this, what else would he do? He'd couldn't stop working. He'd just taken on that beautiful apartment and there was no way he wanted to give that up now.

He closed his eyes. It would be so easy for him to come up with some new copy for the weed killer. It was the kind of thing he used to get a buzz out of and he knew, if he put his mind to it, he could work his magic on this product. The company would be thrilled and his boss would give him a pat on the back and maybe even a promotion at some point. All he had to do was turn a blind eye as so many other people had obviously done for years while selling this product. But Harry knew he couldn't do that. Not anymore. So he took the papers Anthony had given him and went to his office, knocking on the door and waiting.

'Harry! Got something for me already?' his boss said as Harry entered.

'Not exactly.'

'What is it?'

Harry scratched the back of his neck, but then he remembered something – the green aventurine in his pocket. His fingers reached for it and he felt his thumb slotting comfortably into it, calming him, reminding him that he could do anything he set his mind to – even this.

'This weed killer – it's not really my kind of thing.'

His boss frowned. 'If we only advertised products that were our kind of thing, none of us would be in a job for long.'

'I know.'

'We all have a part to play in the bigger picture, don't we?'

Harry didn't like the condescending tone Anthony was using. 'I was thinking that someone else might want to take on the challenge.'

'The company asked specifically for you,' his boss reminded him.

Harry pushed his thumb into the stone in his pocket. 'Tell them I can't do it.'

Anthony didn't say anything for a moment. He was holding an expensive black and gold pen, clicking it on and off in an unnerving manner.

'I'd rethink this if I were you, Harry.'

Harry nodded. 'Yes. I am. In fact, it's not just this product, it's...' he paused, 'it's the ethics of this company actually. I'm not happy working for an outfit that even wants to consider promoting something like this. Have you looked at what it does? It should be banned. It's doing untold damage.'

'That's not our business.'

'No? Well, I'm making it mine and I don't want anything to do with it.'

Anthony frowned. 'What are you saying?'

'I'm saying, I'm out of here,' Harry told him, feeling a rush of blood to his head. His breath was short and ragged and his mouth was suddenly dry. 'I can't work here any longer.'

His boss stared at him. 'Are you mad?'

'Nope. But I really think you all are.' And, with that, he left the office, walking back to his where he quickly tidied his desk, picking up the carnelian Aura had given him and carefully putting it in his pocket before chucking the rest of of his personal possessions into a bag and hurrying through the open-plan office towards the stairs. It was as he was half-way down them that Letitia called.

'Harry! What are you doing?'

He stopped and looked back up at her. 'I'm leaving. I've quit.'

'But why?'

'Scruples, Letitia.'

She laughed. 'It's not over that silly weed killer, is it?'

'Yes, but not only that.'

A strange look passed over her face. 'So you're not working on it?'

'Damned right I'm not.'

She nodded and then she did an about turn and disappeared up the stairs, back into the office. Harry sighed, knowing she was heading straight for Anthony's office to make a pitch for the weed killer account. He shook his head and then, without another glance back, he left the building for the last time with something like relief coursing through him.

CHAPTER SEVENTEEN

It was a strange feeling for Harry to be home in the middle of the afternoon, but he hadn't wanted to go anywhere else. One of his colleagues had stopped him in the car park, astounded at his decision to leave and offering to buy him lunch, but Harry had just wanted to go. Now, sitting in the garden at Winfield, he breathed a sigh of relief so long that he felt sure he must have been holding his breath all day.

What have you done? Those four words kept turning over in his mind. Had he just made the biggest mistake of his life? Letitia obviously thought he was crazy as did his boss, but they weren't exactly his role models, were they? He didn't like what they were doing. They were fine with advertising harmful, horrible products that took away from the world rather than adding something wonderful to it. Well, that wasn't what Harry wanted to do for a living anymore and that's why he found himself sitting on a bench in the walled garden on a Monday afternoon. Actually, it was quite a nice feeling to do nothing and, to get into the true spirit of accepting his decision and being at peace with it, he bent to take off his shoes and socks, feeling the coolness of the grass beneath his toes a moment later.

He still couldn't believe he'd had the courage to do what he'd done. Had the crystal in his pocket helped, he wondered? Or was it Aura's influence? Whatever it was, he liked the person he was becoming. He felt stronger and happier and far more confident than he ever had, and yet he still couldn't help feeling a little anxious – not just about his future, but about how his parents would respond to his news. They'd been so proud when he'd told them about his job in the big city and were especially pleased when he'd been chosen to help set up the Brighton office. His role was just high-flying enough for them to be able to boast to their friends.

Our son's in advertising, you know?

It sounded important – businesslike yet creative at the same time. A step above the run-of-the-mill office jobs. He couldn't help thinking of the disappointment they were bound to feel when he told them he'd quit. His father had had the same job all his life so he wouldn't understand this new restlessness that Harry was feeling, and his mother would no doubt fret about him, believing him close to poverty and living on the street if he wasn't working five days a week.

So what was he going to do now? Did he want to do the same thing or try something new? And was the decision his to make? He had no idea what the job market was like at the moment. He might have to take anything that came his way because he didn't want to lose his apartment at Winfield. One thing was certain, though. He didn't want to rush headlong into another job just like the one he'd had. He was determined to change things around and to learn from his past mistakes. With that in mind, there was one person he wanted to talk to more than anyone else. So he texted Aura.

Are you around? x

He didn't get a reply for half an hour which probably meant she'd been with a client.

I'm on my way home now. Where are you? x

At home. x

You okay?

Got something to tell you.

I'll see you soon. x

Harry smiled, trying to anticipate what Aura would say. She'd be pleased, wouldn't she? Yes, just as he was quite sure of his parents' horror, Harry was sure of Aura's delight.

Aura was home within the hour and sat out on Harry's bench in the walled garden, her bare feet tantalisingly close to his. She'd made them a cup of rosehip and hibiscus tea each and they were nibbling shortbread she'd bought from her favourite bakers in town.

'So you just walked out?' she said after Harry told her what had happened.

'Yep! I grabbed a few things from my office and left.'

'And you're allowed to do that? They won't dock your pay or do anything legal?'

'I've absolutely no idea! I expect I'll get a call from the London office at some point to sort things out. But I left everything in good order. I just couldn't work there any longer.'

'I'm so impressed, Harry. Something like that takes real courage.'

He smiled. 'You know what they wanted me to advertise next?'

'No. What?'

'A weedkiller.'

Aura frowned. 'Oh, Harry!'

'They wanted me to make it *seem* greener.'

'Really?' Aura looked horrified.

'Truly.'

'I can't believe there are companies that'd do that.'

'I know and I'm afraid I've been blind to it for years. I don't know. It's like I just wasn't thinking. I was so wrapped up in my own little role – choosing the words and images, getting a buzz from being part of a team – I never really thought about the bigger picture.'

'But you are now.'

'Yes. Only, what's my bigger picture? I'm not quite sure what I do next.'

'I don't think you have to decide this afternoon,' Aura said gently.

He smiled. 'The trouble is, I feel like I'm half-baked. A sort of non-person.' He paused. 'I haven't become *me* yet. Does that make sense?'

Aura nodded. 'Yes. It makes absolute sense.'

'And I don't know what to do about it. I feel a bit like one of those hydrangeas that hasn't decided what colour it's going to be.'

'You're evolving.'

'Is that what it is?' He laughed. 'Will there be any side effects?'

Aura looked thoughtful. 'Joy, calmness, a deep sense of purpose and fulfilment.'

'Yeah?'

'Yes. But maybe not this afternoon.'

~

The Towner Art Gallery in Eastbourne was not the sort of place to fade into the background. A nineteen-twenties block of a building, it had been recently painted in bright bands of colour from deep purple to bright yellow. Not everybody loved it. Indeed, the colours weren't Abi's favourite, but she admired its boldness and the way it seemed to light up the street.

Oscar had said he'd meet her at the gallery for lunch on Friday and Abi was looking forward to it. The café on the top floor was a lovely low key sort of place where you could relax before taking in an exhibition and seeing the permanent collection. Abi was particularly looking forward to showing Oscar some of the paintings and ceramics on display by one of her favourite artists, Eric Ravilious. His Sussex landscapes in watercolour were mesmeric and his stylised ceramics had provided Abi with hours of inspiration.

It was an awkward thing to wait for someone. Abi had stood outside for the first ten minutes, eager to spot Oscar as soon as he arrived, but she'd soon got bored of that and had gone into the gallery, browsing around the shop in the lobby. She'd checked her phone a dozen times, wondering whether to call him or text him, and wondering why he hadn't got in touch with her if he'd known he was going to be late. But that was the trouble with Oscar – he didn't seem to acknowledge time and she wasn't even sure if he was aware when he was late. So she waited as patiently as she could, picking up a couple of books to flip through and buying a handful of postcards.

Half an hour passed by in this fashion and then Abi took herself off to the ladies where she brushed her hair and gazed at herself in the mirror, giving herself an internal dressing down.

What do you think you're doing? He's not coming. You know he isn't.

She checked her phone again. There were still no messages.

Of course there weren't. She probably wasn't even on his radar. Should she text him? A sensible part of her told her she should, but then the angry, frustrated side of her wanted to sulk and huff and play the victim, storing up all the hurt until she could hurl it his way in person.

With angry strides, she returned to the lobby and stood by the gift shop for a full ten minutes more, just to give him one last chance, just in case he'd been caught up in traffic or something totally out of his control had happened like a little old lady falling down in front of him and needing assistance. But she didn't suppose either of those things had happened. He was probably still in bed or down the pub or flirting with the girl with the pink ponytail.

So Abi left the lobby and went upstairs to the café. Being single, she'd perfected the art of eating alone, but it was quite a different feeling when you'd arranged to meet somebody to share a meal and they didn't show up. With every mouthful, she couldn't help glancing around at the other people who were in the café. There were couples, and groups of friends, an elderly woman with a grandchild, and another woman eating alone, her eyes glued to the screen of her mobile. Abi kept glancing at the entrance, half-hoping that Oscar would show up. There was still time for an explanation and forgiveness. He'd tell her about his tricky journey, the problem he'd had parking or some other unavoidable catastrophe and they would laugh and she'd feel bad for having ever thought he'd stood her up, and they'd go on with their day. But, of course, he didn't show up.

Abi finished her lunch and then looked around the gallery, burying her disappointment and hurt, and taking herself to the glass cabinets where she admired her favourite Ravilious ceramics. They were so familiar to her that they felt like old friends. When she'd drunk her fill of them, she took a look at the new exhibition, wondering what Oscar would have made of it all. She'd been looking forward to sharing the experience with him and she couldn't help feeling disgruntled that he wasn't there. After all, she'd gone to his club and listened to his band, hadn't she? And she would have stayed too if he'd been a gentleman and hadn't sloped off to the bar without telling her.

As she walked around the rest of the exhibition, her eyes only half-seeing the paintings and sculptures, she came to a grim realisation. It wasn't going to work, was it? Oscar and Abigail. It was a match made in purgatory. They simply weren't meant to be together even though they'd both made an effort to cross a cultural divide which Abi had felt from the onset. Her heart had been full of optimism and she'd really given it all she had, but it was beginning to wear her down. She felt emotionally exhausted trying to work out what Oscar was doing and if he was going to keep his word or not. She didn't need that in her life. She'd been bowled over by that incorrigible smile of his and the flattery and attention that had been lacking in her life for so long.

But a few smiles and compliments couldn't make up for the way Oscar was making her feel now and, as much as she didn't want to think about Edward in that moment, she couldn't help thinking that *he* would never have treated her like this.

Harry's first full week not working had flown by. He'd made some calls to friends in the business, asking about vacancies, but coming up with nothing. He'd joined a recruitment firm, but hadn't liked what they'd offered him. He'd also sorted things out with his old company, making a few painful phone calls and sending emails to colleagues. He couldn't quite believe he'd done it. His subconscious still thought he was working there. He was waking up at the same time to go to work even though he'd cancelled his alarm. It was going to take some getting used to.

One thing he did manage to achieve, though, was helping Aura with her website. To be frank, it was a bit of a mess. A well-intentioned mess. It was just a bit, well, naïve. For a start, her home page was a rather startling shade of pink. Harry's eyes had almost popped out of his head when he saw it for the first time on his laptop when they were working together in his apartment.

'It's not quite the shade of rose quartz I was going for,' Aura explained.

'We'll put it right,' Harry told her.

'It's very kind of you.'

'Hey, I've got heaps of time now and it's good to be doing something constructive.'

'I'm not very good at that sort of thing.'

'You just have to set your mind to it. Your *intention*,' he said with a grin.

'Ah, now that's something I *do* understand!' She laughed.

'Find the right words to explain who you are. What kind of impression do you want to make? What can you do that nobody else can? That kind of thing,' he told her.

Borrowing a notebook from Harry, Aura started jotting ideas down. Together, they worked on a brand new welcome page and biography. Harry replaced the much too vibrant pink with a soft blue background and he added an all-important popup to encourage visitors to sign up to Aura's newsletter.

'My newsletter?' she said.

'You've got to communicate with your clients. Keep in touch with them. Tell them about new treatments and any special offers.'

'Harry – that's a great idea!'

Harry beamed. It was fun working with Aura. She got so excited about new ideas and wasn't afraid to start from scratch. The end result was a website that was beautifully fresh and inspiring with a simple layout that was easy to navigate, but which also allowed Aura's full personality to shine through.

'I can't thank you enough,' Aura said.

'But you can – by coming to my parents' on Sunday. You haven't forgotten?'

'Of course I haven't. I'm looking forward to it.'

Harry smiled at her enthusiasm, trying desperately to hide his own reservations about introducing her to his parents.

CHAPTER EIGHTEEN

Sunday came round a lot quicker than Harry wished for. He awoke to a room flooded with sunlight and all he wanted to do was close his eyes against it. But he didn't. He got up, showered and shaved, had a quick breakfast and then took a walk up onto the downs where the summer sky was painfully blue and he was able to clear his head for a few blissful moments, listening to the spiralling song of a skylark. One felt invincible up here, he thought. It was as if by being on top of the world, its problems couldn't touch you.

But, as he descended the hill back towards Winfield, panic assailed him again at the thought of what the day might have in store. There was no getting out of it, though. He'd told his mum he was coming and that he was bringing someone. If he backed out of it now, she'd never forgive him. Besides, he wanted to see his Uncle Arthur. He was one of life's special people even though he didn't say a lot and could be painfully shy around strangers. He lived quietly alone, worked as a lab technician, played golf – alone – every weekend, and holidayed in Tenby every summer, staying in the same bed and breakfast overlooking the sea. One year, he'd surprised everyone by booking a fortnight in Lanzarote, but he hadn't liked it and, the next year, it was back to Tenby.

There was an innate sweetness about Uncle Arthur that stood in stark contrast to his brother, Harry's father. It was funny how two people could come from the same parents and share the same genes and yet be so very different. Harry had seen it with Aura's brother too. One would never have guessed that they were related.

Reaching his apartment, he tidied around, checked his emails and then sat with a cup of coffee until it was time to call for Aura. Since meeting Aura's brother, Harry was now a tad nervous every time he knocked on Aura's door, but he needn't have worried today for it was Aura who answered.

'Hi Harry!' she said with a bright smile.

Harry took in the dress she was wearing in swirling blues and greens, as billowing as the ocean. Her long red hair was loose with two pink diamante hair grips holding it back from her face, and a pair of silver stars were hanging from her ears.

'Harry? You okay?'

He nodded. 'I was just trying to decide whether you look like the sea or the sky.'

'Why not both?' she said.

'Why not?' he agreed, leaning forward to kiss her cheek. She laughed and he thought he detected a little nervousness so he took her hand in his and drew her to him, kissing her deeply.

Then it was time to go. He really couldn't delay it any longer – much as he'd like to spend all day hiding in the hills with Aura, cuddling on the picnic blanket.

'You're very quiet. You all right?' Aura asked him as they got into his car.

'Yes, sure. Just thinking.'

'What about?'

Harry winced as they left Winfield and set off on the short journey. He couldn't tell her what he was really thinking about – that he was anxious about introduce her to his parents. That, as soon as his mother clapped eyes on Aura, she'd be able to read her disapproval. That his father would bark something wildly inappropriate about her bohemian clothes or the little diamante she wore in her nose or the jangle of bangles she favoured or the crystal bead necklace she loved so much. They would make a snap judgement about her, he knew it, and it would break his heart if it hurt her.

'How's your brother?' Harry dared to ask, avoiding answering Aura's question.

'Johnny? Oh, he's okay.'

'I've not seen him around recently.'

'No, he comes and goes.'

'Looking for work?' Harry asked and he saw Aura frown. 'I don't know. I expect so. Work of a kind.'

'What do you mean?'

A pained expression crossed her face. 'He's not one for an office job.'

'Right, well, I can't judge him for that. I'm not sure I'm one for offices now.'

'Have you thought about what kind of work you would like to do?' Aura asked.

'I've been doing nothing but thinking,' Harry confessed. 'I want to get it right, you see. You spend a lot of time at work and I want to do something that resonates with me – that makes it worth getting out of bed in the morning for. But I don't want to do any damage.' He sighed. 'When I think about the products I was putting out into the world for my old company, I feel terrible. I keep having nightmares that I'm personally responsible for climate change.'

'Oh, Harry! I don't think you did *that* much damage!'

'But it preys on my mind, you know?'

'I know. But you've made a change now. A positive change. You're moving in the right direction.'

He grinned. 'If only I knew which direction that was.'

'You'll find out soon enough, I'm sure of it.' She reached across the car and squeezed his shoulder and Harry felt blessed to have her believe in him.

'Well, this is it,' he said as he turned into the driveway which led to his parents' barn conversion.

Aura gasped. 'It's stunning!'

'It's rather impressive, isn't it? Mum loves the garden and the views are rather special. That's what really sold it to them.' He parked the car and looked at Aura. 'You ready?'

She nodded and they got out, walking to the front door which had been left open for them.

'Mum? We're here.'

'Harry? Come on through. I'm in the kitchen.'

Harry took Aura's hand and they went through to the kitchen.

'There you are!' his mother said, greeting him a moment later, her hands briefly touching his arms while her eyes appraised Aura. Maria Freeman was wearing a crisp white blouse and a single strand of pearls and looked so very prim and proper next to his wispy, willowy Aura.

'Mum – this Aura. Aura – this is my mother.'

Aura stepped forward. 'Very pleased to meet you, Mrs Freeman.'

His mother's mouth dropped open momentarily and then closed again. 'Thank you, Aura? Is that right – *Aura*?'

'That's right.'

'That's very... unusual.'

'You have a beautiful home.'

'Thank you. We're quite proud of it.' His mother looked at Harry again as if she'd seen enough of Aura.

'Is there anything you need help with?' Harry asked, handing over a bottle of his uncle's favourite wine which he'd brought with him.

'No, thank you, dear. Go and see your father and Uncle Arthur while I sort out the lunch.'

Harry smiled at Aura. 'Come on,' he said, placing his hand in the small of Aura's back.

They walked through the open-plan house to the far end where the two men were sitting on a sofa facing a picture window.

'Hi Dad. Hi Uncle Arthur. Happy Birthday!'

Uncle Arthur nodded towards him and the two men stood up as they saw Harry's companion.

'Ah, there you are, Harry!' his father boomed.

'Dad, Uncle Arthur, I'd like you to meet Aura. Aura, this is my dad and the birthday boy himself.'

Aura smiled and held a hand out. Both men shook it, Harry's father almost crushing her fingers while Arthur held it gently, hardly shaking it at all. Harry couldn't help noticing the look of consternation on Leonard's face.

'What did you say your name was?' his father asked.

'Aura. It's short for Aurora.'

Harry sighed. Aura must be heartily sick of that question. If she had a crystal for every time somebody asked her it, he was quite sure she'd need the whole of Winfield to store them in.

They all sat down and Harry had to admit that the silence felt awkward.

'It's lovely to meet you both. And happy birthday,' Aura said, addressing Uncle Arthur. 'I brought you a little something.' She leaned towards him, handing him a small bag.

'You didn't need to do that,' he said, genuinely surprised as his hand delved inside, bringing out a piece of purple tissue paper. He put the bag down and slowly unwrapped the gift.

'Oh, look at that!' he said.

'I wasn't sure what you would like, but I'm sure pretty much everybody responds to amethyst,' Aura explained, watching as Uncle Arthur turned the little amethyst cluster around on the palm of his hand.

'It's quite beautiful,' he said.

'What is it?' Harry's father asked, squinting at the thing his brother was holding.

'It's a crystal, Dad. Aura does love her crystals,' Harry said, noticing that his father was frowning and that his mother, who had joined them as Uncle Arthur was unwrapping his gift, was looking deeply uncomfortable, as if she'd sat on a particularly pointy crystal.

'Well, thank you,' Arthur said. 'I'll keep it close to me.'

'That's a good idea,' Aura said. 'It has a very protective energy.'

Harry was used to such talk now, but his parents weren't and he could see them both wincing in horror at one another. He willed Aura not to notice. He could only hope that she had a crystal about her person that would protect her from his parents' negative energy.

'I brought you a bottle of your favourite wine,' Harry told his uncle.

'Yes, we're having it with lunch,' Harry's mother said. 'Talking of which...' she stood up and scooted back to the kitchen.

Twenty minutes later, after Harry's father had been holding court, telling everybody about an amusing incident at his cricket club, everyone made their way to the dining room table. Like the sofas, the table had been placed next to one of the barn's many floor to ceiling windows and the view across the countryside was breathtaking. Harry pulled out a chair for Aura, making sure he was beside her and he clocked the precise moment his mother noticed Aura's bare feet. It only took her a few moments before she'd called him over to her and was whispering in his ear.

'Doesn't she own any shoes?'

He sighed inwardly. 'Yes, of course she does, but she left them in the car.'

'Why would she do that?'

'Because she likes being barefoot.'

His mother pulled a face. 'It's not...' she paused, seemingly struggling to find the right word, 'hygienic.'

'It's absolutely natural, Mum. You should try it,' he told her, taking a bowl of steaming new potatoes from her and carrying it to the table. His mother followed, but Harry could feel the weight of her disapproval.

'What a beautiful spread, Mrs Freeman,' Aura said as she admired the delicious food.

'Thank you. Do help yourself, everyone. Harry – do the honours with the wine, won't you?'

Harry poured the wine for everyone but himself as he was driving. Uncle Arthur, very sensibly, had come by taxi so he enjoyed a couple of glasses over lunch. Unfortunately, the conversation didn't flow as easily as the wine did. It was stilted and awkward. Harry did his best to keep things afloat, telling them about life at Winfield, how beautiful the downs were looking and the abundance of the garden. He told them how interesting Aura's business was, but she seemed a little shy to talk about what she did, and so each of Harry's topics soon floundered.

Thankfully, the mood lifted a little when Harry's mother came through with the cake she'd made for Arthur and what a glory it was with its lemon icing.

'Delicious!' Harry's father announced a few minutes later.

'Yes, really lovely,' Aura said.

'And all vegan,' Harry's mother told her. 'Harry told me you were one.'

Harry winced at the way his mother said that, but Aura didn't seem to mind. Perhaps, like the reaction to her name, she was used to it.

'I usually make it with free-range butter, but Harry said you wouldn't eat that so I apologise if it isn't as good as my usual.'

'Mum, it's absolutely fine.'

'Well, if you're all sure.'

Everybody very quickly assured her that it was the very best cake they'd ever eaten and Harry's mum seemed placated.

It was as they all left the table a few minutes later to sit on the sofas at the far end of the barn that Aura addressed Uncle Arthur. 'May I ask you something personal?'

'Yes,' he said with a shy smile.

'I've been wondering. Is there any special person in your life – if you don't mind me asking?'

'I don't mind, my dear. And, yes, there is.'

There was a pause in which Harry, his father and mother exchanged bemused glances.

'Her name's Maude,' Arthur revealed.

Harry sat forward on the sofa. 'How long have you been together, Uncle Arthur?'

Arthur looked thoughtful for a moment. 'About three years. No,' he paused. 'Four come September.'

Harry's mother did a double take. 'Why didn't you tell us about her, Arthur?'

'Never came up,' he said simply.

'And we never asked you, did we?' Harry said, looking at Aura. 'Only Aura thought to ask.'

A blush crept over Aura's skin. 'I'm sorry, I didn't mean to...' she paused, looking around at everybody awkwardly.

Harry took her hand in his. 'I *love* your questions. You always get to the heart of things.'

'And may I ask you one?' Arthur said to Aura.

'Of course.'

'These dates – all the solstices and pagan festivals and things – do you mark them all? I mean, celebrate them?'

'I try to. It's fun to acknowledge the passage of time, don't you think? It kind of anchors us to the seasons,' Aura said. 'Instead of our days simply passing us by, we stop and give them a little of our attention. It keeps us in touch with nature and our roots. I think that's something we've lost over the centuries,' she paused. 'We've become a race of indoor dwellers, and the outside scares us sometimes. It seems strange and hostile. We close it out and turn the heating up or put on the air conditioning. We don't know what's real anymore, but our ancestors did. They always made time to simply stop and say, this is where we are right now and we're going to celebrate.'

Arthur nodded thoughtfully. 'I like that.'

Harry nodded and smiled. 'She's right, isn't she?' he declared. 'I could listen to her for hours.'

'I'm afraid you have!' Aura teased.

'But you have so much wisdom,' he told her. 'And you're right, we have lost touch with nature and that's something we should be more concerned with. When I think of all the hours I've spent in office buildings with sealed windows and strip lighting and the hum of computers sucking the life out of me, it makes me shudder.'

'But you have to work, Harry,' his mother chimed in, 'and you have such a good job.'

Harry swallowed hard. He hadn't yet told his parents about quitting his job and, if he wasn't going to tell them now, then when was he? After all, he had Aura next to him and hers was a wonderful, protective energy to have beside him.

'I've been meaning to tell you all,' he began. 'I – well – I quit my job.'

A deafening silence greeted him. His mother's mouth had dropped open and his father looked dumbstruck. Even Uncle Arthur looked concerned.

'What do you mean, Harry, you *quit* your job?' his mother asked.

'I mean exactly that. I left. I'd had enough so I walked out.' Harry gave a tentative smile, not quite sure how it would be received, but it felt good to get the words out at last.

'Harry didn't agree with the products the company were advertising,' Aura said.

His mother now directed her look of extreme disapproval to Aura. 'So *you* had something to do with this, did you?'

'It was nothing to do with Aura, Mum.'

'No? Because she seems to have turned your head with all this airy fairy talk about stars and crystals and growing roots and whatever else she's into.'

'Mum!'

'Well, I won't have it! You had a good job, Harry. You just tell your boss you made a mistake. Your father will ring too if you want.'

'Listen, Mum! I don't want to work there and I don't need to beg my boss for forgiveness and I certainly don't need Dad wading in.'

It was then that Harry noticed his mother glancing down at Aura's bare feet again with something approaching disdain. Harry leaned forward, carefully easing his shoes off, followed by his socks. 'Ah, that's better,' he said with an exaggerated sigh of satisfaction. 'You should try it. You know Aura's really on to something with this barefootedness.'

'Really?' his mother said, sounding unconvinced.

'It's a wonderful sort of freedom,' Harry went on, 'and we should embrace it more in our lives.'

'And is that why you've quit your job?' his mother asked. 'So you can prance around barefoot with *her*?'

Harry glared at his mother and then, very quickly, he stood up, taking Aura's hand in his and grabbing his shoes and socks.

'Come on,' he said, marching to the front door and putting his things on.

'Where are you going?' his father cried.

'Uncle Arthur – I hope you enjoy the rest of your birthday,' Harry called back through.

'Harry – it's okay,' Aura whispered.

'It's not okay at all. I won't have you talked to like that.'

'But your mum...'

'She knows exactly what she's doing and I'm not having it.'

'Harry!' his mother cried, but she made no attempt to go after him and Harry could hear the irate voice of his father mumbling something about children being ungrateful as he left the house.

Harry swore under his breath as he opened the car door for Aura.

'Harry, please go back and talk to your mum,' she said as she got in. 'You can't leave like this.'

'I have nothing to say to her.' He got in the car, slamming his door. 'I'm so sorry you had to witness that, Aura.'

She reached out and placed her hand on his knee. 'It's okay.'

'No it's not. She was mean and cruel and that's not on.'

'She was just looking out for her son.'

'Well, I don't need looking out for. I can make my own decisions about where I work and who I see.' Harry started the car and, as soon as they were out of the driveway and onto the road, he put his foot down.

'Harry, I don't want to cause a problem. That's the very last thing I want to do.'

'You're not causing a problem.'

'But I obviously am.'

He sighed. He still couldn't quite believe what had happened. He'd known Aura would cause a bit of a stir, but he hadn't expected his normally very polite mother to be quite so unpleasantly vocal. There was absolutely no excuse for it even if his mother did blame Aura for him leaving his job which was ridiculous.

'I'm sorry,' he said. 'I'm sorry for ever taking you there and putting you through that.'

'You don't need to apologise.'

'I feel that I do. It was horrible.'

'Your uncle was nice.'

Harry laughed at that. 'Yes. You'll never hear him say anything mean even if you punch him on the nose. And I can't believe you wiggled that confession out of him.'

Aura frowned. 'There was no wiggling involved.'

He smiled. 'No, you were just being your own true

wonderful self and I love that. I really do. I'm just really angry that my parents didn't love it too.'

'It's totally fine. I know not everyone understands what I do or agrees with it. Maybe I talked too freely about it all. I'm sorry if I made them uncomfortable.'

'Don't you dare apologise!' Harry said. 'You have nothing to be sorry for. You're a sweet and genuine person who has a unique way of looking at the world.'

'A unique way that your parents hated,' she said, her voice filled with sadness.

Harry slowed the car down and reached a hand across to touch Aura's knee. 'Let's stop talking about them for a while, shall we? We'll go home and I'll make us some tea and we can sit in the garden. I can even take my shoes and socks off again and not be scowled at.'

When they arrived back at Winfield, Harry checked his phone and saw there were five missed calls from his mother. Aura had nipped back to her apartment and he was just about to switch his phone off when it rang again. There was no point ignoring his mother as he knew she could keep this up all day and that he'd have to answer at some point so best to get it over and done with now, he thought.

'What is it?' he asked as he answered.

'Harry?' She sounded distraught. 'I'm sorry,' she said. 'I didn't mean to be, well, quite so blunt.'

'Mum, I don't know what to say.'

'Well, I do. I'm sorry. Really. It was just such a shock to hear you'd quit your job.'

'People quit their jobs every day. It isn't a big deal, but how you treated Aura *is* a big deal.'

There was a pause before his mother spoke again.

'Come and see us next weekend, okay?'

'I'm not sure I want to bring Aura again,' Harry told her.

'Well, that's good that you're rethinking things, darling. You have to admit, she really isn't your sort.'

Harry gasped, not quite believing what he was hearing. 'I'm not breaking up with her! I'm not bringing her because I don't want you hurting her again!'

'Harry, listen to me. You must see how odd you are together. You're so conventional and proper–'

'I don't want to be conventional and proper.'

'You're just being perverse. It's like you're deliberately trying to hurt me.' Her voice was high-pitched again, on the verge of tears.

'I'd never do that. You know that. But you have to accept that I'm with Aura and it's serious, Mum, so you'd better get used to it and, if you want to see me again, at your home, then you'd better be sure that you make Aura welcome.'

He hung up just as Aura entered his apartment. Her face was ashen. How much of the conversation with his mother had she heard exactly?

'Ready for that tea?' he asked hesitantly.

'Actually, I think I might just have a rest,' she said, giving him the faintest of smiles before leaving the room.

CHAPTER NINETEEN

The crystals weren't working their usual magic. As Aura looked down at the crystal grid she'd laid on the coffee table with its large rose quartz centre surrounded by clear quartz points and blue lace agate tumbles, she felt no calmer than she had the night before. The gentle heart-healing energy of the pink crystal didn't seem to be soothing her as it should be. She'd even spent twenty minutes gazing into the soul of a favourite smoky quartz, allowing herself to drift gently into the crystal, looking at its rainbows which winked merrily at her. But even that hadn't dispelled her dark mood. The heavy weight of being rejected by Harry's parents just wasn't shifting. She felt it keenly and she knew it wasn't going to resolve itself easily.

She'd known the moment she'd seen the beautiful barn conversion that she didn't belong there with its pristine white curtains and its matching dinner service. It was all so perfect and conventional. There were no rough edges, nothing casually mismatched. Harry's mother had greeted her with a tight-lipped smile, and the look she'd given Aura when she'd believed she had something to do with Harry walking out on his job had been Medusa-worthy. Indeed, a little piece of Aura's heart had been turned to stone in that moment which was why she was meditating with *her* stones this morning. She'd spent a few moments holding her largest black tourmaline which was meant to dispel negative energy, but she feared there wasn't a black tourmaline in the world big enough for the job.

Aura tried to shake the image of Mrs Freeman and her disapproving scowl from her mind. The more you thought about negative things, the more power you gave them, she reminded herself. Perhaps she needed to work on her aura, she thought. Perhaps hers was leaky, and there was nothing worse than a leaky aura because it allowed negative energies in. You had to create healthy boundaries and protect yourself. So she picked up the smoky quartz again. It had a beautiful polished point and she carefully guided it around the outline of her body, imagining it strengthening her while repelling anything that had no business being there, all the time doing her best to breathe in the crystal energy and exhale anything that she didn't need to carry.

She was glad Johnny wasn't around because she needed to be alone today. In fact, she hadn't seen Johnny for over twenty-four hours which didn't mean a lot really. Ever since he was a teenager, he'd had a habit of disappearing for hours on end, only to turn up again with a black eye or a swollen lip. It was always best not to ask where he'd been or what he'd been doing. Aura hoped he'd been looking for work, but he was always vague on such matters, mumbling something about having enough to be getting by on. She never probed, but only hoped he wasn't spending any time with his old buddies – the ones that seemed to get him into trouble.

Feeling that she wasn't really getting anywhere with her

energetic hygiene, Aura put her crystals away and was just about to update her blog when there was a knock at the door.

'Aura?'

It was Harry. Of course it was Harry. He'd called late the night before, gently knocking on her door for several patient minutes, but she'd ignored him. But she could only ignore him for so long.

Slowly, she made her way to the door and opened it.

'Hey,' he said.

'Hello.'

He leaned forward and kissed her cheek. 'I've been worried about you. Are you okay?'

'Of course I am.'

He took in her expression. She looked wounded somehow.

'You're not okay, are you?' he asked gently, reaching out to touch her arm, but she backed away. 'Aura?'

'I'm sorry. I'm just feeling... a little fragile.'

'Can I come in?' Harry asked, trying to look around the door. 'Is your brother...?'

'He's out.'

'He's not good for you, Aura.'

'What do you mean?'

'He's draining you. You look exhausted.'

'I'm fine,' she said, not bothering to add that it was Harry's parents who'd been draining her of her energy as well as Johnny.

'Well, you don't look fine,' he added.

'Thanks very much!'

Harry sighed. 'I'm worried about you.'

'Well, you don't need to be.'

'Don't I?'

Aura bit her lip. She couldn't remember the last time

anybody had cared for her in this way and it felt strange. She could feel herself getting emotional, which was very silly. Perhaps she was just tired. That would be it.

'Where is he now?'

'Johnny? I don't know. He's going through a rough time,' Aura told him, not adding that Johnny always seemed to be going through a rough time.

'Well, I hope he gets himself sorted both for you and for himself.' He paused for a moment. 'Listen, Aura, I spoke to my mum last night. I think you might have heard some of it actually?'

Aura nodded. 'A little. Enough.'

Harry raked a hand through his hair. Now that Aura looked at him properly, she could see that he was tired too, maybe even more than she was.

'She said she was sorry for the way she spoke to you. And she means it too. It was so unlike her. I'm still shocked actually.'

'Did she say anything else?' Aura asked, knowing that she had, but wondering if Harry would share it with her.

Harry hesitated. 'Not really.'

'Are you sure?' Aura pressed. 'She didn't say something about me not being welcome there again?' As soon as the words were out, she saw Harry flinch. 'She did, didn't she?'

'No. Not in as many words. Look, I need to talk to her.'

'I'm not sure she's going to listen or even if it's worth it.'

'What do you mean?' Harry asked.

'I mean, she doesn't want me in your life, Harry. I'm not a part of the world you were brought up in. I don't fit.'

'Well, that makes two of us because I don't fit in that world either now.'

'But it's different with me.'

'How?'

'Your parents want you there and I'm imagining they want you with some lovely neat girl who wears crisp clothes and court shoes and not – well – me.'

'But I want you there, Aura!'

'I don't think that's enough.'

'What are you saying? Are you giving up on us?'

'No, of course not,' she said as he stepped forward and she felt his arms closing around her.

'Because it sounds as if you are.'

'I'm just worried that this is going to cause a problem and the last thing I want to do is to come between you and your parents.'

He shook his head. 'Look, I'm going to talk to Mum and make her see just how important you are in my life and, if she can't see that then, well, I don't know. But I'm not giving you up,' he said, kissing the top of her head. 'Not ever.'

As much as Abi immersed herself in her work, she couldn't push Oscar Townsend completely from her mind. The rat still hadn't rung her to explain what had happened on Friday when he hadn't shown up at the gallery and she certainly wasn't going to chase after him. As far as she was concerned, it was over. Whatever had gone on between them had been a mistake. Albeit a very pleasurable mistake at times, but a mistake nevertheless.

Just that morning, she'd seen Edward in the garden on his phone, marching up and down as he'd talked. She'd watched, trying to catch his eye so that she could wave and wondering if she should tell him about Oscar and how she wasn't seeing him now. Perhaps he might invite her swimming again if she wasn't seeing his brother. But, even though he had caught her eye as he'd ended his call, he didn't smile or wave back. He simply went back inside.

So, that was it, she thought. She'd made her decision and it had been the wrong one and now things would be forever awkward in Edward's presence just as she'd dreaded. Maybe she'd have to move, but the idea of leaving Winfield was too painful to contemplate even for a minute. No, she thought. She'd just have to live a torturous life, forever trying to avoid Edward in the hallway and garden, and she really didn't want to have to do that because she liked him so much.

Oh, why was life so difficult, she mused, putting far too much ink on her roller and ruining the print she was working on. She cursed, putting the roller down. It was too hot to work anyway. Perhaps she should go out in the garden and see if there was a shady corner somewhere where she could sit and brood. Yes, that sounded like a plan.

It was late on Tuesday night as Aura was sitting just outside her open French doors enjoying the cool night air of the garden when she heard her front door slam shut.

'Johnny?' She got up and went inside and there was her brother.

He looked terrible. His eyes were bloodshot as if he hadn't slept in days and he had a sort of jitteriness about him like he was unable to keep still. Aura swallowed hard, instantly knowing that he'd been using again, but she was too afraid to say anything.

'Have you eaten?' she asked at last.

He nodded, but then shook his head. 'Can't remember.'

'Are you hungry?'

'Yes.'

'Let me make you something,' she said, disappearing into the kitchen. It was late, but that didn't matter. All that mattered was giving Johnny something nourishing and trying to pull him out of the hole he'd obviously fallen into. Again. Why did he do it to himself? Why did he find it so hard to turn things around and make a good and happy life for himself?

Aura whipped up a quick pasta with plenty of fresh vegetables and presented it to him a few minutes later, sitting down opposite him at the table.

'You're not going to watch me, are you?' he asked.

'Yes. I want to make sure you eat it all.'

'God, you're like a little mother.'

For a moment, Aura wondered if she could surreptitiously wave a crystal wand around him to clear his negative energy. Instead, she asked, 'Where've you been, Johnny?'

He shrugged as he shovelled pasta into his mouth. 'Here and there.'

'Have you been looking for work?'

'I've been working.'

'Have you? Doing what?'

He didn't reply and Aura didn't push because she probably didn't want to know.

'Anna? You couldn't lend me a few quid, could you?'

She sighed. 'Oh, Johnny! Don't ask me that.'

'I'm not asking for much. Just – I don't know – fifty to tide me over.'

'Fifty pounds?'

'Well fifty pence wouldn't get me very far, would it?' He snorted at his own humour, but Aura wasn't laughing.

'I don't have that kind of money,' she lied.

'Don't your clients pay in cash?'

'Only some of them,' she said, thinking of the little bundle of notes she'd squirrelled away over the past few weeks. She'd been meaning to take it all to the bank, but hadn't got round to it yet. 'Anyway, I thought you said you were working.'

'Yeah, well, I've got expenses, haven't I?'

'And are you looking for somewhere to live?' Aura dared to ask.

Johnny sniffed and mumbled something about a friend's sofa which had broken springs and a bad odour.

'You can't stay here forever, Johnny.'

His fork clattered onto the plate and he pushed it away. 'I'm going out.'

'But you've just got back.'

'You don't want me here.'

'Don't be like that – Johnny!'

But he was gone, slamming the door behind him and leaving his unfinished pasta and very bad energy in the room for Aura to clear.

CHAPTER TWENTY

The Lewes farmer's market was a favourite haunt of Edward's, but even that wasn't lifting his mood this week. He felt sluggish and despondent as if his life was missing a vital ingredient and he knew exactly what that ingredient was. Abigail. He missed her vibrant friendship, her laughter, her humour. He missed their little outings together and their casual conversations in the hallway or the garden.

As he walked around the stalls, buying a bagful of fresh herbs and some mixed salad leaves, he recalled seeing Abi in the garden earlier in the week when he'd been on the phone. She'd waved at him and he'd ignored her.

You stupid fool, he cursed himself. What would it have taken for him to wave back? Even to walk over to her and strike up a casual conversation. She seemed to want that so why couldn't he give it?

Oscar, that's why, he told himself. Every time he saw Abi now, he thought of Oscar. His little brother had come between them as surely as if he'd been a big old brick wall and Edward simply couldn't get over it. As far as he was concerned, Abi had made her choice.

And just when he'd been working up the courage to reveal his feelings towards her. Well, he told himself, that's what happened when you kept putting things off. Edward tortured himself as he thought of all the opportunities he'd had when he and Abi had been alone in the most glorious settings. If he hadn't been able to tell her then, maybe it wasn't meant to be. Maybe she was destined to be with Oscar.

He shook his head. Abi and Oscar. The idea of them being a couple was preposterous and the painful thing was that Abi seemed to be blind to the fact. He couldn't blame her really. He'd seen the way his brother had of charming the ladies, but it baffled him that he'd gone for a woman like Abi. Edward still believed it was because his little brother had got wind that *he* liked her. He was quite sure that, ordinarily, Oscar would run a mile from someone like Abi whose interests were so very different from his.

He was just pondering all this when he caught sight of a sandy-coloured head of hair and heard a laugh that could only be one person's. Edward stopped walking and watched as the man moved into the centre of the path between the stalls. It was, indeed, Oscar, and he wasn't alone. His arm was draped around the shoulders of a young woman with a pink ponytail. Edward frowned. What was he doing? Had he and Abi broken up? Or was Oscar up to his old tricks again, seeing how many women he could date at once?

Edward watched as the woman with the pink ponytail gently elbowed Oscar in the ribs. Oscar laughed and then drew her towards him, kissing her fully on the mouth. It was all Edward could do to stop himself from charging over to them and demanding to know what was going on. But it wasn't his place and he certainly wasn't one for making scenes, especially not in public, and so he let them drift off into the crowded street before making his way home.

Abigail, he told himself, wasn't his business. He couldn't be responsible for her choices and, as much as he wanted to, he couldn't protect her from his brother if she truly wanted to be with him. It was frustrating and he felt utterly helpless. He cared about Abi and he knew in his heart that Oscar was not good for her, but what could he do?

'Nothing,' he told himself. 'Absolutely nothing.'

Edward wasn't the only soul from Winfield Hall at the farmers' market that morning. Aura was there too. No matter how trying a week had been, Aura could always make herself feel better with a trip to Lewes's farmers' market. She loved the variety of stalls: the fruit, the vegetables all locally grown, the artisan loaves of bread, and wild mushrooms fresh from the fields come autumn. The colours and the scents were always inspiring even if you didn't have enough to buy bagfuls of produce, and Aura was often quite content just to look without buying.

It was as she was walking towards one of her favourite stalls that she saw her. Although she'd only met her once, Mrs Freeman was someone whom Aura wouldn't forget in a hurry. Harry's mother was standing next to the vegetable stall that Aura favoured for its fresh seasonal produce and, before Aura could change direction, Mrs Freeman spotted her too.

And there was that look again. The deep disapproval etched all over her face, making Aura feel as if she'd committed some atrocious crime. It took every fibre of Aura's being not to turn and flee. Why should she, after all? She had as much right to be here as Mrs Freeman, and so she stood her ground as Mrs Freeman stared her down.

'Aura,' she said, sounding the name as if it was something unpleasant she was trying to spit out.

'Mrs Freeman. How are you?' Aura said, deliberately trying to disarm her with charm. It didn't work.

'Harry not with you?'

'No.'

'Good. Because there's something I want to say to you and it's easier if it's just you and me.'

'Oh? What's that?' Aura said, but she knew Mrs Freeman wasn't about to ask Aura's advice on recipes for the enormous bag of tomatoes she'd just bought.

'You seem like a nice enough young woman,' Mrs Freeman began and Aura could hear the approaching 'but' a mile off. 'But I think you realise that you're just not right for our Harry. You must see that.' It was a statement rather than a question and Aura was rather blindsided by it. 'So I think the sooner you end things with him, the better. I always think a little bit of fun with someone outside our – well – *circle*, can bring a bit of entertainment, but these things never last. And Harry needs someone by his side who will help him in his career. He's a very bright young man, you see, and he needs a woman who's accomplished and polished. A professional.'

By the time Mrs Freeman stopped to draw breath, Aura had lost count of the number of insults that had been heaped upon her and she had no idea how to respond to any of them. For a moment, Mrs Freeman glanced down at Aura's feet, safely inside a pair of sparkly sandals today, and Aura guessed what she was thinking. Harry's future partner would be somebody who wore sensible shoes and who never went barefoot.

Aura took a deep breath. 'I'm sorry you feel the way you do,

Mrs Freeman, but Harry and I are very happy and I rather think it's up to him who he chooses to see, don't you?'

'No I don't. Harry's always been a little immature when it comes to matters of the heart and he turns to me for guidance in such matters.'

Aura frowned. That sounded very unlikely to her. Not for one moment could she imagine Harry consulting his mother before dating somebody. The idea almost made Aura laugh out loud, but she managed to curb the impulse.

'Does he?'

'Yes he does. We're very close, you see, and it would be very uncomfortable if somebody came between us. Harry would take it badly if, for example, he couldn't visit us because of his choice of partner. That would hurt him immeasurably.'

Aura blanched at the barely disguised threat. Indeed, she didn't know how to respond and so she did the only thing she could and reached inside her tote bag, bringing out a little bag of tumbled stones, opening it up and taking out a rose quartz.

'I'd like you to have this,' Aura told her. 'It's only small, but it might help you to see the good in people. *All* people.'

And, with that, she turned and left the market as quickly as she could.

When she got back home, Aura wrestled with whether to tell Harry about her meeting with his mother at the market, but decided it was probably best if she didn't. She didn't want to cause any more pain than she had to, and the horrible little scene by her favourite vegetable stall had been between her and Mrs Freeman – no one else. And yet, what was she going to do? This problem wasn't just going to go away, was it? As long as she was with Harry, his relationship with his parents was going to be strained and Aura knew she couldn't be responsible for that.

Opening one of her drawers, she pulled out a favourite amethyst point. It was raw at the base with a polished top and, when you tilted it to the light in just the right direction, there was a beautiful rainbow trapped inside. Aura took it outside and sat on the little chair she'd placed in the walled garden just by her French doors. She held the crystal lightly in her hands, gazing into its purple depths. As well as being a very calming stone, it was associated with intuition and decision making, and Aura hoped it would help her now.

What should she do? What was the right decision to make? She closed her eyes, listening to the beat of her heart, but she knew what it was telling her: she loved Harry. She'd never felt this way about someone before, but they'd become so close so wonderfully quickly. He was the sweetest, tenderest soul and she could so clearly see him in her future. Okay, so they weren't an obvious match. That was one of the few points on which Aura agreed with Mrs Freeman. But obvious matches were highly overrated. Wouldn't life be very dull indeed if you always went for the obvious option?

She opened her eyes, staring into the amethyst's depths, its rainbow winking at her. It hadn't helped at all.

Harry had been busy, but not very productive. He'd scoured websites, papers, called in favours with friends and made phone calls to companies he thought suitable, but there was nothing out there. He'd even been looking at jobs in London but, now he'd made the break from the capital, he really didn't want to go back unless he absolutely had to. But the truth was, there was very little in the local area that inspired him jobwise.

He sat back in his chair and rubbed a hand over his jaw. His shoulders ached and his eyes were sore. He'd had enough job hunting for today. What time was it anyway? He'd thought Aura was coming over to see him for lunch, but she hadn't called. He hadn't seen her for a couple of days now. They'd texted each other, but she'd said she was working whenever he suggested getting together. But what had happened today?

He got up and made his way to her apartment, knocking lightly on the door in case she had a client with her.

'Who is it?' her voice answered.

'It's me. Harry.' There was a pause and then she opened the door. 'Were we going to have lunch together today?'

'Oh, Harry! I'm sorry. I forgot.'

He peered closely at her. She looked pale. 'Are you all right?'

'I'm fine. Just tired. This heat.'

'Yes, it's pretty hot, isn't it?'

'I've been sitting outside then coming back inside. I can't seem to get comfortable anywhere.'

'I drew the curtains in my apartment. Try that – keep the sun out,' he advised.

'Yes.'

He frowned. 'You sure you're okay?' He took a step closer to her and reached out to touch her face, so soft, so warm. She closed her eyes and her cheek pressed into his hand. A natural fit.

'I was in the market on Saturday,' she said, her eyes opening and fixing their gaze on him.

'The farmers' market? Mum loves that.'

Aura nodded. 'Me too.'

'And?' he prompted. 'Was there something you were going to tell me?'

She stared at him, her lips slightly parted and her eyes looking suddenly fearful. 'No.' She gave a nervous laugh.

'No?'

'Just – well – you should go sometime.'

'Okay. Maybe we could go together,' he suggested.

'Yes.' There was a pause and Aura seemed to know that Harry had something to say. 'What is it?' she asked him.

'I spoke to my dad.'

'How is he?'

'He sounded stressed actually. I'm worried about him.'

'What's the matter?' Aura asked.

'He's upset about us. I think he liked you, you know.'

'Really?'

Harry smiled. 'But he said Mum's still having a hard time about it all.'

'Do you think she'll come round?' Aura asked. 'I mean, if I've a vote of confidence from your father.'

Harry leaned forward and kissed her. 'I guess we'll have to wait and see,' he told her.

The weather was unbearably hot during the first week in July. It was difficult to work during the day and even harder to sleep at night. Aura didn't like to leave windows open, but the heat was too much for her and she was desperate for whatever breath of air the downs could give her. Anyway, Winfield felt wonderfully safe to her so, for just one night, she'd take a chance.

Aura wasn't sure what time it was when she woke, but it

was still dark and so she turned over, kicking her legs out from under the bedding in an attempt to cool down.

It was as she walked into the living room in the morning that she saw something odd. There was a mug on the floor. Was that what had woken her in the night, she wondered? She went to pick it up, tutting when she saw the chip in the pretty porcelain. She put it on the little table and then frowned. How had it come to be on the floor in the first place? There had been only the lightest of breezes during the night, but it would take a gale of some force to have knocked the mug from the table. Perhaps a cat had come in through one of the windows she'd left open. Yes, that would be it.

But then she saw something else that made her change her mind. Her handbag was on the sofa instead of hanging up behind the door. Aura's heart plummeted, knowing what it meant. It hadn't been a cat who had come into her apartment the night before; it had been her brother, hadn't it? He even had his own key after he'd persuaded her to give him one so he didn't need to keep using the intercom.

Dreading discovering the truth, Aura opened her handbag and, sure enough, the little money she'd had in her purse had gone. She tried to remember how much it was, but it certainly wasn't more than twenty pounds. And then something dawned on her and she looked across to the set of drawers where she kept her crystals. Her crystals and her cash.

'Oh, no,' she said, rushing towards the chest and opening it. A moment later, she knew the truth. The money was gone. Of course it was. She closed her eyes, thinking about the roll of notes she'd been saving up and how very careful she'd been in not spending it. Her heart plummeted as she thought about what had happened in her apartment the night before. Johnny had been living with her and knew his way around the place although he must have forgotten the coffee table and knocked into it. He certainly knew where her savings were though. He'd most likely discovered them before he broke in, but he'd been hoping she'd give him a handout when he asked her. Would he have stolen from her if she'd given him something? Could she have saved herself the heartache? She wasn't entirely sure. One thing was certain, though. Prison had never reformed Johnny. He was back to his old ways and there was nothing she could do about it. It was awful to admit, but the real pain came from knowing that he could do what he'd done to his own sister when she'd shown him nothing but love and support. She didn't matter to him. She was only a provider of funds, someone who had a sofa he could kip on rent-free. And that hurt because she truly cared about her brother. No matter how old he got or what he did, he'd still be the little brother she'd grown up with.

Aura had just been straightening the throw over the sofa when there was a knock at her door. She froze. It wouldn't be Johnny, would it? No, of course not. He was long gone and she'd probably not see him again for months if, indeed, he ever dared to show his face again.

'Who is it?' she called.

'It's Abi.'

Aura opened the door.

'Hi Aura. I'm sorry to bother you. I'm just checking on you. Is everything okay?'

Aura panicked. Did Abi know something? 'Why?' she asked.

'It's just...' Abi pulled a pained face. 'I'm afraid my apartment's been broken into. Or rather, someone's been in. It was my own fault, really. I left the French doors open last night. I don't normally do that, but you know how hot it was.'

'Yes. It was. Gosh, Abi. What was taken?'

'Jewellery mostly and a bit of cash I had lying around. But there was a little gold brooch that's missing now and it's breaking my heart. It was a gift, you see, from a friend and I'm frantic about it.'

'Oh, I'm sorry,' Aura said, her own heart breaking a little at the thought that it was her own brother who'd taken it. She felt like she'd betrayed Abi by letting Johnny into Winfield and a part of her wanted to confess now, but what would Abi do? She'd call the police if she hadn't already and they'd find out who Aura was and soon put the pieces together.

'Is anything missing from yours?' Abi asked.

Aura nodded, deciding it was best to tell the truth. Or at least some of it. 'All the cash I had.'

'Oh, no! Was it a lot?'

'Yes. I'd been meaning to bank it, but just hadn't got round to it,' Aura told her, cursing herself for her oversight. That money represented a good portion of her wages for the past few weeks and she'd been going to buy a new computer with it. Now, it was gone.

'But there isn't any damage anywhere?' Abi asked.

'No.'

'That's good. There isn't any in mine either. It looks like an opportunist who just sneaked in and out, grabbing things they could pocket.'

'Are you going to call the police?' Aura asked, dreading Abi's response.

'We should really, although I suppose there's little they can do now. Are you around if they come over to ask questions?'

Aura nodded, feeling flustered. 'I'm so sorry,' she told Abi.

'It's not your fault!' Abi said. 'Although I suppose we're not totally blameless if we left windows and doors open. Is that how the thief got into yours?'

'I think so. I left most of my windows open, I'm afraid,' Aura said, shuddering inside at her brother being referred to as a thief. But that's what he was, wasn't he?

'Leave it with me. It's still early, isn't it? And we should check with Edward and Harry and see if anything else has been taken.'

Aura panicked. The thought of her brother causing so many people so much trouble was almost unbearable.

'Don't look so worried,' Abi said. 'We'll get things sorted.'

But Aura was worried. She was worried about her brother being caught. He'd be back in prison quicker than you could say smoky quartz and it would probably be for longer this time because he just kept on offending.

'I don't know what to do,' Aura said, not realising she'd spoken her fears out loud until Abi responded.

'I'm so sorry this has happened. It was stupid of me to leave those doors open.'

'No – no. You weren't to blame,' Aura said quickly.

'At least nobody was hurt. We're still here and we've learned our lesson, haven't we?'

'Oh, yes,' Aura said, 'we've definitely done that.'

CHAPTER TWENTY-ONE

Abi felt bad for her tenant. While Abi had plenty in the way of savings and wouldn't miss the money that had been stolen, she felt sure that Aura would probably feel the loss of hers keenly. Perhaps she could help her out. Maybe she could stop charging her rent for a couple of months. Yes, she'd offer that.

As Abi went back to her own apartment, she couldn't help feeling a little sullied. It was horrible to think of her beautiful home being invaded by a burglar. But, as she'd admitted to Aura, she had practically invited them in by leaving her doors and windows open. And yet a part of her cursed a world where you couldn't do just that. Why did things have to be locked and secured all the time? Abi thought back to the night before. She'd been working at her dining room table until late and there had finally been a cooling breeze through the doors she'd left open into the garden. She'd walked outside for a few minutes, her feet sinking softly into the lawn as her skin cooled and, when she'd come back inside, she hadn't been able to bear the idea of closing the doors.

Had the burglar been waiting then? Hiding in the shadows,

watching, waiting? Abi shuddered at the thought. She cursed whoever it was too for the loss of her pretty gold brooch. She didn't believe it was worth a lot of money but, being a gift from Ronnie and having belonged to his beloved wife, it was priceless to Abi and it pained her that it had been so callously stolen from her. What right did somebody have to break into someone's private space and just take whatever they wanted? Abi was furious and felt deeply wounded that the special place she'd found, her little sanctuary, had been invaded and violated in such a way.

Leaving her apartment, she knocked on Harry's door, hoping against hope that the same thing hadn't happened to him and Edward.

'Abigail. How are you?' he said when he answered.

'I'm okay. I'm just checking in with you. You haven't had anything stolen, have you? It appears we had a break-in during the night.'

'Oh, no! Really?'

'Mine and Aura's apartments, I'm afraid.'

'What did they take?'

'Just jewellery and cash we think.'

'Was there any damage done?'

'No, luckily. It seems they came in through the windows and doors we foolishly left open in the heat, took what they could carry in pockets and left quietly.'

'I'm so sorry.'

'So nothing's missing from yours?'

'No. I've just checked my wallet too. Needed a card for an online payment. Everything was in place.'

'Well, that's good.'

'What about Edward's?'

'I'm going to check with him now.'

'I'm really sorry, Abigail. That's a horrible thing to happen.'

'I know. Do take care with security, won't you? Let's hope it's a one-off, though.'

Harry nodded and Abi went to Edward's door, taking a deep breath before knocking. It felt an age since she'd spoken to him properly, as something more than people sharing a house and, when he answered, he gave her a look that made her feel not altogether welcome.

'Hi,' she said awkwardly. And then she cleared her throat. She was here on official Winfield Hall business and so she told him the same thing she'd told Harry.

'I'm sorry to hear that,' he said. 'It seems it was just your half of the hall that was targeted. There's nothing amiss here.'

'I'm glad to hear it.'

'So, what are you missing exactly?'

'Most of my jewellery.'

Edward cursed. 'That's awful.'

'Yes. There was a little gold brooch too set with flowers. I'd just been given it as a gift. The other pieces don't matter so much. I don't wear a lot of jewellery other than this locket which, luckily, I was wearing in bed as I usually do, but the brooch was special.'

Edward nodded in sympathy and there was a pause between them.

'Well, I'm glad you're not missing anything.' She turned to walk away.

'Abigail?' he called.

'Yes?'

'Is everything else all right?'

She frowned. 'You mean between me and Oscar?'

He nodded again.

'You don't need to worry,' Abi told him. 'We're not together anymore.'

Before Edward could respond, Abi returned to her apartment to call the police.

As soon as Harry heard Edward's door close, he left his apartment and headed towards Aura's.

'Hey!' he said as she opened the door. 'Are you okay?'

'No!' she cried.

Harry stepped inside, noticing Aura's red eyes. She'd been crying.

'Oh, sweetheart!' He caught her in his arms and hugged her. 'I'm so sorry. What an awful thing to happen. If I ever get hold of who did this to you...'

'It was Johnny!'

'What?' Harry took a step back.

'I know it was him! He knew where everything was and just took it. All my savings are gone and some of my rings and necklaces too – the ones that he thought were worth something to him, that is. But thank goodness he didn't take any of my crystals.'

'How can you be sure it was him?'

'Because he asked me for money and I wouldn't give it to him. So *stupid* of me!'

'Don't say that!'

'He's always just used me, Harry, and I fall for it every time. I can't help hoping he's changed, you see, but he never does.'

Harry held her close again, trying to imagine what it felt like to have a sibling do something like that to you.

'Listen,' he said, 'I'm popping round to see Dad later. You

know he's not been feeling so good? And Mum's going out so I thought you might want to come with me. It might cheer you up a bit.'

Aura pulled away from him and wiped her face with a tissue. 'Cheer me up? To sneak into your parents' house while your mum is out and hope that your father's actually happy to see me?'

Harry was shocked to hear Aura's tone. She sounded almost spiky. It was a side of her he'd never seen before.

'Look,' he said, 'I know you're going through a lot and that my family hasn't exactly made things easy on you–'

'No, they haven't. You don't know how it feels, Harry, to be rejected all the time. It's bad enough in my professional life, but at least I'm used to that, but it's quite different when it's personal – when it's your boyfriend's family or your own brother.'

He sighed, unsure of what to say to try and make things better. 'I'm sure my dad would love to see you.'

Aura shook her head. 'Harry, this is all too much.'

'What do you mean?'

'I mean, I'm not sure we should go on. It's hurting too many people.'

Harry swallowed hard. 'What are you saying?'

She looked up at him, her bright eyes swimming with tears. And that's when Harry's phone went. He took it out of his pocket, looking at the screen.

'It's Mum,' he said. 'I'd better take this.'

Harry stepped outside Aura's apartment to take the call, hearing the shrill voice of his mother a moment later.

'Mum! Slow down. What's going on?' He listened to the strange sound of his mother crying, her words only partially coming out and often in the wrong order. But Harry got the gist of it and, as he hung up, he turned to face Aura who had stepped out into the hallway now.

'Harry, what is it?'

Harry blinked, afraid he was about to cry. 'It's Dad. He's had a heart attack.'

Harry was racing around his apartment. What did he need? Keys, wallet. Anything else? What did you take to see your father in hospital?

Aura was watching from the door, feeling helpless.

'What can I do, Harry?' she asked. 'Do you want me to go with you?'

He stopped and looked at her and then crossed the space between them and hugged her tightly.

'I want you with me more than anything, but...'

Aura took a deep breath. 'Your mother will be there.'

'Yes.'

'It's okay. I'll stay here. You know where I am if you need me.'

He kissed her and she could see tears in his eyes. And then he hugged her again, holding her oh so close.

'Don't leave me, Aura,' he whispered.

Aura's own eyes pricked with tears. 'I won't,' she told him.

It was almost impossible to work after Harry had left. Aura added a few things to her website, but postponed an appointment she had with a client. She was in no position to heal anyone when she herself was in such turmoil.

She sat in the garden for a while, wondering how Harry was getting on and hoping that his father was okay. She'd only met Leonard Freeman once, but Harry had told her that he wanted to see her again. She thought about that now. Did he see something in her that his wife didn't? She'd been a little scared of him when she'd been at Harry's parents'. Leonard was a big man and his deep voice boomed and his manner was brusque. He was so very different from the gently-spoken Harry, but Aura so wanted to be able to reach out and help him now.

She looked at her phone. There were no messages from Harry. She sent him a quick text and waited. It was over an hour later when she got a reply.

He's weak but alive! Mum frantic. Harry x

Aura texted back. *Send him my love.* She paused. *And your mum. X*

It was late when Harry got home and he looked exhausted. Aura had left a note on his door to call round no matter what time it was.

He almost fell in to her apartment and she sat him down and made him a cup of chamomile tea which he sipped gratefully.

'I've never seen Dad look like that,' he told her. 'He was so weak. So helpless.'

'How's your mum coping?'

'Not well. She was in and out of the room trying to find answers. She wouldn't settle and that wasn't helping Dad. He needs calm and he's never been the calmest man. Maybe that's why he's there now.'

'Oh, Harry!' Aura sat down next to him and put her hand

on his and then her eyes settled on her favourite rose quartz. The stone of love, of calm, of healing.

'Harry?' she said after a moment. 'Could I visit him?'

Harry put his tea down. 'You'd visit Dad?'

'If you think it would be okay.'

Harry smiled. 'Are you thinking of taking crystals along?'

Aura smiled back. 'I might be.'

He laughed and it was so good to see his mood lift if even for a moment. 'You're wonderful, Aura,' he told her. 'Dad might not know it, but you're *exactly* what he needs right now.'

CHAPTER TWENTY-TWO

Aura lay awake for most of the night knowing what she had to do. It was one of those times in life when she knew what was right and, even though she was scared to do it, she had to push herself because it was the only thing to do. Besides, she'd told Harry she was happy to do it and she *wanted* to.

After an early morning session with a client online, Aura got ready to leave Winfield. She tied her hair back because she thought that would suit the situation better, choosing a simple hair band rather than a ribbon or piece of lace, and she dressed in the most conservative dress she had which was sky-blue covered in tiny silver stars. Some might say that it was as far removed from conservative as you could get, but at least it wasn't tie-dyed and it didn't feature rainbows or unicorns. But she couldn't do without her crystal jewellery. She always felt naked if she left home without at least three pieces about her person. This morning, she chose her large oval blue lace agate pendant to remind her to keep calm, a silver ring set with a tiger's eye crystal for courage, and a bracelet made of smoky quartz beads to help absorb any negativity she might encounter although she sincerely hoped that Mr Freeman may be slightly happier to see her than Mrs Freeman would. She thanked her lucky stars that Johnny had only taken some of her silver and gold pieces and had left her crystal jewellery, obviously deeming it worthless. But it was so very precious to Aura especially at stressful times like this.

Last, but not least, she picked up a rose quartz palm stone, feeling the cool weight of it in her hand and then holding it up to the window, gazing at the delicate pink swirled with fine lines of white. It was a beautiful piece – a piece that had brought her so much comfort and joy over the years, but it was time to pass it on now. It was needed by somebody else.

Harry had told her the visiting hours and when his mother intended to go so Aura could avoid running into her. He'd also given her the address. Leonard Freeman had the privilege of his own room in a private hospital and Harry had told her that it was all very pleasant and quiet. Still, she couldn't help feeling nervous.

When she arrived, she made her way to the main reception and was directed to Mr Freeman's room. She took a moment to still herself before knocking on the door which was ajar.

'Mr Freeman?' she said gently as she entered. There was no reply. She walked inside, noting the large window which looked out over a pleasant courtyard with a tree. It had its own en suite and there was a table full of cards and gifts. It was, as Harry had said, a very pleasant room. And then Aura looked at the figure lying in the bed. For all his barking and brusqueness, Aura could see just how frail and vulnerable he looked now, his skin as pale as the white bed sheets, and her heart swelled with compassion for the man who had scared her so.

She was about to sit down when his voice called faintly from the bed.

'Who's that?'

'It's Aura.'

'Eh?'

So, he could still bark then, she thought. 'It's Aura,' she said again. 'Harry's friend.'

'That girl? That fairy girl?'

Aura smiled at his term for her. 'That's right.'

He barked out a laugh. 'What are you doing here?'

'I've come to see how you are.'

'Did Harry tell you to come?'

'No. I wanted to come myself.'

'He's not here?'

'No. It's just me.'

It was then that Leonard opened his eyes and fixed them on her. 'Is my wife here?'

Aura blanched. 'I don't think so.' She turned around anxiously, as if Mrs Freeman might walk in at any second.

'She doesn't like you,' Mr Freeman stated without apology.

'I know.'

'And I'm not sure if I do yet.'

'Oh.' Aura was taken aback by his honesty.

He attempted to sit up and Aura sprang forward, helping him with his pillows. 'Good grief,' he complained. 'Everything hurts.'

'Does it?'

'Yes it does!'

'I'm sorry you're going through this.'

He stared at her. 'Why?'

'Why?' Again, he surprised her. 'Because you're Harry's father and he loves you. He's worried about you.'

'But you're not worried about me on your own account? Just as Harry's father?'

'Of course I'm worried but...'

'But what?'

'Well, I haven't decided if I like you yet either.'

There was a dreadful pause when she wished she could take her words back but then he barked a laugh out. 'Ha! Touché!'

Aura smiled. She was heating up with embarrassment, but it had felt good to say that to him, and it was a relief that he'd taken it so well.

'Listen, I wanted to give you something,' she said, reaching inside her handbag and bringing out the rose quartz palm stone she'd wrapped in tissue paper for safekeeping.

'What is it?' he asked, peering closer.

'It's a crystal. I brought it for you. It'll help.'

'How? *How* can a bit of rock help me? I've had a bloody heart attack!'

She bit her lip. His sudden anger scaring her. But she persevered.

'I'll put it on your bedside cabinet here so you can reach it.'

'Eh?' he said.

'It's a palm stone. Or comfort stone. They're wonderful to hold. I hope you'll try it.'

He muttered something under his breath, but Aura wasn't sure she wanted to know what it was.

'Listen,' he said after a moment. 'I don't agree with all this crystal business and my wife – well – I think you probably know how she feels about it all. But I think I'm beginning to like you! And I like how my son is these days. He's...' he paused, 'he's more relaxed since he met you. I can see the change and that's good. Especially after what's happened to me. I'd hate him to follow in my footsteps and end up here.'

Aura nodded, watching as Mr Freeman reached for his glass of water.

'Here, let me,' she said, passing it to him.

'Thank you.'

Aura waited for him to finish his drink and then put the glass back on the bedside table.

'I should let you rest. I don't want to tire you.'

'You're not,' he said, but his eyes gave him away. He looked exhausted.

'I hope you find some comfort with the crystal.'

'Hah! How? By throwing it at that bothersome nurse who keeps prodding me?'

Aura tried not to laugh. 'Probably best not to,' she told him. 'Just hold it and take some deep slow breaths. Don't think about anything else other than your breath. Perhaps you can look at the tree in the courtyard as you're breathing or you could close your eyes and imagine a place that you love.'

He looked at her, but she couldn't quite tell what he was thinking. His expression was quizzical. Or disdainful. She couldn't quite tell which.

'Well, goodbye,' she said as she stood up.

'Aura?' he called as she reached the door. 'Are you coming to see me again?'

'Do you want me to?'

His face seemed to soften a fraction, but he didn't say anything. Instead, she watched as his eyes slowly closed and he fell asleep.

'I had a visitor,' Leonard announced once Harry and his mother had sat down.

'Oh, yes?' Harry's mother said.

'That fairy girl.'

'Her name's Aura, Dad.'

His father gave a small smile. 'I know what her name is.'

Harry smiled back. His father was still pale and he looked like he had sunk deeply into himself, but there was something remarkably improved in him today, Harry thought. A lift in his mood.

'What's that in your hand, Dad?' Harry asked, noticing he was clenching something.

'A gift!' He held up the pale pink crystal and his wife gasped.

'What are you doing with that?' she demanded.

'I've been holding it. It's a comfort stone,' he informed her.

Harry watched in amusement as his mother squirmed visibly in her chair. 'I don't want that girl taking advantage of you. You're quite helpless here and if she's been filling your head with nonsense–'

'Mum!'

'I'll make sure reception knows not to let her in.'

'Pipe down, woman!' Leonard said.

'I just don't like it. She's got no right to be here. Harry – I thought you two had broken up.'

Harry bristled. 'Whatever gave you that idea?'

A loud groan came from the bed.

'Mum – your stress is stressing Dad out. If anyone should be banned from visiting, it should be you!'

Her mouth dropped open in shock, but Harry's father laughed.

'Look, let's leave Dad to rest, okay?'

'Well, I'm not happy about this,' she stated, getting up and giving her husband a kiss. 'Don't be taken advantage of, do you hear me?'

But he'd closed his eyes. It was only as she was leaving the room that Leonard's eyes opened again to give Harry an encouraging wink.

Mr Freeman was sleeping when Aura visited for the second time. She sat down in one of the chairs by the bed, putting her handbag on the floor and looking around the room. There were some new cards today and the sun was streaming in through the window. But, as she glanced at his bedside cabinet, she saw that something was missing. The rose quartz. He'd probably thrown it in the bin, she thought, sincerely hoping that he hadn't because it was a very pretty stone. Perhaps he'd given it to one of the nurses, passing on the magic of the stone that he wasn't able to feel, but which somebody else might.

Aura was tempted to take a peep in the bin, because she couldn't bear the thought of it being thrown away, when Mr Freeman opened his eyes.

'Aura?'

'Yes. How are you?'

He wrestled with his body, trying to get more upright. Aura helped him with his pillows once again and, after he'd had a sip of water, he looked at her.

'What's happened to your hair?' he asked.

'Nothing,' she said.

'What's that in it?'

'Oh, just some beads and crystals.'

He leaned forward, trying to see them better and Aura moved an inch closer to him.

'Ah, I see them now. I thought something terrible had happened to your hair like you'd had an accident with a paint can.'

'No. I just like colour everywhere.'

'Yes, you do.'

There was a pause during which Aura didn't know what to say. Maybe it was a mistake her coming here. Maybe she was causing him more distress than doing him good. Still, she couldn't help asking him something, curiosity getting the better of her.

'You didn't like the crystal, did you?'

'What?'

'The rose quartz. It's not on your cabinet.'

'No,' he said. 'It's here.'

Aura gasped as he opened his hand.

'I've been holding it.'

'So I see!' She beamed a smile.

'Tell me about it,' he said.

'About what?'

'This rose quartz.' He held it up to the light, its perfect pink softness almost glowing.

Aura bit back a smile because she could tell from the tone of his voice that he was genuinely interested and he wasn't making fun of her. Had the stone worked its magic, she wondered?

'Well, it's one of the most common quartzes on the planet, but it's also one of the most adored. It's thought of as a stone for love. All kinds of love – self-love, compassion for others, friendship, romantic love.'

'A good all-rounder, eh?'

'Yes. It works hard. But you've got to work with it. It's a tool, you see. All crystals are. Like a power drill or a knife and fork, they won't magically work on their own – you have to hold them and work with them.'

He nodded and she could see he was genuinely listening to her.

'Have you been working with it?' she asked.

'Yes, I think I have.'

'And has it helped?'

He took a moment before replying. 'My doctor says I've got to relax more. Take things easy. Not get so worked up about things.'

Aura nodded, recognising those traits in Harry.

'Well, holding this stone here seems to help with that,' he continued. 'Does that make sense?'

'Oh, yes.'

'Holding it makes me feel...' he paused, searching for the words. 'Calm. Peaceful.'

Aura smiled.

'You're laughing at me.'

'No!' Aura said. 'I am the very last person to laugh at such a thing. Remember, I brought this to help you.'

'So you did. And you knew it would do that?'

She shrugged. 'I couldn't possibly know how you would react. For all I knew, you could have thrown it out of the window.'

He barked out a laugh at that. 'Well, it did cross my mind when I first picked it up, but there was something about it.'

Aura watched him closely. His face seemed to have softened a little along with his voice.

'What?' she asked.

'I'm not sure,' he said. 'Just... something. So I held it for a while and looked at its colour.' He gave a little chuckle. 'Now,

I'm not the sort of man who goes for pink. Too girly. Too romantic. But that wasn't the vibe I was getting from it at all.'

Aura felt her heart leap at his use of the word *vibe*. Had he noticed too?

'It made me feel...'

'What?' Aura pushed, anxious to know now.

'This is going to sound daft.'

'It won't.'

He took a deep breath and then coughed.

Aura got to her feet and poured some more water into the glass, passing it to him and watching as he took a sip. He nodded and handed the glass back to her.

'It made me feel happy.'

Joy swelled inside Aura and she was just about to tell him some more about rose quartz when she saw that his eyes were closing again.

'You look tired. I'd better go.' She stood up to leave.

'Aura?'

'Yes?'

'You will visit me again, won't you?' he asked.

She nodded. 'I'll bring you another crystal if you like. I have a nice piece of Auralite 23. It's a nice companion crystal to your rose quartz.'

She saw him smile and, for a brief second, she thought he was going to laugh at her. But no. The time for laughing at her was over. He believed in her now. Or, if he didn't quite believe in her, he believed in her belief.

CHAPTER TWENTY-THREE

'You know,' Leonard Freeman began the next day, 'lying in a hospital bed all day gives you time to think.'

'Yes?' Aura said, wondering what he'd been thinking about, but believing it impolite to ask.

'Yes. I don't think I've ever thought so much in my life.' He chuckled. 'All sorts of things have been coming back to me, but it all comes down to just two things really. Things I've done that I shouldn't have, and things I haven't done that I should.'

They sat in silence for a moment.

'It's good to think,' Aura said at last, 'but sometimes, you just need to be.'

'To *be*?'

'To not think. To just exist. To breathe, to drift, to look and hear without judging anything or needing it to have a purpose.'

'Well, that all sounds easier said than done.'

'Actually, I've brought you something that might help with it.' She reached into her handbag and retrieved a small glass bottle.

'What's that?'

'Lavender essential oil. I've diluted it so it's safe to put on your skin if you like. You can use it on your brow if you have a headache or massage it into your hands. Or you can just take the top off and inhale it.' She passed it to him and watched as he undid the top and sniffed.

'Well, well! It's like a summer's day.' He chuckled. 'You've brought summer to me!'

'It travels well with the Auralite I've brought for you. You're really tapping into that wonderful deep purple magic.' She paused, wondering if she'd gone too far with the word *magic*. But he didn't say anything. He was simply watching her take the crystal out of her bag.

'This is the Auralite,' she said, handing him the stone that was the length of the palm of her hand and gently tapered at one end. It was a mix of purples – some so rich that they almost deepened into black and others so pale that they were translucent. The piece was also threaded through with white lines in chevrons, making it very appealing to the eye as well as to the fingers with its surface that was rough in some places and smooth in others. She handed it to him.

'It's a kind of amethyst,' she said. 'Although it has many other minerals in it too. It's a very relaxing stone. Amethyst is a natural tranquiliser.'

'So I won't need to take some of my medication, eh?'

'Oh, I'd never suggest that!' Aura said.

'Don't worry. I wasn't going to stop it,' he told her.

Aura looked at him. She still could never quite tell when he was joking with her. 'Anyway, it's just nice to hold.'

She watched as he weighed it in his hand and then something happened. His thumb moved across it and he gasped.

'My thumb fits!'

Aura laughed. 'I call that plugging in to a stone.'

'It's smooth here too. Feels nice and snug.'

Aura smiled. It was the exact same place that she'd often plugged in to the stone too. In fact, she'd probably helped to smooth that particular place over the years, making it feel glassy and cool.

'Does it feel good, then?'

'Surprisingly so.'

'Because I don't want to force any particular stone or crystal on you. It's important that you have your own connection. Perhaps I should bring a selection in for you to choose from.'

'That might be fun,' he said.

Aura nearly did a double take at the word *fun*. It was most definitely a word she'd never have associated with him before.

'Pass me my glasses there, will you?'

Aura did so.

He put them on and examined the stone. 'It really is a beautiful thing,' he said, holding it up to the light.

'I'm glad you like it.'

'And it's very kind of you to bring it here.'

'It's my pleasure,' she told him. 'I love sharing the crystal bliss.' She bit her lip, again feeling self-conscious using such phrases in front of him, but he didn't react in a negative way.

'Hey!' he suddenly said. 'Look at this.'

Aura peered closer as he pointed to something in the stone. There was a seam of clear quartz within a purple chasm and he ran a finger along it.

'It's like a glacier in a mountain landscape,' he said.

'Yes! I've always thought that too. With purple mountains.'

'Hah! Yes! Why not? Purple mountains.'

'That's one of the things I love most about crystals – they totally absorb you. They take you to another place just by looking at them. The normal world slips away and your mind slips with it – into a different realm. A realm of dreams and possibilities. They give so much and yet they ask nothing of you in return. It always seems like such an unfair exchange to me.' Aura's gaze had softened into the stone, which was totally normal, but she came out of her trance quickly and saw that Leonard was looking at her. 'Sorry. I got lost there for a moment.'

He nodded and, for a second, he looked so like Harry did when he was listening to her.

'There's a jacket in the cupboard over there. Will you bring it to me please?' he asked.

Aura got up and went to the cupboard, finding the jacket and passing it to him, watching as he reached inside one of the pockets.

'What's that?' she asked as he brought out a silver object.

'I was hoping you might be able to tell me.' He passed it to her and Aura saw that it was a silver keyring fob, round in shape and featuring the symbol of an eye. She recognised it at once.

'It's a kind of talisman,' Aura told him. 'Egyptian. The Eye of Horus, I believe.'

'My mother did go to Egypt once.'

'Did she?'

He nodded. 'A holiday. Oh, it was years and years ago. It's just a cheap trinket she brought back with her, but it has a nice weight about it.' He paused. 'Does it *mean* anything?'

'Well, if it *is* the Eye of Horus, it's for protection and good luck,' Aura explained. 'Have you heard of the Evil Eye?'

'Yes.'

'It's for keeping you safe from the ill wishes of others,' she said. 'It's a lovely thing. The eye itself is made of lapis lazuli.'

'Is it?'

She handed it back to him. 'See the wonderful blue flecked with gold? The gold is pyrite.'

'Fool's gold?'

'That's right. Lapis was valued and revered in Ancient Egypt. It was used on the famous gold death mask of Tutankhamun.'

'Well, I never!' He shook his head. 'I've carried this thing around with me for years and yet I've never really looked at it, and I've never stopped to think that it might mean something until you began explaining about stones.'

'But it *does* mean something if you've carried it with you all these years,' she told him. 'It's been a silent companion which you've kept close to you.'

'Ah,' he said with a sigh. 'Now you're being kind.'

'But it's true – you don't have to *know* what something means in order to appreciate it. I mean, you don't have to have an intellectual relationship with it. You just have to feel that it's right. Does that make sense?'

'It does actually.'

'And you obviously felt right carrying that with you all these years.'

He gazed at it for a long time.

'Do you believe in talismans?' he asked her at length.

'I believe that they can give you confidence.'

'Do you wear one when visiting me?'

Aura could feel herself blushing and decided that she couldn't hide behind a denial now. 'I did on my first visit.'

He barked out a laugh. 'Hah! What was it?'

'A smoky quartz bracelet.'

'Why smoky quartz?'

'It's meant to absorb negative energy.'

'So you think I'm a bad sort? Bad energy to be warded off, eh?'

'No, I...'

He frowned. 'What? I want to know. Do I genuinely frighten you?'

Aura thought carefully before answering. 'You did. When we first met.'

He made a noise of disapproval as if he was chastising himself. 'Well, I'm sorry I scared you. I hope I don't now.'

'No, you don't. Not much anyway.' She gave a little laugh.

'And do you think I can change? Do you think there's any hope for me and that I might be able to stop scaring people in the future?'

'Of course! There's always hope! And I think you already are changing.'

'I am?'

'Yes! I don't think we'd have been able to have this conversation a couple of weeks ago, would we? I don't think you'd have been holding a rose quartz and inhaling lavender oil.'

He laughed and it was a gentler sound than his usual bark and it made Aura laugh too.

When they stopped laughing, they held one another's gaze and then Leonard shook his head.

'Has it really taken a heart attack to mellow me?' he asked.

'They don't call these kind of things life-changing experiences for nothing, I suppose,' Aura said, 'and I've heard that it sometimes takes a bit of chaos before we can find order and that a physical breakdown can often lead to a spiritual breakthrough.'

'You think I've found some kind of spirituality now?'

'I don't know. How do *you* feel?'

He rested his head back on his pillow, closed his eyes and

sighed. 'Calm,' he said and then his eyes snapped open. 'And I've never felt calm in my entire life.'

Aura gasped. It was a very sad admission, she thought, trying to imagine the inner as well as outer chaos that he must have dealt with for so many years.

'I'm glad you're feeling calmer,' she told him. 'Would you like to do a meditation with me? Just something simple you can remember to come back to whenever you feel you need a little bit of calm?'

He sighed and it was a sigh of contentment. 'That sounds wonderful, my dear!'

'You don't have to visit him *every* day,' Harry told Aura.

'But I like to!'

'Well, it's very kind of you. Are you sure he appreciates it?'

Aura was thoughtful for a moment. 'I think he does, yes.'

Harry looked amused. 'So what exactly do you talk about with my father?'

'Hmmmm, I'm not sure if it's ethical for me to say. I mean, what happens between a healer and her client–'

'Oh, is he a client now? I hope he's paying you well!'

Aura laughed. 'I'm just teasing. He's not a client and of course I'm not charging him anything. But I'm not sure if he'd want me talking about the things we're doing.'

'Okay, okay!' Harry held his hands up.

'Suffice to say that he is finding value in some of the same things that you are these days.'

'You mean *you*?' Harry said. 'I hope he's not flirting with you!'

Aura gasped. 'Harry Freeman – what a thing to say!'

'I couldn't blame him if he was.'

'Oh, stop!' She laughed and then said more seriously, 'How's your mum doing?'

Harry pulled a face. 'Not so good. She just wants him home.'

'Of course.'

'But the doctors want to keep an eye on him. He's a big guy and his body's been through a lot.'

'But he's getting there, isn't he?' Aura said, suddenly feeling anxious. 'I haven't spoken to the doctors like you. It isn't my place and I don't like to talk to your father about that when I'm with him.'

Harry took her hands and squeezed them. 'He's better than he was, I can see that, but there's still a long way to go. There was a lot of damage to the muscle and tissue around his heart.' Harry's face fell as he told her this and she leaned forward to kiss him.

'I think everyone's doing all they can to help him recover well,' she told him.

'I know.'

'These things just take time, don't they?'

Aura was spending as much of her spare time at the hospital as she could. She was on first name terms with the staff and had even given a small bag of crystals to one of the nurses who'd expressed an interest in what she did for a living. Mr Freeman was highly amused by it all.

'My doctor says you're a good influence on me,' he told her one day. 'Says whatever you're doing, keep it up!'

Aura laughed, delighted to hear it and thrilled to see the

colour beginning to bloom in his cheeks at last. He was looking so much better than that grey, sunken man she'd seen on her first visit.

They spent a little while meditating together, the window open, allowing a light breeze inside the room which stirred the curtains and brought with it the sound of birdsong. And then they chatted and the lovely thing was it wasn't just about crystals. Mr Freeman told her stories about Harry growing up, tales Aura felt sure Harry wouldn't necessarily want her hearing – like the time he fell in the pond and came out with his head covered in slime and wouldn't stop crying for an hour. He told her about how he felt like he'd wasted so many of his years in a job he didn't love and that's why he supported Harry's decision to leave his now, despite his wife's fury over the whole business. And he told her how, once he was home, he was going to spend far more time doing nothing. Nothing with purpose, he called it. He was even thinking about giving up marching boys.

'Now that you've taught me how to breathe properly and just to be able to sit, well, I'm going to do a lot more of that,' he vowed.

It was on her fifth visit to the hospital when Aura saw Mrs Freeman. Had she mistimed her visit? She did her best to make sure she didn't run in to Mrs Freeman or intrude on her time with her husband, but there she was in the corridor outside her husband's room, and the doctor was stood next to her. Both looked up as she approached and Aura knew that it was too late to back out now.

She stopped for a moment, watching as the doctor whispered something to Mrs Freeman and nodded towards Aura. Panic assailed her. Had something happened to Mr Freeman? And was the doctor blaming *her* for it?

'Aura!' Mrs Freeman cried, coming towards her. She looked

fragile and so unlike the forthright woman Aura had met at the market that day.

'Hello, Mrs Freeman' Aura said anxiously.

'You've come to see my husband again?'

'Yes. Is that okay? Is he all right?'

Mrs Freeman nodded, her eyes looking to the left and the right, but not quite able to focus on Aura directly.

'He says you've given him things. Crystals.'

'Yes.'

'He says they've helped him.' She gave a strange sort of shrug. 'I don't know about that sort of thing, but if Leonard says they've helped him then they have. That's all I know. And the doctor is very pleased with his recovery.'

Aura breathed a sigh of relief. 'Then he'll be able to go home with you soon?'

'Yes! Yes, he will!'

Suddenly, Mrs Freeman lunged towards her, wrapping her arms around Aura. 'Thank you!' she breathed. 'Thank you!'

CHAPTER TWENTY-FOUR

Edward was finding it hard to concentrate. He kept thinking about Abi. So, she wasn't with Oscar. Well, he couldn't pretend that wasn't a relief. He wondered when they'd broken up and why, and did it have something to do with the girl with the pink ponytail? It wasn't any of his business, though, was it? He should just be thankful she was no longer involved with his good-for-nothing brother.

He was just about to make some calls when his phone went and he frowned as he saw Oscar's name come up. Had his brother sensed he was thinking bad thoughts about him? No, that wasn't possible, was it? Still, it was odd he should be ringing just as Edward was thinking about him.

'What is it, Oscar?' Edward said impatiently as he answered.

There was no preamble. It was straight down to business. 'It's Dad,' Oscar said. 'He's in a bad way again.'

'He's always in a bad way.'

'Yeah, but he's not eating properly.'

'He's a grown man, Oscar. He can take care of himself if he wants to only he doesn't want to.'

'Yeah, well I've just come from there and there's no food in the house and everything's a mess.'

Edward sighed. That it should be his problem annoyed him intensely for the man had done nothing but bring misery to his life. Why should Edward now be expected to take care of him? It wasn't fair.

'Can you get some food in for him at least?' Oscar asked.

'Why can't you? You see him more than I do.'

'I've got a job interview. I wouldn't ask if I could go over again, but he really needs help. Straightaway too if you can.' There was a pause. 'You can, can't you?'

Edward relented. 'Yes. I can.'

'Right away? I'm worried about him.'

'I'll go and see him now. I'll pick up some shopping first.'

'Good man!' Oscar hung up.

Edward left immediately, silently cursing as he got in his car for the trip to see a man who hated him. As promised, he stopped off at the supermarket and picked up a few things he deemed as essentials but which his father would probably sneer at. At least he could tell Oscar that he'd done his bit.

He let himself in at his dad's when he arrived. Sure enough, the house was a mess. But then it always was. Once again, the television was blaring and Edward was surprised to see his father slumped asleep in an armchair. How on earth could he sleep with that racket on, Edward wondered, turning it off.

'What the hell are you doing here?' his father asked as he awoke abruptly.

'Oscar said you needed some shopping.'

'What?' he barked. 'I don't need nothing!'

'He said he was just round here and that you weren't doing great.'

'Goddamn liar. I haven't seen him in days. Anyway, there's nothing wrong with me.'

Edward stared at the old man: his hair was a mess, his eyes were bloodshot and he hadn't shaved for at least a week, but he didn't look any worse than usual.

'Well, I've brought you some things.'

'Don't expect me to pay you for them.'

'I don't,' Edward said as he made his way through to the kitchen, his feet sticking to the linoleum floor. He didn't even want to think what it might be. Spilt beer probably.

He put the shopping away as quickly as he could and did a quick tidy around in the kitchen.

'Don't go moving things around like last time!' his father shouted through.

'I didn't,' Edward shouted back. 'I simply cleaned them.' He sighed, wondering exactly why Oscar had sent him round here with such urgency. His father clearly wasn't expecting him. Still, he was here now so he might as well do his bit.

'Get out!'

Edward jumped, turning round to see his father in the kitchen behind him.

'I didn't ask you to come here.'

'No, and I didn't volunteer,' Edward told him, putting one last handful of rubbish into the overflowing bin before leaving the house, cursing Oscar for piling on the guilt and sending him round there. Well, it would be the last time, Edward promised himself. The emotional damage was just too much to bear. And what exactly was going on anyway? Oscar said he'd just been round, but his father said he hadn't seen him for days.

Edward sighed. If he spent any more of his day trying to

fathom his father and brother, he'd go crazy. So he did his best not to think about them and drove directly home.

∾

Abi picked up her jewellery box and looked inside, remembering the few pieces of gold and silver she'd had in there, including the pretty brooch Ronnie had given her. She still felt its loss keenly and was hugely disappointed by the response of the police who, when she'd rung them, had told her to fill in a form online. They weren't going to visit Winfield and take fingerprints and make an immediate arrest, she'd discovered. It all felt so dispiriting.

She tried to get on with some work, opening the French doors to let in a little bit of breeze, and thinking about trying one of her prints in a new colourway, and that's when she heard the sound of a car horn. It startled her at first, but she ignored it. Or she tried to, but it sounded again. And again. It couldn't be for her, could it?

'ABI!' a voice suddenly shouted. It *was* for her. She leapt up from her table and ran out of the French doors and through the walled garden, spying Oscar standing in the driveway beside a new car.

'Oscar!' Abi cried. 'What are you doing here?'

'What do you mean? I've come to see you, silly!'

Abi stared at him, disbelievingly. 'But you...' She didn't actually have the words to express how cross she was with him.

'Look, I know it's been a little while and I'm sorry. I've been busy. But I've really missed you. Have you missed me?' he asked with a cheeky grin.

'You've missed me – really? You missed our date, Oscar!'

'What date?'

'At the gallery.'

'Gallery?' He looked blank.

'You were going to meet me at the Towner Art Gallery!'

'Nah!' He laughed. 'I don't think so. I'd never have agreed to go to a gallery. I can't stand them!'

Abi gasped at his ability to not only lie but to forget so callously. She put her hands on her hips. 'Look, I think it's best if you go, okay?'

'Oh, don't be like that! Come on. I'm here now, aren't I? And I wanted to take you for a spin in my new car. Well, it's a few years old, but it's got less dings in it than my old one.'

Abi turned to go back inside. She wasn't going to listen to him. Not this time.

'Abi!' he shouted after her. 'I've got a surprise for you. Come on! Come and see it.'

'Oscar, I really don't think–'

He was next to her now, his arm around her shoulder, propelling her back towards the car. 'Just come and look. It won't take a minute. It's for you.'

'And then you'll go?'

'If you really want me to.'

He led her back towards the car, opening the back door and gesturing grandly. 'Ta da!'

Abi peeped inside and couldn't help smiling at the sight. The whole back seat was full of flowers. She'd never seen so many except in a florists'.

'Oh, Oscar! These aren't for me, are they?'

'Well, of course they are! Who else? Come and get inside – they smell wonderful.'

'No. I can't.'

'Why not? Don't deny me the fun of taking you out for a

spin in the new car. We can go out to the coast, see some sights. I'll even buy you lunch. How's that? Come on, Abi!'

Abi looked at his funny, sunny face and then looked at the flowers gracing the back seat. They really were very impressive. She couldn't remember somebody ever making such a grand gesture to her before.

'Only a quick spin,' she told him.

'Whatever you say!'

She ran back inside to grab her bag and lock the doors and was back out with Oscar a moment later.

'Come on, let's go!' he called, flapping a hand madly at her as if he couldn't leave fast enough.

Abi got into the car and they set off through the village and onto the main road towards the coast. It was a definite improvement on the last vehicle and she smiled as she turned around and gazed at the blooms on the back seat. 'Can I take them with me when you drop me off?' she asked.

'Of course! They're no use to me.'

Abi nodded, thinking of the joy she'd get from painting them. The colours were wonderfully subdued – whites, pale lemons and delicate pinks. He'd chosen so carefully, hadn't he? She smiled, looking closer at one of the bunches in the shape of a dome. And it was then that she spotted something. It was a card. At first, she assumed it was to her, but she read the printed message: "In Loving Memory" above the handwritten note below.

Aunt Gladys. We will miss you so much. Love John and Daphne.

Abi's mouth dropped open as she looked at the other flowers. There were no more cards visible, but it was obvious to her that Oscar had not bought them from a florists at all. He'd stolen them from somebody's grave. As soon as she realised, she noticed that some of the flowers were definitely past their best, their pale petals crinkling and shrinking. Abi stared at Oscar. He caught her eye and grinned back at her.

'I do love spoiling you,' he said.

She felt sick. She'd been given Aunt Gladys's funeral flowers.

'Oscar?'

'Yes?'

'I really can't go far. I'm in the middle of something at the moment.'

'Work?'

'Yes.'

'Well, I've got the day off,' he said as if that was the only important thing.

'But I'm working so we mustn't go too far because I've got to get back,' Abi said, making it absolutely clear.

'Yeah, yeah,' he said, laughing lightly and putting his foot down as he drove.

Abi felt distinctly anxious. At first, it was a vague kind of feeling – a just under the skin sensation of unease. Perhaps it was the funeral flowers, their scent now a sickly mix of perfume and rot which wouldn't leave her. She opened her window a tad and breathed in the heady coastal air with its refreshing salt tang.

'It's good to get out, isn't it?' Oscar said.

Abi nodded.

'We should do this more often.'

Abi didn't reply. She was thinking about how to break up with Oscar once and for all. When they got back to Winfield, when she was safely out of the car. She'd do it then. He could keep his flowers. *Gladys's* flowers. But he wasn't going to keep on seeing her in his oh so casually destructive way.

It didn't take long to reach the coast and Abi's heart lifted a little as she saw the wondrous blue of the sea. Oscar had chosen to drive along the famous stretch of road high above the dazzling white cliffs where the road wound its way dangerously close to the edge. It was a magical landscape where the land felt suspended between the sky high above and the sea far below. There were great banks of yellow gorse and scrubby areas of grass leading out to the sheer drop. It had a wild, untamed feel that Abi would normally have revelled in. But she couldn't relax today.

'I think it's time to try this little beauty out, don't you?' Oscar said mischievously. 'Let's see what she can do?'

Abi glanced at him. He surely wasn't thinking of...

Oscar put his foot down again.

'No, Oscar!' Abi cried.

He laughed. 'It's like being on the French Riviera or something, isn't it? Wind your window down more!' he said as he opened his. A blast of breeze entered the car.

'No, it's too windy here.'

Oscar opened her window anyway and Abi's long hair flew out in a hundred different directions at once.

'Oscar, slow down! You're going too fast!'

He put his foot down again and overtook a car which blasted its horn as they pulled in with just inches to spare before a bend.

For the second time that day, Abi felt physically sick as Oscar took the bends in the road at a terrifying speed, not slowing down at all. Her mind felt out of kilter as she saw glimpses of road and glances of sea through a veil of blonde hair and she knew she had to get out of there.

'Stop the car!' she cried. 'Right now!'

'Don't be silly, Abi!'

'I mean it! I need to get out!'

Oscar wasn't listening. In fact, Abi could have sworn he put his foot down even more and he was laughing again, the wind blasting his face from the open window. Abi wanted to close her eyes against it all, but felt compelled to keep them open and it was as they were approaching the next bend that she screamed. She knew they weren't going to make it. They were going too fast. She saw the deep blue of the sea, the white edge of the cliff and the sheer drop. It was all so close and they were heading straight towards it.

She heard the screech of brakes as the car spun off the road. The circular bouquet came crashing into the front, the little card with the printed message, "In Loving Memory", resting at Abi's feet. And then the world went black.

CHAPTER TWENTY-FIVE

Edward couldn't remember the last time he'd felt this nervous. Perhaps it had been that day in the auction room when he'd been bidding on Winfield and not entirely sure of the outcome. But one thing was sure – he felt nervous now as he approached the ward in the hospital where Abigail was.

Abigail. His Abi. And he'd never had a chance to tell her. Well, he had, only he hadn't made the most of it, had he? He'd let so many chances slip by and what if it was too late now? The thought of losing her made Edward feel ill. Then he thought of Oscar and his anger rose. What the hell had he been doing? Edward could hazard a guess, judging by what he'd heard from the police and what he knew of his brother. He'd been driving too fast – speeding along a dangerous coast road with no regard for the passenger beside him or anyone else who might have been on the road that day.

Edward entered the ward now, anxiously looking at each bed in turn. Where was she?

'*Abigail!*' His voice left him in a hoarse sort of a cry as he reached her.

'Edward?' Her eyes slowly opened at the sound of his voice.

'How are you?' Relief surged through him as he saw that she was going to be all right.

She managed to get herself upright and pushed her hair out of her face. 'I'm fine. It all looks worse than it is. I've got two breaks in my arm and some whiplash. The worst thing is it's my right arm so I won't be able to draw or paint for a while. But I feel fine. Just a bit shaky. They're keeping me in for observation in case there's any head trauma, but I've told them there's nothing wrong with me.'

'You'd better do as you're told,' he said.

'Yes, I suppose you're right, but it's very frustrating just lying here. I feel such a fraud.'

'Abi, you were involved in a serious car crash.' He could barely disguise the emotion in his voice.

Abi's face fell. 'Was it really that bad? I thought Oscar was okay?'

'He is. Just a few cuts and bruises.'

'Good.'

Edward shook his head. 'God, Abi! How can you be so kind?'

'What do you mean?'

'You could have died! My brother might have killed you!'

'But he didn't. I'm alive.'

'Well, you both got incredibly lucky this time. You know how close that road is to the cliffs?'

'Yes, I was very aware of that,' Abi said with a nod and then winced. 'Ouch. That hurts.'

'What happened? Oscar conveniently can't remember a thing,' Edward said with some derision. 'Do you remember anything?'

'Bits and pieces. It all seems a bit of a blur. We were on the coast road. Oscar wanted to show off his new car. But, well, I suppose you know what he's like. He always wants to show off.'

'Yes, I know.'

'Then you'll probably know that means going a bit too fast.'

Edward cursed under his breath.

'I kept telling him to slow down, but he was laughing and telling me I was worrying about nothing.'

'I had a word with the doctor taking care of him. The police have already questioned him and he's been breathalysed.'

'Had he been drinking?'

'No. Not this time. But he'll likely be fined or worse for dangerous driving. I'm hoping they ban him for life this time.'

'You keep saying "this time",' Abi pointed out. 'Has he done this before?'

'Once or twice.' Edward sighed.

'I'm afraid the police asked me some questions too,' Abi confessed. 'I had to be honest about your brother's driving. There were witnesses, I'm told.'

'Yes, I believe so,' Edward said. 'Oscar deserves all that's coming his way.'

'But he has a good heart,' Abi said sadly. 'Doesn't he?'

Edward shook his head. 'You don't know him, Abi. He's dangerous. What were you doing in his car anyway?' he asked now, frustration fuelling his voice. 'I thought you said you'd broken up with him.'

'I meant to. And I was going to. I just hadn't told him in so many words.' She winced again. 'And I didn't plan on getting in the car with him, but he turned up in that new one, which I'm guessing he's written off now, tooting his horn and making a right song and dance about it.'

'Did he?'

'Yes! And then there were the flowers.'

'What flowers?'

'He'd filled the entire back seat with them. Although, I don't think he paid for them.'

Edward frowned as something occurred to him. 'When was it Oscar turned up?'

Abi looked thoughtful. 'Erm, just before lunch. Around eleven, I think.'

Edward nodded. The double-crossing liar! So that was why Oscar had rung him asking him to see their father. He'd wanted him out of the way when he turned up at Winfield, tooting his bloody horn and flaunting his flowers. Oscar had known he couldn't do that without Edward coming to see what was going on and he'd also known that Edward would never have let Abi get into the car with him.

'I wish you hadn't gone,' he said, knowing it was ridiculous to say such a thing now, but needing to say it all the same.

'Yes, well, you're not the only one.'

'Can I get you anything?' he asked, looking around as if there might be something within reaching distance.

'No, thank you. I'm hoping they'll let me out tomorrow after some tests and, to be honest, I'll probably sleep until then. I'm so tired.'

He nodded. 'I'd better leave you to it.'

'Edward?' she said as he turned to go. 'There is one thing you could do for me.'

'Name it.'

She smiled. 'You could take me home once I get the all clear.'

'Absolutely. Have you got your phone?'

'Yes.'

'Just call me as soon as you're ready, okay?'

'I will. And thank you for coming.' She gave a yawn.

Edward nodded and edged a little closer to the bed, swallowing hard. 'Abi? There's something I've been meaning to tell you.' He lowered his gaze to the floor, determined to win the battle with his nerves this time but, when he looked up again, Abi's eyes had closed and he could hear the gentle sound of her breathing as she slept.

Abi wasn't sure how long she slept for, but the next voice she heard was one she recognised even with her eyes closed.

'It's not *fair* that we can't bring Pugly! He wanted to see Aunt Abi!'

Abi opened her eyes and there were three people standing around her bed.

'Rosie!' she cried as her young niece launched herself onto the bed to hug her.

'Careful!' Ellen screamed. 'Careful! Oh, my god, Abi! Look at you!'

'I'm fine. Really.'

Ellen came forward and kissed her quickly on the top of her head and then Bethanne moved anxiously towards her.

'Does it hurt?'

'My neck and back do a bit, but my arm's all plastered up – look!'

'Can we draw on it?' Rosie asked excitedly. 'Noah Jones at school had one and we all got to draw on it with felt tips.'

'I think that sounds like a wonderful idea,' Abi said. 'After all, I won't be able to draw for a while.'

'What will you do?' Bethanne asked, understanding at once what this loss meant to Abi.

'You know, I haven't dared think about it yet.'

'Well, you should probably be resting,' Ellen told her sternly. 'What happened?'

Abi told her briefly and Ellen's face turned white as she listened.

'Were you scared, Aunt Abi?' Rosie asked.

'Of course. But it was all so quick that I didn't really have time to think about it much.'

'Did you have long to wait for an ambulance?' Ellen asked.

'No, not long. Thank goodness someone stopped to call one.' Abi looked at the anxious faces around her and noticed that there were tears in Bethanne's eyes. 'Come here, you!'

Bethanne gently climbed onto the bed, joining her sister there and Abi embraced her with her one good arm.

'I'm all right, do you hear? I'll be going home soon and you can come and visit me.'

'But you won't be able to paint,' Bethanne complained.

'You can paint for me then, can't you? I can watch you.'

'And I'll draw Pugly on your arm,' Rosie declared.

'And I'll cook you some meals,' Ellen said.

'Thank you,' Abi said, feeling the waves of love washing over her and thinking just how lucky she was to not only be alive but to be loved.

It was the next day and Aura had just returned from a walk when she heard the front door open and saw Abi enter with Edward.

'She's back!' Edward announced with a smile.

'Abi! How are you?' Aura rushed forward to greet her. 'Edward told me what happened. Oh, your poor arm!'

'It's fine. Just a little broken here and there.'

'Can I help you with anything?' Aura asked.

'I should be okay. But I'll let you know if I'm struggling,' Abi promised. 'Oh, there's a delivery van outside. Anything to do with you?'

'I shouldn't have thought so,' Aura said.

Abi shrugged and made her way into her apartment with Edward, and Aura was just about to return to hers when Harry appeared in the hallway.

'Aura?'

'Harry?'

'Can you come outside? I think you're going to want to see this.'

'What is it?'

Harry grinned. 'Come and see.'

Aura accompanied him, thinking how mysterious he was being, and then she saw the white van Abi had mentioned.

'What's this?'

Harry shrugged, but she could tell he was hiding something. She watched as two men got out of the van and opened the back doors. Inside was a large wooden crate.

'What is it?' she asked.

'Search me, love. Something heavy mind,' one of the men said and she watched as they slowly manoeuvred it out of the van onto a trolley.

Aura looked at Harry. 'Do you know what this is?'

'I have an idea.'

'Where do you want it?' one of the men asked.

'Follow me,' Harry said, leading them indoors and straight to Aura's apartment.

'Harry! Tell me what's going on!'

'How about this corner?' Harry suggested. 'You don't want it too close to the windows.'

'Is that a clue?' Aura asked.

'It could be.'

Slowly, the men removed the crate and, once they did, a mountain of bubble wrap was revealed.

'Help me with it,' Harry said, making a start unwrapping it.

'Harry – this is crazy! What's going on?'

'You'll see in a minute.'

And she did. As the last piece of bubble wrap fell away, Aura gasped, her hands flying to her mouth and her eyes filling with instant tears.

'No, no, no!' she cried.

'Don't you like it?' one of the delivery men asked.

'Don't worry – she loves it,' Harry told them. 'Thank you.'

After Aura signed for the delivery, the two men left and Aura stared in wonder at the sight before her. It was a pair of gigantic angel wings fixed to a silver pole running between them. But they weren't ordinary angel wings made out of feathers or wood. These had been carved from amethyst – huge amethyst geodes each filled with individual crystals the size of pound coins.

'I don't understand,' Aura said. 'Where has this come from?'

'Brazil,' Harry said.

'No – I mean who sent it here?'

'Oh!' Harry exclaimed as if he thought she might have guessed. 'It's from my dad. It's a present for you, Aura.'

She shook her head again, tentative steps moving her towards the dark sparkling crystals, her fingers reaching out to touch them.

'It's beautiful,' she whispered. 'I've never seen anything like it. Not in the flesh so to speak.'

'It is pretty amazing. Dad was trying to describe it to me, but I couldn't quite imagine it.'

'So you knew about it?'

He nodded. 'He's been planning it for a while. He wanted to get you something super special, but he didn't know much about crystals so he got in touch with someone in London, I think. Said he wanted something that was big, beautiful and bold. He was thrilled when he found this.'

'But I don't understand why.'

'He kept saying that you were his angel,' Harry told her.

'But this is too much!' Aura protested.

Harry laughed. 'Dad told me that it actually wasn't enough. He said you saved his life.'

Aura stared at Harry in confusion. 'But I didn't. He was doing fine. The doctors–'

'The doctors were only a part of it. They said that his recovery really began after your visits.'

'But I didn't really do more than give him a few crystals. I think they helped to calm him down, but I...' she stopped.

'You do more good than you know,' Harry whispered softly into her ear. 'And I don't think the crystals can take all the credit here.'

'But, Harry–'

'No more *buts*!' he insisted. 'You gave something special to my father and he's simply returning the favour, okay? Don't deny him this. He can't stop talking about you now. It's Aura this, and Aura that. Honestly, he's a different man. He's even signed up for a local meditation class in the village hall.'

'Has he really?'

'Yes! He's making Mum go with him. Funnily enough, she's not too sure, but doesn't want to give him an excuse for not going because she can see the difference all this is making in him. Honestly, Aura. He's a new man. It's as if...' Harry paused.

'What?'

'He's suddenly woken up to all the possibilities in life and can see the colours and the beauty of it all for the first time.'

Aura smiled. 'Like you did?'

'Yes. Just like I did. And we both have you to thank for that. Only I wouldn't let my dad thank you quite like this.' And, with that, Harry placed his hands gently on Aura's face, cupping her as if she was the most precious thing in the world, and then kissed her.

Aura closed her eyes, feeling the lightness and the brilliance of his kiss as if she were swimming in diamonds.

'There's one other thing,' he said. 'You've been invited over for Sunday lunch this weekend.'

Aura frowned. 'Really?'

Harry laughed. 'Don't look so worried. Mum's quite desperate to have you there again. You're her new favourite person.'

'I am?'

'Yes! She's so grateful for what you've done for Dad and she's even mentioned having you give us all a family meditation session.'

'With crystals?'

'Well, let's take it one step at a time,' Harry said with a laugh. 'But really, Aura, she wants to thank you for all you've done and, well, to say sorry. She feels awful about the way she treated you.'

Aura took a deep breath. It was rather a lot to take in. 'So does this mean she's okay with me being with you?'

Harry nodded. 'I think I'd have a riot on my hands if I broke up with you now.'

'Don't ever do that,' she said, snuggling into him in a tight cuddle.

'And did I tell you that Dad's bought a pair of sandals? He

hasn't quite embraced barefootedness yet, but he's getting there.'

'Now, that's something I'd *love* to see!'

'And there's one more thing,' Harry said, leaning back so he could see her face. 'I may have a job.'

'Oh, Harry!'

'Now, don't get too excited. It's a new company and I'll be taking a pay cut, but they're ethical and smart and it's in Brighton so I won't have to travel far.'

'It sounds great!'

He nodded. 'Yes. I think I'm going to be happy there. And you know what else?'

'What?'

He kissed her fully on the mouth before answering. 'I think I love you,' he whispered.

'Well, that's a relief, Harry Freeman,' she whispered back. 'Because I'm a little bit in love with you too!'

CHAPTER TWENTY-SIX

It had been a very trying week since Abi had left hospital. The hot July weather had broken and there was a delicious cool breeze playing around the walled garden, but Abi wasn't happy because she wanted to throw herself into it all, only couldn't. There was so much to do and she got no pleasure from paying somebody to do it for her. She wanted to be out there herself, weeding and hoeing and gathering the fruits of her labour, staking floppy perennials and supporting growing tomatoes.

So far, Ellen had visited twice, each time with a basket full of meals for Abi to pop into the oven. It was extraordinarily kind of her. She'd also dropped the girls off one afternoon and, after drawing all over Abi's cast, they'd gone for a walk together, but had had to turn back at a very tall stile which Abi hadn't been able to climb over safely with one arm out of action. So they'd returned to Winfield and made lemonade together which they drank while sitting on the grass under the sunflowers.

Having her right arm out of action was a terrible bore. She was also getting annoyed at not being able to draw or paint. She was just deliberating if she could train herself to sketch with her left hand when there was a knock on her door. Answering it, she saw Edward standing there.

'Abi, how are you?'

'I'm okay. How are you?'

'Good. Can I come in?'

'Of course.'

She watched as he entered her apartment. 'And you're coping okay? You're sure you don't need a hand with anything?'

'Actually, there is a jar of jam I can't get open.' She led him through to the kitchen and handed it to him but, before he took it, he slipped something into his trouser pocket.

'There you go,' he said a moment later. 'You should have called me.'

'I didn't want to bother you over some silly jam.'

'It's no bother,' he said.

'Thank you. That's kind. I'm afraid everything's a bother with this!' She raised her arm up in its sling. 'It's so heavy and hot. But I know I shouldn't complain. Things could have been far worse.'

Edward nodded. 'I'm sorry this happened to you. I'm sorry Oscar hurt you so badly.'

Abi smiled at him reassuringly. 'You don't have to apologise.'

'I feel I do.'

'It's not your fault. It's mine. You did warn me about him and, well, I didn't listen.'

There was an awkward pause between them.

'Do you know what's happening with him?' she dared to ask.

'The police are still processing everything, but it looks like he could be banned from driving for at least two years.'

'Poor Oscar. He'll hate that.'

'He shouldn't ever be allowed to drive again. I don't know how you can still feel sorry for him.'

Abi sighed. 'I can't help it. For all the wrong he does, there's something rather vulnerable about him. He's like a little boy, don't you think?'

Edward made a derisive noise. 'No, I don't.'

Abi suddenly remembered her manners. 'I'm sorry, Edward, would you like a cup of tea?'

'No, thank you.'

'Just as well. I make lousy tea with one arm.' She laughed.

'Do you want me to make you one?'

'No, I'm good, thanks.'

They walked back through to the sitting room and sat down by the French doors which were open onto the garden.

'I see you've been coloured in,' he observed.

'Ah, yes. My nieces got quite creative. This is Pugly,' Abi said, pointing to the little felt tip drawing of the dog. 'And that's Pugly too – in pink. And that's Rosie's drawing of Bethanne sporting a large green nose, and Bethanne's revenge drawing of Rosie with blue hair and a spider crawling out of it.'

Edward smiled and then shifted uneasily, his hand diving into his trouser pocket.

'I have something for you. I might have forgotten if it hadn't just stabbed me.'

'What is it?'

'I found it in the walled garden this morning. It was just sitting there, glinting gold in the grass. I wasn't sure what it was at first, but I believe it belongs to you.'

He opened his hand.

'You found my brooch! Oh, Edward! Thank you! I can't tell you what it means to me.'

'I guess the thief must have dropped it. You might want to wash it. It's a little mucky, I'm afraid.'

Abi gasped. 'I don't suppose it will have fingerprints on it, will it? You know – the burglar's?'

'I think you'll probably find that the only fingerprints on there now are mine and I'd hate to be arrested. My family's in enough trouble with the police at the moment.'

Abi sighed. 'I suppose you're right. Well, I'm just so glad to have it back.'

'Here, let me wash it for you,' Edward offered. Abi handed it back to him and followed him into the kitchen where he washed it carefully under the tap and then dried it with a piece of kitchen paper.

'Will you pin it on me?'

Edward came closer to her and gently pinned the brooch on to her cotton cardigan, frowning in concentration. She took in the dark sweep of his eyelashes and the golden lights in his sandy hair where the summer sun had kissed it.

'Thank you,' she said, her left hand flying up to check it and catching his as he withdrew.

He took a step back. 'There. Safe with its rightful owner again.'

'It's a pretty thing, isn't it?'

'Very lovely,' he said, his eyes never leaving hers.

Abi broke the tension by walking back through to the living room.

'I see that Aura and Harry are a couple,' Edward said.

'Yes! Isn't it wonderful? They're so cute together.'

'The first Winfield romance,' Edward said. 'I mean of two people living here. Not, erm, of residents with others from – you know – outside.' He stopped, a faint blush creeping over his face.

'I've broken up with Oscar.'

'You have?'

'Yes. Properly this time. I don't know what I was thinking really. I mean, we weren't exactly made for each other, were we?'

They held one another's gazes for a moment and then Abi swallowed hard, suddenly feeling embarrassed by the whole thing and glancing out of the window.

'So, when does your cast come off?' Edward asked.

Abi turned to face him, glad that he'd changed the subject. 'The beginning of October, all being well.'

Edward's eyes suddenly filled with light. 'Will you be up for a swim after that?'

Abi gasped. 'In *October*? Won't it be horribly cold by then?'

Edward laughed at her response. 'Probably.'

Abi considered it for a moment, looking at Edward's kind face and the eyes that were looking at her with such tenderness. It was a look, if not of love then of the very sweetest of friendships and Abi felt incredibly lucky to have that, remembering the time earlier that summer when she'd thought she'd lost it forever.

'Okay then,' she said. 'It's a date!'

'Good. I've found a new place I want to share with you.'

They walked out into the walled garden together, the sun full on their faces.

'Where is this new place then?' Abi asked.

Edward looked coy for a moment. 'Well, that's a surprise,' he told her, 'but I'm sure you're going to love it.'

END OF BOOK TWO

ACKNOWLEDGEMENTS

I have been very lucky to have met and bought crystals from some wonderful sellers while researching this novel. All of them have been so helpful, answering my questions and providing inspiration. So huge thanks to Candy at Pretty Stones Wholesale in Cambridge, Ruth at Stone Rose Crystals at Stonham Barns, Sammie at Crystality and India at Enchanted Malas. I have also enjoyed learning about the world of crystals from Hibiscus Moon.

Thank you also to Celia Hart and Anne Townsend for answering all my questions about Abigail's art and for letting me handle some of the tools of your trade!

As ever, thanks to Roy who is such a vital component in my books being created, polished and published.

ALSO BY VICTORIA CONNELLY

The House in the Clouds Series

The House in the Clouds

High Blue Sky

The Book Lovers Series

The Book Lovers

Rules for a Successful Book Club

Natural Born Readers

Scenes from a Country Bookshop

Christmas with the Book Lovers

Other Books

The Beauty of Broken Things

One Last Summer

The Heart of the Garden

Love in an English Garden

The Rose Girls

The Secret of You

Christmas at The Cove

Christmas at the Castle

Christmas at the Cottage

The Christmas Collection (A compilation volume)

A Summer to Remember

Wish You Were Here

The Runaway Actress

Molly's Millions

Flights of Angels

Irresistible You

Three Graces

It's Magic (A compilation volume)

A Weekend with Mr Darcy

The Perfect Hero (Dreaming of Mr Darcy)

Mr Darcy Forever

Christmas With Mr Darcy

Happy Birthday Mr Darcy

At Home with Mr Darcy

One Perfect Week and Other Stories

The Retreat and Other Stories

Postcard from Venice and Other Stories

A Dog Called Hope

Escape to Mulberry Cottage (non-fiction)

A Year at Mulberry Cottage (non-fiction)

Summer at Mulberry Cottage (non-fiction)

Secret Pyramid (children's adventure)

The Audacious Auditions of Jimmy Catesby (children's adventure)

ABOUT THE AUTHOR

Victoria Connelly is the bestselling author of *The Rose Girls* and *The Book Lovers* series.

With over a million sales, her books have been translated into many languages. The first, *Flights of Angels*, was made into a film in Germany. Victoria flew to Berlin to see it being made and even played a cameo role in it.

A Weekend with Mr Darcy, the first in her popular Austen Addicts series about fans of Jane Austen has sold over 100,000 copies. She is also the author of several romantic comedies including *The Runaway Actress* which was nominated for the Romantic Novelists' Association's Best Romantic Comedy of the Year.

Victoria was brought up in Norfolk, England before moving to Yorkshire where she got married in a medieval castle. After 11 years in London, she moved to rural Suffolk where she lives in a thatched cottage with her artist husband, a springer spaniel and her ex-battery hens.

To hear about future releases and receive a **free ebook** sign up for her newsletter at victoriaconnelly.com

.

Printed in Great Britain
by Amazon

18459521R00181